LEE BROOK

The Blonde Delilah

MIDDLETON
PARK PRESS

First published by Middleton Park Press 2022

Copyright © 2022 by Lee Brook

All rights reserved. No part of this publication may be reproduced, stored or transmitted in any form or by any means, electronic, mechanical, photocopying, recording, scanning, or otherwise without written permission from the publisher. It is illegal to copy this book, post it to a website, or distribute it by any other means without permission.

This novel is entirely a work of fiction. The names, characters and incidents portrayed in it are the work of the author's imagination. Any resemblance to actual persons, living or dead, events or localities is entirely coincidental.

Lee Brook asserts the moral right to be identified as the author of this work.

Lee Brook has no responsibility for the persistence or accuracy of URLs for external or third-party Internet Websites referred to in this publication and does not guarantee that any content on such Websites is, or will remain, accurate or appropriate.

Designations used by companies to distinguish their products are often claimed as trademarks. All brand names and product names used in this book and on its cover are trade names, service marks, trademarks and registered trademarks of their respective owners. The publishers and the book are not associated with any product or vendor mentioned in this book. None of the companies referenced within the book have endorsed the book.

First edition

This book was professionally typeset on Reedsy. Find out more at reedsy.com

*My daughter Charlotte—
For your inspiration. Thank you.*

Contents

Chapter One	1
Chapter Two	5
Chapter Three	20
Chapter Four	28
Chapter Five	34
Chapter Six	39
Chapter Seven	45
Chapter Eight	55
Chapter Nine	65
Chapter Ten	76
Chapter Eleven	83
Chapter Twelve	93
Chapter Thirteen	98
Chapter Fourteen	105
Chapter Fifteen	109
Chapter Sixteen	122
Chapter Seventeen	130
Chapter Eighteen	138
Chapter Nineteen	147
Chapter Twenty	156
Chapter Twenty-one	160
Chapter Twenty-two	167
Chapter Twenty-three	176
Chapter Twenty-four	184

Chapter Twenty-five	194
Chapter Twenty-six	203
Chapter Twenty-seven	210
Chapter Twenty-eight	224
Chapter Twenty-nine	229
Chapter Thirty	236
Chapter Thirty-one	246
Chapter Thirty-two	255
Chapter Thirty-three	260
Chapter Thirty-four	266
Chapter Thirty-five	273
Chapter Thirty-six	278
Chapter Thirty-seven	285
Chapter Thirty-eight	294
Afterword	300
Also by Lee Brook	302

Chapter One

The soft sound of music came from Alec Rawlinson's mobile phone on the coffee table near the window in the cheap B&B bedroom. He'd made sure the volume was turned low so that he could hear the moans and shallow breaths he hoped would soon come from his companion. Beyond the window, April showers battered the city of Leeds. Inside, it was warm, so warm that condensation had misted up the single window.

Alec was laid on the bed on his back, looking up at the mirror on the ceiling and was pleased by what he saw, especially for a man in his fifties. His head of black hair was still full despite greying at the edges, and his teeth were straight and white. Alec frequented the gym and had a firm square jaw. Alec was a handsome, powerful man, a man who looked as if he had been born to wealth, even though nothing could be further from the truth.

As a boy, he'd lived in a dingy two-bedroom flat in Beeston with a mattress on the floor and threadbare carpets. There was never enough heating in the winter. His mother was a housekeeper and a cook for a care home around the corner from the flat. His father—well, he was nothing. He'd fucked off whilst Alec had still been in nappies, and he could barely remember the man he'd been named after. His mother tried, but she couldn't cook or clean very well. She did her best, but her best was never good enough. It was probably why her husband fucked off; it was probably why she got sacked from the care home.

His father, Alec Rawlinson Sr., drifted in and out of the traces of his memory, a shade, a shade that always wore a crumpled suit and cheap aftershave, with eyes that were always angry and usually too drunk to commit to whole sentences. It was his paternal grandmother who'd had the most significant input in his life. He'd tried to spend every waking moment at her detached house in Headingley with his cousins, eating sweets and cakes, watching her massive television, and riding their bicycles around the claustrophobic streets. And when he'd been old enough to pick his GCSE options, which college or university to study at, it was always his grandma who had helped him decide.

Because of those decisions, Alec Rawlinson had become a man of great wealth and self-assumed impeccable taste. But as with all tastes, it came in both good and bad. He craved luxury, the kind of luxury afforded by his wealth. Expensive watches were his vice, but so were powerful drugs and young women. He'd been off the drugs for a while, but as a handsome, fit man who didn't look his age, he could have had any woman he wanted. Yet, for him, it was all about age. The younger the woman, the better.

The young woman straddling him was beautiful. Blonde curls cascaded down over her pale shoulders, ending just before each pink nipple of her perfect breasts. They hung like ripe fruit just above his face, tantalisingly out of reach. How desperately he wanted to nibble them, to take them in his

CHAPTER ONE

hands. "You still haven't told me how old you are," he said.

"Old enough. But only just."

He smiled. Like Eve, he knew the fruit was forbidden, that the young blonde who was smiling above him was young enough to be his daughter. But like Eve, he'd decided to take the forbidden fruit, anyway.

Enough was enough. The temptation was too much. He couldn't wait any more. Alec took control. He wanted her then. He was ready. The young woman groaned as he nibbled her nipples. He bent her head down and forced her to lower her crimson lips to his, kissing her voraciously, his tongue darting between those crimson, bulbous folds.

His hands went towards the ripe fruit that was her perky breasts, but she gripped him by both wrists and pushed them towards the metal headrail. "Close your eyes," she told him as she slid further up his abdomen. "Keep your hands still." The young blonde woman pulled two pairs of silver handcuffs from under the spare pillow and gently tethered him to the railing. "Ah, ah, ah, keep them closed," she commanded.

"I just need to remove my knickers," she told him and rolled off him, retrieving another two pairs of cuffs from her bag. "Keep your eyes closed until I say. OK?"

He nodded his consent as the young blonde snapped the cuffs to his ankles, cuffing him to the two metal posts at the foot of the iron frame. It wasn't an unusual sight for her, nor a unique situation. This wasn't the first time she'd seen a naked, middle-aged man cuffed to all four posts, his erect penis ready and waiting. This also wasn't the first time she'd bent down to retrieve the knife from her bag. She'd done this before and would definitely do the same again.

"Time to open your eyes," she whispered.

And he did. Alec had expected to see an angel when he opened his eyes, a naked one with firm breasts and long, golden curls. He desperately wanted to know whether she'd shaved as he'd requested; the less hair down there, the better. What he saw made him recoil. His back arched. Alec strained against his bonds and buckled as he tried with all his might to get free.

There was nothing he could do. The blonde stepped closer and, with a manicured hand, pulled his head back with his black hair, exposing his pale throat. Then the porcelain blonde goddess smiled, and Alec saw another glint of silver. The blade looked sharp and deadly. He saw her grip the knife even tighter. Then suddenly, she plunged, hard and fast, the blade puncturing his throat, his pale skin awash with crimson. Alec convulsed, but she wasn't done yet. The young blonde gripped the knife with two hands and plunged down, and down, and down, each plunge more frenzied than the last until Alec's pain finally faded away, and he drifted into death. When she was finally finished, the white sheets below him were stained crimson.

Chapter Two

DI George Beaumont was leaving his video link interview with Boris Jarman, the paedophile uncle of the Bone Saw Ripper, Alexander Peterson, at HMP Leeds when his mobile phone rang. He glanced at his phone and answered. "DI Beaumont."

"I've got a case for you, George. There's been a murder at a bed and breakfast in Headingley. Uniform's already there, and it's yours if you want it." It was his Geordie boss and head of the Homicide and Major Enquiry Team based at Elland Road Police Station, Detective Superintendent Jim Smith. George's team wasn't on call that week, but there was an unwritten rule that the team not on call would pick up any work overflow.

They must be inundated, he thought. There were three Detective Chief Inspectors above him in the pecking order, but clearly, they were all tied up with other cases. George didn't need to think about it. Being SIO was ingrained in him now and something he looked forward to. "Absolutely."

"Great," Smith said. "How soon can you get there?"

It was Monday afternoon. He glanced at his watch. "Headingley?" Smith grunted a confirmation. "Twenty minutes. I'm at Armley nick."

"Ah, the Boris Jarman interview. Of course. DS Wood will be

your deputy," Smith confirmed. "I'll text you the address of the B&B and get her to meet you there."

George breathed a sigh of relief. Three months ago, he'd been accused of abusing his position for a sexual purpose by a whistleblower. He'd thought initially the whistleblower had been Alex Peterson, but he'd told George it had been the 'rotten seed' in his team, one that needed 'weeding out'. And despite Alex being a psychopath, he believed him. George had desperately tried to fathom who the 'rotten seed' was but, despite his detective skills, was no nearer to knowing.

He called DS Isabella Wood on his way down, wanting to know as much as possible about the case before he got there.

* * *

"It's a bit of a mess in there, George," DS Wood warned as he got out of his Honda. He'd had to park halfway down the street at the junction of Langdale Avenue, and Canterbury Drive as a fleet of ambulances, police vehicles and forensic vans had blocked his way. Wood had agreed to meet him and talk him through her first impressions. The street had been cordoned off with police tape. Despite that and the cold April showers, several nosy neighbours were hovering around the tape, squinting their eyes and craning their necks to see what was going on. Uniform was keeping them back, but they could do nothing about the nosy parkers watching from their first-floor windows.

"Get back inside," Wood told a nosy neighbour who was loitering by his gate, craning her neck around for a good look. "We'll be around later today to take your statement." The grey-haired older woman huffed and shuffled back inside, slamming her door.

"As I left, a Crime Scene Co-ordinator and their team of SOCOs went in to process the scene."

George nodded at her and thought about Stuart Kent, the usual Crime Scene Co-ordinator, and shuddered. DSU Smith had told George it would take a lot of rehabilitation before Kent was back on the job. It was a shame as he was the consummate professional and incredible at his job. And overall, a nice guy. Even if he did support Newcastle United.

Wood handed George a protective coverall, blue latex gloves, and shoe covers, all disposable. "Tell me about the victim." He asked her as they headed towards the B&B.

"He's a fifty-three-year-old IC1 male named Alec Rawlinson." George took in the sturdy triple-storey property, noticing a red metallic sign stating the place was called 'The Boundary B&B'. George thought it was named that because of it being so close to the Yorkshire Cricket Ground.

"How do you know that?" he asked Wood. "From the booking, or was there any ID on the body?"

"His wallet was in the back pocket of his trousers."

George nodded.

They were met at the tape by a uniformed officer who took their names after they showed him their warrant cards. George could see from the log she'd been signed in and out twice already.

The B&B was lovely inside, nicer than George had been expecting. Whilst the carpet wasn't new, it wasn't threadbare and was clean. An acrid tang indicated to George that the walls had been freshly painted. It was all pastels and soft edges. *Sleek,* George thought, and the recessed lighting added to that effect. For a B&B with a name like The Boundary, he hadn't expected it to be so stylish.

"When I first saw it, I expected it to be a bit of a sordid place that would have been filled with cricket memorabilia," George said to Wood. "But I take it back. It's quite nice in here." She grinned at him, and he smiled right back. "Was Rawlinson married?"

Wood nodded her head. "Wedding ring on the correct finger, though that finger isn't where you'd expect it to be." George raised his brow at her cryptic words. "DS Fry is at the station looking into his next of kin."

There was a Do Not Disturb sign hanging on the open door, which George thought was somewhat ironic. Somebody had obviously disturbed the dead man.

Heart pounding, George entered the room, followed by Wood. He always mentally prepared himself for the worst, as even though he'd seen quite a few dead bodies, he knew deep within that the initial shock never diminished. Loss of life affected him deeply, right down to the bones. It was something he was sure he'd never get used to.

A young female crime scene photographer that he recognised was taking pictures, her camera flashing every few seconds. The incessant click always got on George's nerves. There was something about it that seemed to induce anxiety. He just wasn't sure what. Wood nodded to a dark shape that George assumed was a metal four-poster bed. "His body's on the bed. This is how he was found."

George walked over and looked down to inspect the victim. A faint metallic smell pervaded the air around the corpse. He was a well-muscled, tall guy, over six foot at least, who lay on his back on crimson sheets. A pool of his blood had formed on the floor where it had cascaded over the edge. His face was

CHAPTER TWO

twisted with pain, and his eyes were devoid of life. There were multiple stab wounds to his body, and from what George could see, they were concentrated around his neck and his torso. He looked at the SOCO taking photos.

"Anything you want me to get in particular, sir?" she asked.

Wood explained to George that she'd ordered the young photographer to take photos before he arrived. "No. Whatever DS Wood told you to get is fine." He knew he needed to trust his team more if he wanted to make Detective Chief Inspector. But it wasn't only that. He trusted Wood like he trusted no other. She was the yin to his yang; she was everything he wasn't, and in truth, she completed him. "We could do with some extra light in here, though," he said with a smile.

She nodded and left the room. And not even a minute later, a young male SOCO set up a portable spotlight and switched it on. Immediately, a bright light illuminated the dead man. George turned to the young man to say thank you and noticed it was Hayden Wyatt, a Blond American with an overbearing personality. He used to be part of Stuart's team. He wondered who the Crime Scene Co-ordinator was when a voice interrupted his thoughts. "Nasty, isn't it?" Wyatt said over his shoulder.

He nodded and circled the body.

"Good afternoon, detectives." There was an abrasive tone in the voice.

Both George and Wood looked towards the doorway. Looking at them was a young, blonde woman with cascading curls and intelligent blue eyes. "You're in the way, and I've got a lot of work to do."

"I'm DI Beaumont, and this is DS Wood," George said as he straightened up to move away from the victim and give her room. He moved towards the other side of the bed—a different vantage.

She looked at both detectives. "Lindsey Yardley. A pleasure." She offered no shake, not that George had expected her to. He'd never worked with Lindsey Yardley before but knew her by reputation. At twenty-six, she was young but experienced. She was terse but efficient. He'd been told not to ask any stupid questions; otherwise, she'd shut you down. One of the DCIs had apparently learned that the hard way.

She set her tools on the carpet and placed two stepping plates on the ground. She used them to kneel on and got close to the corpse, her mask tight on her face. "This is terrible—multiple stab wounds. I haven't seen anything this bad in ages," she said as she inspected the puncture wounds that covered Alec's torso.

George nodded his agreement. "I could smell the blood as soon as I walked in. There's a lot of it."

"Aye. It's potent. But then, the victim *has* been stabbed *multiple* times," said Lindsey. "To hazard a guess, I'd say the fatal stab was probably this one." She pointed towards a large gash in his neck. "The carotid artery is close to the surface. If breached, it will spray blood under pressure from the heart out from the wound into the air and land everywhere." She looked up. George followed her line of sight and saw blood spatter on the ceiling. "Whoever stabbed him would have been drenched in blood. Yet, by all accounts, there are no bloody footprints anywhere. That's strange if you ask me."

Wood scrunched up her nose. "Why didn't they stop there? Why stab the victim again, and again, and again?"

A thin smile broke out on Lindsey Yardley's face. She didn't meet Wood's eyes but said, "That's your job, isn't it, detectives? How am I to know the killer's mental state? All I can tell you is how many wounds he has and give you a possible murder weapon, but even then, Dr Ross will probably take over back at the mortuary. But I can tell you that whoever did this was strong. The force required to pierce the breastbone is rather large."

"Can you tell us the time of death?" George asked.

"Until I take his temperature, no. But, from the viscosity of the blood and the colouration of the body, I can advise it was last night. That's it, I'm afraid, but you'll know more after the post-mortem. Dr Ross will call you, OK?"

A small yellow sign with a number six on it stood on a coffee table beside the only window. On the floor was a plastic evidence bag.

"What's this?" George said to a young, blond SOCO.

Hayden Wyatt turned and smiled. "Evidence of a stolen phone, sir," the young man said. "From the silhouette, you see. Whoever stole it stole it whilst it was covered in blood."

George scanned the room and, without looking at Wyatt, said, "What about inside the bag?" He walked over to another yellow sign numbered five without waiting for a reply.

Wyatt grinned his usual grin and, in his American drawl, said, "Nothing, sir. It's waiting for evidence."

"Waiting? What do you mean?" George asked, raising his brow.

Wyatt nodded. "We're struggling to find anything. All the appropriate swabs have been taken, and we'll look for prints later, but places like this are awful to process."

Lindsey walked over and added, "It's because of the number of guests these places have. The cleaners clean, yes, but not enough. There could be ten or twenty lots of different DNA in the room alone. If not more." She shrugged. "Same for the prints. It'll be expensive to extract profiles from every swab, but it's your call, DI Beaumont. Tell me how you want to proceed."

George looked at Wood, who smiled. He wanted her opinion, but he didn't want to seem lacking in front of the new Crime Scene Co-ordinator. "Our priority is Alec Rawlinson's body. Whoever killed him got close. We can go down the route of testing everything for DNA if we get stuck later on." George sounded more upbeat than he felt.

His DS nodded. So did the Crime Scene Co-ordinator. It looked as if he had made the right decision. "OK, good," Lindsey said.

"What's number five?" DI Beaumont said, pointing towards the floor.

Wyatt's Cheshire grin returned, but his superior spoke before he could. "That is—"

"The deceased's finger," Wyatt said, interrupting Lindsey. "Left ring finger."

"Well, where is it?"

"It's inside his anus," Lindsey explained. "The ring is visible. I'm leaving it there until the post-mortem, OK?"

George looked at his DS, who grimaced. That was why she had been cryptic earlier. She'd known his finger had been removed and was lodged up his arsehole. "Nice," George said, nodding at Lindsey. The removal of his ring finger had to be significant, as did the location it had been left. He looked around the room, looking for other opportunities they could harvest for DNA. In the corner was a leather chair. "Have we processed this chair for DNA?"

The young blond SOCO nodded. "Yes, sir. We found very

little, but we took samples anyway."

He nodded at Wyatt and looked at Lindsey. "Good. Put that on priority, too." The killer may have sat there before they'd launched their frenzied attack on their unsuspecting victim, and hopefully, a hair follicle or skin sample was left behind.

There was a shout from the en-suite.

They filed in, first George, then DS Wood, then Lindsey, and the young SOCO at the back. The young female who had been taking pictures was bent over the sink. "There's a lot of blood in here. Maybe the killer used it to wash the blood off their hands or clean the murder weapon. There's also evidence of blood in the shower cubicle, too."

A thought hit George. "Swab it. It could be the killer's blood." He knew from experience that during frenzied attacks, offenders would often lose control of the blade once it became slippery from their victim's blood. It was how they'd tied the Miss Murderer to the murder of Beeston Park Academy headteacher, Eileen Abbott. And if it wasn't, then they could confirm part of the killer's MO.

"OK, sir. I'll take samples." She bent down and fetched the appropriate equipment from her bag. "We'll get them tested for you."

"Thanks." George glanced at Wood. "It would be extremely convenient if the killer cut himself in the process. There could be a DNA goldmine in the sink or shower."

She shrugged and muttered, "True. I doubt it, though. They probably just cleaned Alec's blood off themselves before they left the B&B." She twisted her head to nod back towards the room. "Killing somebody like that would have made a proper mess."

George thought the same but hoped otherwise. "We can

hope, DS Wood, we can hope." George cast his eyes around the en-suite, aware it was becoming crowded.

When they reached the door to exit the room, George turned to DS Wood and said, "I need you to speak to the receptionist and get her to give you the names of every worker who has access to this room, and if possible, a schedule of when they did."

Wood nodded and said, "Mr and Mr Lancaster are the owners. They hire Sylvia Gordon to cook the breakfasts in the morning, and she's also the housekeeper. Matthew Lancaster runs the reception, and James Lancaster runs the business from the small office downstairs."

George knew Wood would have researched the place ahead of time, but he was still impressed by her knowledge. "Great work. We need to speak with Matthew urgently."

"I agree. I already spoke with Matthew's husband, James, and he tells me there's no CCTV."

"When's the post-mortem?" George asked Lindsey, who had momentarily left the B&B room.

She brushed a blonde curl away from her face. "I spoke with Dr Ross, and he can't do it until tomorrow. He's had a busy weekend. He'll call you."

George nodded. He would have liked it done today, but there was nothing he could do. Dr Ross was always there when George needed him, so he must have had his hands full.

"Can we bag the Do Not Disturb sign up, please, Lindsey, and check it for prints and DNA?" George asked.

She nodded. "Hold your horses, Inspector; I was getting to it."

The woman was very brusque, and rumours around the station suggested she was challenging to work with. He could see why those rumours were rife. He nodded to her and smiled. With the crime scene under control, he led the way back down to a small empty room opposite the check-in desk. The guests had been asked to leave for the day, and no one was allowed back in until they were finished processing the scene.

DS Wood came back two minutes later with Matthew, a man in his mid-thirties with brown curly hair, who she'd found sitting in the back office with his husband, crying. Matthew's eyes were red, and he spoke in a Lancashire accent. He'd been the one to discover the body, it seemed. He knew how the man was feeling. Seeing a corpse was not a fun experience.

"Mr Rawlinson was supposed to check out at ten this morning," Matthew told them, his voice trembling. "As is usual protocol, when a guest who is supposed to check out doesn't come down, one of us goes up to check that they're OK. Sometimes our customers sleep in and forget to check out. It's more common than you think."

He knew all about sleeping in and forgetting to check out. Not that long ago, he and Isabella had spent all night together at the Holmfield Arms Hotel in Wakefield. He smiled as he thought about it.

George nodded but said nothing, inviting Matthew Lancaster to speak.

"First, I called to him through the door after knocking, but there was no answer. Sometimes customers have left without settling their bills, so I opened the door with my key and—" He whimpered. "That's—that's when I found him lying handcuffed to the bed." His eyes filled up with tears whilst he shook his head. "I don't think I've ever seen so much blood."

Isabella Wood leaned forward and squeezed his arm. "You're

doing great, Matthew. Seeing a corpse is difficult for anybody, even us, who sees them more regularly than we want. What happened next? Did you touch the body at all?"

"No," he said. "I watch a lot of crime shows. I turned and fled and immediately called triple nine."

"Good," George said with a nod. "You did the right thing, Mr Lancaster." He wrote a note in his pocket notebook. At this moment, every person was a suspect. "Had Mr Rawlinson stayed in the B&B before?" George asked.

Matthew shook his head. "No. Though if he did, I didn't recognise him."

"How long have you owned this place?"

"Six or seven years." He sniffed and rubbed his nose on a tissue. "When you buy a place like this, you don't expect things like this to happen."

"True," said George. "Were you working yesterday?"

"Yes. We have Sylvia, Sylvia Gordon, to assist us. I have a weekend girl. We also have a night manager. James' brother, Steve." He'd get DC Blackburn to interview all the staff later that day.

Wood leaned forward in her chair and gazed directly at Matthew. "So you were on reception duties yesterday?" He nodded. "Did you notice anyone come into the B&B yesterday? Somebody who shouldn't have been there?"

"What do you mean?"

"Well, anyone, really. You checked Alec in, right?" He nodded again. "Did he check in alone or with a guest?"

"Alone," he confirmed.

"And after he checked in, did you see anybody else enter the B&B? A visitor or a guest, maybe even a stranger?"

He thought for a moment, nibbling at his lips. "The cricket

isn't on until the end of the month, so we've been fairly quiet. And most of our guests go out after breakfast if they're not checking out. I was here all day, and I don't remember anyone coming in."

"Were you at your post all morning?" George asked. Matthew nodded but didn't quite meet his eye. He wrote that down in his notebook and thought about pushing him but then decided against it. He'd been through enough. "If you were at your post all morning, and you didn't see any strangers enter, then it means one of three things. One, your killer got into the B&B by a different entrance, two, it's a customer at the B&B, or three, the killer works here."

He glanced at George in surprise and shook his head erratically. "I don't believe for one minute that my husband or Mrs Gordon are capable of killing anybody. And Mr Rawlinson was the only guest yesterday, so it couldn't have been anybody else."

George let Matthew's sentence hang in the air. *It could have been you,* George thought. *That, or you're telling lies about not leaving your post.*

When Matthew said nothing, George said, "OK, Matthew, you've been great." From the corner of his eye, he saw Isabella Wood glance at him in surprise. "Just one more thing. You mentioned earlier that guests sometimes leave without paying. How do they do that if there's always a person at the reception desk?"

Matthew Lancaster looked down in shame. "We have a fire escape at the back of the building for legal purposes. Each floor has access to it. We can't lock it; otherwise, it invalidates our insurance."

"OK. So he could have gotten in via the fire escape. Thank

you." George got up and went to find Crime Scene Co-ordinator, Lindsey Yardley. He wanted to make sure they took swabs and prints from the doors leading to the fire escape, as well as looking for any evidence from any railings.

"He?" Matthew asked.

"It's just the pronoun we usually use," Wood said. "Did you take a copy of Mr Rawlinson's ID and other documents when he checked in?"

He straightened up. "Of course. And his card details."

"OK, we'll need a copy of those," said Wood. It didn't hurt to be thorough, even though they had the contents of his wallet. It'd probably give them the same information. "Do you have any records of any calls made from his room?"

"I can check that for you."

"Please."

Matthew Lancaster got up and walked across to the front desk, then disappeared into the back office. After five minutes, he was back with his husband in tow. "This is a copy of everything we have." DS Wood accepted it. It was a printout of the guest register, complete with Rawlinson's driver's licence and debit card details. "I'm sorry, but he didn't make any phone calls from his room."

"Perfect," George said as he walked down the stairs. "We're leaving now, but I'll be sending over DC Blackburn later to take statements from you, as well as prints and DNA, for elimination purposes."

Matthew went to protest until his husband James clamped his hand on Matthew's shoulder. George wrote another note in his book before saying, "Thanks again." He turned to Wood, who was talking to a member of the SOCO team about the importance of the fire escape. "Let's head back to the station,

CHAPTER TWO

Wood. There's nothing else we can do here."

Chapter Three

George stood at the front of Incident Room Four, the largest of their five glass-panelled incident rooms, waiting for his team to filter in. DS Wood, as usual, was pinning photographs of their victim onto the whiteboard behind him.

"Come on; we need to get cracking. Not only do we have the Jack the Butcher case to close, but now we have this." He pointed to the board and tried to keep his voice light, but even he could hear the impatience in his tone.

DS Elaine Brewer and DS Joshua Fry, two experienced sergeants, were sitting at the front next to DS Yolanda Williams. All had worked on both the Miss Murderer and the Bone Saw Ripper cases with him last year. There was nobody new on his team, and next into the incident room were DC Tashan Blackburn, DC Jason Scott, and DC Oliver James. George was about to ask Tashan to close the door when he realised one of his team was missing. He scanned the room and counted. There should have been nine of them, yet he counted eight, including himself.

Then suddenly, there was a ruckus from outside, and DC Terrence Morton bounded in. "Sorry I'm late, sir," he said, his face red and sweaty. Terry was the most recent transfer to his team, a man in his fifties who, it seemed, didn't have the ambition to climb the ranks. He'd been a DC for twenty years yet was quite a decent detective. Why he lacked ambition was anyone's guess, but George had an inkling it was because in between tasks, all the bulky man did was complain.

By that point, Wood had finished attaching the photographs and walked around to stand by his side. "Thanks, Wood," George said. "Right, crack on, shall we? The victim is fifty-three-year-old Alec Rawlinson from Headingley. He was found by the owner of the B&B where he was staying, Mr Matthew Lancaster, who entered the room after assuming he'd left without paying, spotted him lying on the bed covered in blood and called the police. He was stabbed a lot, and the knife wounds were widespread. I'm not sure exactly how many there were—the post-mortem will confirm, I'm sure—and even at first glance, I couldn't be sure. It was a frenzied attack."

There was a gentle murmur around the incident room.

"The murder weapon wasn't left at the scene, and SOCO Hayden Wyatt advised there was a lack of forensic evidence left behind, so we don't know too much so far." He turned to the whiteboard and pointed at the images. "Alec Rawlinson, as far as we can tell, was married. We know this because he wore a wedding ring." He paused, unsure how to relay the information to his team. "His ring finger was cut off and left inside his anus."

"Wedding ring still on?" Jason Scott asked.

"Wedding ring is still on," George confirmed.

He could hear the gasps from his team. He remembered only months ago how they'd reacted to the dismembered torsos and limbs the Bone Saw Ripper had left behind. "DS Fry, did you manage to get in contact with Alec's next of kin?"

"Not yet, sir. I'm working on it."

George nodded. "OK, keep at it." He turned and faced the entire room, looking for detectives who seemed disinterested. There was nobody fitting that description. He'd been looking for the 'rotten seed' for months now, not seeing anything. It was frustrating. "The owners, Mr and Mr Lancaster are adamant Alec was the only guest that day and, with a small staff roster, believe a stranger must have come off the street."

"How could a stranger get into a B&B without being noticed?" Yolanda asked.

She was their CCTV expert, an invaluable detective. "Good question. They have fire escapes on the first and second floors, which they have to keep unlocked for security purposes. Apparently, people can get in and out as they please."

"But surely if they leave by the fire escape, an alarm or something sounds?" Yolanda said.

George hadn't thought of that, but it made sense. Why would they allow guests to leave that way, especially if they were worried about non-payment of bills? It sounded fishy. "Exactly. DC Blackburn is heading there after the briefing. Put that to them, yeah?" The young DC nodded, and George noticed he was taking notes. *Good lad.* "Check the fire escapes, too. In my experience, they open from the inside only. Not the outside. If that's the case, ask them why they believe a stranger got in. And how?" Now that George thought about it more, it made no sense to him. Fire escapes let you out, not in. And Yolanda was right. There should have been an alarm. "This is important, Tashan. I asked the SOCOs to take prints and DNA from both doors leading to the fire escapes outside. It'll tell us whether or not Alec let anybody in. But in the meantime, we need answers, and I don't trust Matthew Lancaster. Interview them all separately. Take Oliver with you, yeah?"

In unison, the two male detective constables said, "Yes, sir."

"I want the usual searches done on Rawlinson. DC Scott, I want you on that. We found no mobile phone at the scene, but a guy like that most likely had a contract. Find who it was with, and get hold of his phone records. I also need information on his social media accounts, emails and such. We need to find anyone who can give us a better idea of who this guy was. Do you need any help with that, Jay, or are you OK?"

"I'm fine, sir. I'll liaise with Josh as and when," Jason said, scribbling notes down on his tablet. He'd noticed a change recently, had George. Many of the younger detectives used such devices to store everything they needed. Tashan was obviously the anomaly, still using paper and pen as he did. He also noticed Wood hardly ever used one, managing with just her memory alone.

"We need to find out everything about Alec. I especially want to know what he did for a living. On the way over, I received a call from Lindsey Yardley, the new Crime Scene Co-ordinator, who told me they found watches worth tens of thousands of pounds each. It's clear to me that this was a violent attack and not a burglary. Yolanda, I need you in Incident Room Five on CCTV. Once Tashan has finished his tasks, he'll be with you."

Yolanda sat up straight. "Headingley is good for CCTV on the main roads, but not so good anywhere else. The Boundary B&B is in a backstreet, right?"

"Right. Do what you can, yeah?" She nodded and made notes on her tablet. Trawling through hours of footage was hard work, but it was hard work that got results. With the amount of CCTV available to them these days, both private and from the council, often it was the footage that led to a winning trial.

"Elaine, coordinate a door-to-door. Take DC Morton and some uniforms. Maybe the neighbours or someone in the local community saw something. They certainly seemed the nosy type. Oh, and organise an interview with Cassandra Broadchurch, the weekend girl. She's seventeen, so she needs an appropriate adult. We urgently need to talk to her as she would have been on shift yesterday when the murder happened."

"I got her address from one of the owners," Wood cut in.

George smiled and nodded at Elaine. "OK, we've all got tasks to do. DS Wood is my deputy, so if you need more tasks, speak with her first."

"Yes, sir," they said in unison, with nods all round

"Before you go, I want to talk to you all about the nature of the attack. He was handcuffed to the bed with no sign of a struggle. We're still waiting on forensics, but this was vicious, and from the removal of his appendage, it was personal."

Tashan leaned forward in his seat. "So, Alec Rawlinson knew his attacker?"

"Yeah, that's what I think, too," said George. "There was no sign of a forced entry, either. To be blunt, this was an execution, and we need to know why. It's why it's so important to know what Alec did and who he knew. It's why we need to know who his family and friends were."

Were. George hated speaking about people in the past tense.

"That doesn't mean he knew his killer, sir," Terry said. "The guy could have snuck in, knocked on his door and threatened him. Knives are scary. If a man came at me brandishing a knife telling me to lie down on the bed, then I'd do it. Any evidence of sexual assault?"

CHAPTER THREE

"True, Terry." George was impressed. It was rather astute of him. The first rule they taught you in policing was to assume nothing. "No, no evidence of sexual assault, but Lindsey said she wouldn't know until the post-mortem. Dr Ross is calling me later, so keep an eye out on HOLMES for updates. And whilst I agree knives are scary, I'd be shouting and making a ruckus. I'd be trying to defend myself. No defensive wounds were found. From what we saw, Rawlinson knew his attacker."

Terry nodded slowly. "OK, sir. Maybe his mobile phone records will show us who came to his room."

"That's what I'm hoping for." George sent a look in Jason's direction. He nodded. "He made zero calls from his B&B room, so if he did, then it would have been from his missing mobile—"

"Maybe that's why he took the phone with him when he left," Jason said.

"I believe exactly that, that the attacker stole the phone to keep the information from us. Maybe it was a WhatsApp call instead of a normal call. We don't even know if he had the app, and without his mobile number, we're stuck." He looked at Jason Scott once more, who made more notes on his tablet. "Anyway, back to the method. Stabbing someone continuously means something," George continued. "This was not a calculated attack; it was frenzied. Though I'd say it was pre-planned, and the attacker wanted that man dead, and he wanted it done as violently as possible."

"Are we assuming the attacker's a he, then?" Yolanda asked.

An important question. "No, we're not. We can't assume anything. Not yet. Forensics should help with that; however, it's a B&B room, and according to SOCO Wyatt, they're tough places to process. Rawlinson was over six foot and, looking at him, a regular at the gym. I don't like saying this, but unless he was taken by surprise, I can't see a woman being able to. Plus, Lindsey Yardley stated the attacker was powerful as it takes a lot of force to pierce a breastbone. Also, women killers are usually calculated, not frenzied."

"Maybe he booked an escort, and when he didn't pay, she drugged him and murdered him?" asked Terry.

"There's no sign of any sexual activity. As for the drugging, it's a possibility. Again, we'll have to wait for the toxicology report for that."

He hated advising his team they had to wait, but forensics took time. He couldn't snap his fingers and have the results, though he would if he could.

"It was definitely premeditated," said Wood from George's side. All eyes turned to her. George motioned for her to go ahead. "They brought the knife with them. And the cuffs, presumably. DI Beaumont has ordered priority forensics on them because we assume they belonged to the killer."

He liked to give Wood free rein, let her do her own thing. It was why the accusation of him abusing his rank for a sexual purpose was absurd.

"Then, there's the blood found in the en-suite. From what the Crime Scene Co-ordinator told us, the attacker pierced the carotid artery. As it is close to the surface, it sprays blood everywhere. We both saw blood spatter on the ceiling, so whoever stabbed Rawlinson would have been drenched in blood. Yardley said it herself when she advised there were no bloody footprints anywhere. It looks like the killer cleaned themselves and their weapon before leaving the room at the B&B—"

"Maybe they wore a coverall and shoe covers like the Bone

Saw Ripper?" Terry chimed in.

"Maybe they did, Terry, but we'll know this for sure once we get the blood results back. DI Beaumont, like myself, hopes the attacker cut themselves in the frenzy. It isn't uncommon for that to happen. If we have his DNA, then bingo."

"That's if it's his blood and not Rawlinson's," said Terry.

"True," said George rather bluntly. "But all this evidence proves the attack was premeditated. What I need now is for you lot to complete the tasks I've given you whilst we wait for further updates. I spoke to DSU Smith on the way over, and he's got uniform searching the bins and skips in the area looking for the murder weapon or any items of clothing with blood on them. Luckily, their bins don't get emptied until the end of the week."

Chapter Four

"George, a word," came Detective Superintendent Smith's Geordie voice from the other end of the squad room. He didn't sound mad, despite his voice rising above everyone else's.

George made his way to his boss's office, and when he got there, Smith said, "Close the door, son."

George did as he was told and noticed the blinds were down. This was unusual for Smith, and suddenly, George was nervous he was about to receive a bollocking. Yet, unusually, the Detective Superintendent's veins weren't standing out in his thick neck like they usually were when he was pissed off. "Everything OK, sir?"

"Fine. You know how I feel about murder, Beaumont. Anyway, I just wanted to let you know that DCI Shelly Arnold was working on a case that went cold with an MO similar to yours. Well, it was her DS, Luke Mason, who was looking into it for her. Nathan Patterson was the victim's name."

George had worked under Luke when he was just a DC, and under his guidance, George had made DS and had moved to Elland Road. Luke moved to Elland Road six months later but was put on a different team. They still had beers now and again.

"Patterson? As in DC Nate Patterson, sir?"

"That's right."

Nate Patterson was a DC who George worked with a couple of years ago. They were good friends until Nate changed his number and started avoiding him. He had no idea the man had been murdered. He took a deep breath to calm himself. "Thanks, sir. I'll look into it."

"Good. How's baby Jack?" He leaned back in his swivel chair and smiled.

"Growing by the minute, sir," said George with a huge smile on his face. He knew where this was going. George hadn't been SIO of an active case since Jack had been born, and Smith was clearly worried about his ability to commit to the investigation.

"Good, I'm glad to hear it. And his mother?"

Smith was asking about Mia, his ex-fiancée and the mother of his son. The first month after Jack had been born went smoothly, even after having spent an entire week in the hospital. But after that, Mia struggled and had what George thought was a full-blown nervous breakdown. It wasn't. It was post-partum psychosis, a severe mental health illness that can affect someone soon after having a baby. Initially, Mia had looked and sounded well, but he quickly realised she was behaving in a way that was out of character. She'd begun talking and thinking too much and too fast, saying she felt 'high' and 'on top of the world'. But then things changed rather rapidly. She was withdrawn and often tearful. Whenever he was around, he noticed she lacked energy and wasn't eating. Mia also became easily agitated. That's when George called the doctor, and he felt guilty for not seeing it before. A point came where her mood would change rapidly, and sometimes she displayed a mixture of both a high mood and a low mood. There was a scary point where she got very suspicious, fearful that

George was going to take Jack away from her. He'd never do that, not without good reason. Then she'd wake up confused about why he was there.

In the first week, Mia was treated at a hospital in a mother and baby unit and was prescribed a cocktail of drugs. Once the initial week was over, he stayed with her for five weeks, supporting her with her CBT—cognitive behavioural therapy—until the middle of March, when she thought it would be good if he moved back into his flat.

Those six or seven weeks were awful for George, but he knew it must have been a hell of a lot worse for Mia. He couldn't imagine what she had gone through, and he felt guilty because she told him regularly how much she needed him. She was a single mother, despite begging George to take her back. He considered it for Jack's sake, but he was happy with Isabella. Jack's life would be better if his parents weren't in a romantic relationship. He'd used his annual leave, guiltily leaving the Jack the Butcher case to DS Wood and his team. He'd obviously explained to DSU Smith the circumstances, but this was the first time he'd broached the subject with George.

"Mia's doing OK, now. She's been living alone with Jack for three weeks now. I pop in every other night to make sure she's coping. She has her aunt and her grandparents for support, too. And Ryan." Ryan Jarman was Mia's half-brother who had been involved in the Bone Saw Ripper case late last year. Mia and Ryan both didn't know they had any siblings, and it was nice to see how close they had become.

Smith sighed. "Listen, George. You know I'm the type of boss to tell you straight. With Mia struggling as she is, are you sure you're able to commit a hundred per cent to this case? Because if you can't, I can assign—"

CHAPTER FOUR

"She's fine, and I can commit," George cut him off. "We're not romantically involved, sir. She knows this. We spoke about me taking over custody of Jack, and whilst that would have meant a break from work, if that's what it took, then that's what it took, you know? But we decided it wasn't fair on any of us. You know how badly I want to make DCI, don't you sir?"

Smith exhaled and nodded his head. It was then that George realised how relieved his boss was. "Your aspirations to be a DCI have been noted, Beaumont. Anyway, I'm glad to hear Mia's better and that you two are in a better place. It's good to have you back fully, son."

Even though he'd been at work since Jack had been born, he'd been working the Jack the Butcher cold case and light duties only, which, from a professional point of view, was incredibly frustrating, but from a personal point of view, necessary. It hadn't been the first time he'd had to sit back while Isabella Wood and his team dealt with serious crimes.

After surviving attempted murder, George had given several interviews to the press and had somehow become something of a temporary media star. Not only had he survived the Bone, Saw Ripper after being locked down in the dingy cellar, but he'd got a confession out of the man and had saved Crime Scene Co-ordinator Stuart Kent's life, too. Luckily, he had contacts within the press, Johnathan Duke and Paige McGuiness, who, despite being relatively quiet during the Bone Saw Ripper case, had helped suppress the media swarm.

"When's the PM?" his boss asked.

Crime Scene Co-ordinator, Lindsey Yardley, had rung him after the team briefing earlier and had explained Dr Ross couldn't do it until Thursday, but she could do it Tuesday. "It's at four tomorrow. Crime Scene Co-ordinator Lindsey Yardley's doing it instead of Dr Ross." George wondered whether he'd made the right decision by allowing her to do it.

Smith read his mind. "She's highly qualified, George. Very skilled. A bit mardy, but don't go telling anyone I said that." George grinned. "Any DNA from the scene yet?"

"Not yet, sir." George shook his head and grimaced. "Tomorrow will be the earliest."

Smith nodded and stuck his tongue through his lips. He was obviously frustrated by how long forensics took, too. "I've spoken with the Chief Super, and he's emailed, Calder Park. Chase them up. They know it's a priority, but that means nothing. Every detective asks for priority, and the entire West Yorkshire Police force sends their stuff there. We've been lucky YappApp hasn't gotten wind of it yet. But they will soon. Trust me. We need something you can give them once they inevitably find out."

"Great..." He'd been lucky with the Bone Saw Ripper case, as the DCI in charge of the case at the time, the Bone Saw Ripper himself, took all press-related interviews and conferences. He suffered after, of course, being the 'hero'. But this time, George was on his own and was well aware that once the media realised who was in charge, the old 'hero detective' news articles would soon resurface.

"Juliette Thompson is available whenever you require. I'll speak with her soon, get her to write you a statement. We can add to it once we know more," Smith said with a dry grin. "At least the public will be pleased to hear you're in charge."

George grimaced. "Whoever decided I was a hero was an idiot."

Smith chuckled. "What you did was heroic, George, whether you like it or not. And anyway, it helps us. With the funding cuts and the bad press from the recent police cover-ups, it's about time the public had a little faith in the police."

George stood up and smiled. "Thanks, boss."

Smith grunted. "No problem, Beaumont. Keep me posted, yeah?"

Chapter Five

Lindsey Yardley rang and said as long as George was still happy for her to do it, she could squeeze in Rawlinson's post-mortem later that day. Lindsey had all the necessary experience, as she had often deputised for Dr Ross, as well as a five-year degree in medicine. Despite only being twenty-six, that meant Lindsey was more than qualified for her job as a Crime Scene Co-ordinator and should have been making the big bucks as a pathologist. With her obvious skills and intelligence, he knew it would be foolish for him to underestimate her. Yet why was she a Crime Scene Co-ordinator and not a pathologist?

He thought about the question as he made his way to meet Lindsey Yardley. As usual, George was late, but this time, it wasn't his fault. He'd spent valuable time with Juliette, their press expert, writing a statement he'd deliver later. As he looked down from the viewing gallery, Lindsey had already begun inspecting the body from all angles. Lying naked on the metal table, George could see the extent of the vicious attack that Alec Rawlinson had suffered.

Lindsey clicked the button on the recorder and spoke. "The victim is a well-nourished fifty-three-year-old IC1 Caucasian male identified as Alec Rawlinson. Initial observations show...

thirteen stab wounds to the throat, chest and abdomen causing evisceration."

Thirteen? Evisceration? Jesus Christ.

She had no assistant to pass her any equipment, so the fresh-faced young woman retrieved her ruler herself. She laid it across Alec's chest, measuring multiple wounds, meticulously recording each one. "The entry wounds are smooth and measure thirty-eight millimetres across. The murder weapon had a sharp tip and was non-serrated."

George pressed the button that allowed his voice to carry down to the room below. "Were all the wounds made by the same weapon?" he asked.

Lindsey glanced up at George and nodded. He depressed the button so he could hear her speak. "Yes, the same weapon, though some wounds aren't as deep as others."

He thought about the size of the wound and the fact it lacked serration and was caused by a sharp tip. "What are we thinking? A knife?" George asked.

"Yes. A chef's knife."

That didn't help much. Chef's knives were easily available. Shops readily sold them, and most homes carried them. He wondered how the uniformed officers were getting on with their search of the skips and bins. A murder weapon was extremely helpful in that they could tie it to the murder and then tie it to the Killer. He doubted they'd find anything, however. It was never that easy.

"Do we know whether the ring finger was removed ante-mortem?"

"Post-mortem," she said. "As was the evisceration, which is strange as that's usually done ante-mortem."

"Any signs of sexual activity?"

She shook her head. "Evidence of sperm and semen inside the foreskin, which suggests arousal. There's zero evidence a condom was used. Also, there are no foreign skin cells around his penis, suggesting a lack of vaginal or anal sex. His mouth was bleached. Take that as you will. I'll check the contents of his stomach for you."

"No signs of any damage to his anus other than whatever the decapitated finger would have caused?"

She raised a brow. "No."

No sexual contact at all, then. "Time of death?" George asked.

"Between 7 pm and 9 pm on Sunday," she replied.

Lindsey took samples from beneath Rawlinson's fingernails and explained to George that they were clean, and it didn't look like there were any skin samples there. She also confirmed his earlier suspicion that there were no defensive wounds either, so Rawlinson hadn't put up a fight. It surprised him, though, given the size of Alec. He must have known his attacker. He told Lindsey as much, who shrugged.

"Could he have been drugged, then?" he asked the young Crime Scene Co-ordinator.

"I've no idea, but I've taken samples for toxicology. Until the results come back, I won't know."

"Any idea when that will be?" He was wary of putting pressure on the young woman, but he needed something, anything.

She shook her head and ignored him for a moment, making notes. When she finally looked up, she arched an eyebrow, and George saw her tongue poke through her lips. "It's getting late, so probably tomorrow now. Tomorrow afternoon I'd say unless the lab rushes it through."

George thought about the Super, who told him the Chief

CHAPTER FIVE

Super had asked for their results to be the priority. "Thanks, Lindsey. As I'm sure you can understand, as SIO, I'm under pressure to get results."

"Aren't we all?" There was an abrasive tone in her voice.

* * *

Before going home, George wanted to speak to DCI Shelly Arnold, the detective in charge of the murder of his ex-colleague, Nate Patterson.

She was in court most of the week and would probably be there for a while yet. Still, she might be able to take a ten-minute call and answer some questions for him. Plus, she may have even had some information she could send him.

"Hi DCI Arnold, it's DI Beaumont."

"Now then, George. How're you?"

"Yeah, good, Ma'am, thanks. Listen, I'm SIO on murder—"

"Heard all about it, young man. Sounds similar to Nate's, eh?"

"It does, Ma'am. DSU Smith asked me to look into it whilst you're in court. Is there anything you can tell me?"

"Not really. Files are on HOLMES. But to be succinct, we got fuck all. The young man liked visitors to his flat. We got a shit-ton of DNA but got nowhere with it—no signs of sex. Nothing stolen. He was tied up, but we got no prints or DNA from the cable ties."

"How did he die, Ma'am?"

"Like Rawlinson, love. Stabbed to fuck. Chef's knife, Dr Ross said. He was experienced by the look of the wounds. Scary stuff. We looked at the usual people: exes, family members, friends, and colleagues. All had alibis. It's why you weren't questioned, as you were at the station during the time of death. The case went cold immediately."

"Amber Jones, too. I'm sure you remember her."

Like he could forget. The one that got away and broke his heart in the process.

"All I can say, George, is good luck."

"Thanks, Ma'am," he said. She'd been no help whatsoever.

Chapter Six

After tea, which consisted of a microwaved mushroom linguine, he took the case file and opened a bottle of cider and sat in his favourite armchair to read. After speaking with DSU Jim Smith earlier about Mia and his baby son, he desperately wanted to see them both. But, as it wasn't his day, he knew the best option was for him to stay home and keep to the schedule they'd both agreed on. It meant Mia wouldn't get used to seeing him, and it meant George got used to not seeing his son every day. He didn't like it, but it was for the best.

The press conference had been a success, primarily down to Juliette and her help writing a statement, and witnesses were asked to contact HMET and provide statements.

Before each detective on his team had left, he'd reminded them to type up everything they'd done into HOLMES 2. They'd all complied, and George had taken the printouts home with him. He liked to spread out the pages on his living room floor and look at the entire picture as if the printouts were pieces of a puzzle. Like that, he could move them around and consider them from all angles.

He picked up the report from the crime scene. The Crime Scene Co-ordinator, Lindsey Yardley, had signed off on the report. It wasn't complete—they were still waiting on some lab results—but it had come in just before he left, and so he hadn't had the chance to read it yet.

In Rawlinson's room at the B&B, they'd found prints belonging to the B&B owners Matthew and James Lancaster, B&B cook and housekeeper Sylvia Gordon, weekend girl Cassandra Broadchurch, as well as Alec Rawlinson and four other unknowns who weren't on the database. Three sets of prints were found on the fire escape door, those of Rawlinson, Broadchurch and a further unknown person who wasn't on the database. One of the unknowns could be the killer, but without a match on the database, it could have been anybody.

The handcuffs had been cleaned, and they had no prints on them at all, which George found odd. He assumed the attacker had brought them with him and had rather worn gloves or wiped and cleaned them after Rawlinson was dead. With the number of books and TV shows on crime and police procedure now readily available, people were more forensically aware, not that it usually stopped the SOCOs from finding anything. This was very unusual. Very unusual indeed. The DNA from the blood in the en-suite hadn't come back yet, but it would. Same for any DNA on the cuffs, door handles, and the Do Not Disturb sign.

Josh was on Rawlinson's accounts, awaiting a warrant from DCS Mohammed Sadiq. Hopefully, they'd find something that would shed some light on why he'd been murdered. DC Scott had spoken with the providers, and they should have the call and text information from Rawlinson's phone tomorrow. From Rawlinson's licence, DC James had spoken to his wife, Christie Cauldwell Rawlinson, who was coming down from Wetherby tomorrow to make a complete statement and to identify the body formally.

Next, he read the preliminary lab report. They'd been busy and had matched the blood type found in the en-suite to Rawlinson. Calder Park will have a DNA profile for them tomorrow. George leaned back in his chair and took a swig of cider. It was sweet but tangy. Refreshing. He thought about Lindsey's working theory. After killing Rawlinson, he left him lying on the bed and went into the en-suite and washed the blood off the knife and cleaned themselves—which would have been risky considering the risk of skin cells and hair follicles being left behind—or he did what Terry had said, and changed out of whatever clothes he'd been wearing whilst he'd murdered Rawlinson. George tried to put himself into the attacker's shoes and couldn't help but think those were both strangely relaxed actions considering what had happened and a complete contradiction to the frenzied attack he'd just committed.

George wondered what his childhood friend Mark Finch would make of it. Mark was a renowned criminal profiler who had worked for most of Britain's law enforcement agencies during his glittering career. He made a mental note to ask Mark to meet him for a drink. He'd thought about him during the Bone Saw Ripper case but had been so busy being manipulated by the psycho ex-DCI that he didn't have time to call him. It would be helpful to run this past him unofficially; see what he made of it.

Taking out the crime scene photographs the young SOCO had taken, he spread them out across the floor. He studied the image of Rawlinson lying on crimson-stained sheets; his blood pooled beside him, his arms and legs outstretched, cuffed to the iron bed frame.

There was no trace of sperm or semen in or around the body, other than the tip of his own penis, but it was interesting that there were traces of bleach in his mouth, as if somebody had tried to wash something away. I reminded him of the Bone Saw Ripper. Was somebody messing with him? And why? He could only think of one reason—body fluids. Whether that was sperm, semen or saliva, somebody had attempted to destroy that DNA. George had left before Lindsey had cut up the cadaver, and she hadn't rung or messaged him about anything interesting. That meant she didn't find any sperm or semen inside Rawlinson's stomach.

From the images, the B&B room contained lots of expensive items other than the watches they'd found in his draw. Rawlinson owned a lot of earrings and other pieces of jewellery made from precious metals. Their victim, it seemed, liked the expensive things in life.

It wasn't a burglary, just as George had expected. This was a personal, premeditated attack. Somebody had it in for Rawlinson; that was clear. And now he had to find out why. Once he did that, it would lead him to who.

Next, George read through the reports DC Tashan Blackburn had compiled for him. George had sent him down to interview Mr and Mr Lancaster, Sylvia Gordon, Cassandra Broadchurch and Steve Lancaster. They all saw and heard nothing. In a separate report, Tashan advised he'd taken prints and DNA from them for elimination purposes and had asked about the alarm on the fire escape.

He was told there was no such alarm.

George yawned loudly and, to his surprise, was ready for bed. He stood up from his chair, and as he did so, his phone beeped. It was an email from Calder Park. The toxicology results.

He sat down again and opened the report, his eyes straining from the small font. The report told him nothing he didn't know or nothing he hadn't assumed. There was zero evidence of any sedatives or anything else nasty in the man's bloodstream. He'd definitely not been drugged, which meant the attacker had to have relied on the element of surprise to attack his victim. George kept going back to it, and all he could think about was that Rawlinson was a tall, fit, well-muscled man. He wasn't old at fifty-three. He thought back to what Yolanda had said. Was their culprit a he or a she? A he, he decided. Definitely. It had to be a man. It was the strength to subdue him and then cuff him, the strength to pierce the breastbone. There was no way it was a woman, but then—

George thought about Lindsey Yardley's working theory again. There was no evidence Rawlinson was attacked as he opened the door, and there was no evidence of Rawlinson defending himself. So, he must have gotten onto the bed willingly. That also meant he must have been cuffed willingly. Was this a sex fetish gone wrong? And who was involved? There were no bodily fluids other than his own, male or female. He thought about the bleach in Rawlinson's mouth. That was a trick adopted by Jack the Butcher and the Bone Saw Ripper to remove traces of their DNA after they'd had sex with their victims. They were both males. Was Rawlinson a gay or bisexual man, and was that why he was naked in a B&B room in Headingley when he should have been at his home on Linton Lane in Wetherby with his wife?

It was certainly an interesting idea, but an idea with no evidence. He mulled it over in his mind before putting it to one side. George would discuss it with DS Wood in the morning. He also wanted to bring Yardley into a briefing to explain her working theory to his team.

Chapter Seven

George left his flat early the following day and drove the five miles to Elland Road Police Station. It was a crisp, April day that threatened showers, but it would be May soon, and he thought about how much he loved the month of May as he turned his face towards the sun, knowing it wouldn't be long before he'd be enjoying the warmth. April had been a dreary rain-drenched month, one of the worst rainfalls on record, and George couldn't wait for it to be over.

Detective Superintendent Smith was in his office. George grinned. He found it funny that no matter how early he got in, the DSU was there. George put the case file on his desk, took off his jacket, and slung it over the back of his office chair. He had only one thought on his mind. *Coffee.*

He passed Smith's office on the way to get coffee, raising his hand in greeting at his boss as he passed. Smith was on the phone and responded with a nod of his head. The squad room was relatively quiet that morning without the humming of the electronics and staccato of chatter, more peaceful than he'd expected, especially as they had a new murder case to get their claws into.

The coffee machine sputtered into life quietly as it poured him a semi-decent latte. It was nowhere as good as Starbucks nor as good as McDonald's, but it was decent enough, especially the smell that he inhaled before taking his first sip.

On his way back to his office, a deep, grumbling Geordie voice cut through the silence. "George, I need you for a minute. Come here."

Smith's deep rumble had startled him. They were the only two people in the office. He followed his boss into his office, the shades still drawn. It wasn't good news, whatever it was, especially by the look on Smith's face.

"Is everything OK, sir?"

The Detective Superintendent's office was fitted with the same computer and desk as the rest of the squad room and the same as everyone else with offices, such as George and the other detectives of rank Inspector and above. He hadn't wanted any special treatment, despite being the boss. George respected him for that. Opposite the desk were two small chairs that faced it, and George took the one on the left nearest to the door, as he usually did. On his desk were the pictures of his wife, Alexa, and their twins, Brad and Jenny.

Smith studied the brilliant blond detective in front of him, seeing his hungry green eyes, and frowned. "I've got some news that I'm not sure you're going to like, George."

His stomach sank, and he closed his eyes. Was he being taken off the case, after all? Had he performed that poorly in the last twenty or so hours? "What is it, sir?" He sat down, balancing his coffee on a knee, and waited for his boss to explain.

"I've just been on the phone with the Detective Chief Superintendent. He knows the victim, Alec Rawlinson, personally."

"Rawlinson? Really? How?"

"Rawlinson's a close personal friend, apparently. He wants the bastard who killed him found immediately."

CHAPTER SEVEN

George stared at him. "You're serious? Shit..."

"He's pissed, George. I've never heard him as irate. He wants more detectives on the case, more resources, everything. You name it; we got it. If you need overtime, all you've got to do is ask."

"Wow. Could have done with this during the Bone Saw Ripper case," George said, which received a frown from his boss. "So what does that mean, then?" asked George, his eyes locked with Smith's.

"For now, it means he's sending a personal representative to work with you on the case."

He rolled his eyes. Every time he was SIO on a case, there seemed to be some kind of threat to his position. First, it was Wakefield and a hotshot DCI taking over; then, it was a hotshot DCI who took over the Bone Saw Ripper case and turned out to be the culprit... It was clear why his boss had thrown that in there in such a way, almost like an aside. "A representative? What kind? Who?"

"Someone you know, actually. She's gone up in the world since she last worked here, though." For some reason, George felt his stomach lurch. He wasn't sure who it could be. Who had he worked with before? The look on his face must have prompted Smith to continue as he said, "It's Catherine Jones." His tone even.

"I don't know a Catherine Jones," George said, confused.

"What? Of course, you do. You worked with her when she was a young DC." George raised his brow, still not knowing who he was talking about. "At least it's not a stranger," Smith added. "I'm sure whatever happened between you two can just be water under the bridge."

And then it clicked. DC Jones. DC Amber Jones, the pretty

blonde detective he'd slept with before Mia, the result of too much alcohol and an empty stomach. The entire station had known about it, yet it had been Smith who had approached him directly. "Amber?"

"Yeah, though she goes by her first name now, which is Catherine. If I remember right, before she transferred, you two worked well together, right?"

He was right. They had worked well together. Too well, and that was the problem. As were the tequila shots downed on empty stomachs.

George forced a smile, but he couldn't keep it going. Such was the sheer shock. His smile turned into a grimace. "I don't need another DC on my team, sir. DS Wood is my deputy. Putting a DC who is expected to be a representative of the DCS is going to screw up the rank dynamics in my team. I have to refuse, sir. I'm sorry."

Smith was shaking his head whilst George spoke. He didn't interrupt him, however, and George had great respect for that. "She's not with the police any more but is now a well-respected criminal psychologist. DCS Sadiq thinks Catherine being around will help drive the investigation forward."

George couldn't argue with his boss, not when he'd also thought about speaking to a well-respected criminal profiler himself. "Fair enough. When is she arriving?"

"Today." Smith looked at his watch. "Soon, actually. The DCS isn't wasting any time on this. He wants the bastard locked up. Rawlinson has a wife and two young kids. They're mortified, as you can imagine."

George understood. Put him in their shoes, and he'd feel the same way. It just wasn't as easy. Even with a criminal psychologist, any profile they created was still just an educated guess. They still had to commit to the gruelling police work and leave no stone unturned. It could take weeks, especially as they had zero clues. He hated to think this way, but without another murder, they may never find this guy.

"OK, sir," he said. "But this is still my case, right? I'm not handing it over to the DCS or her?"

Smith didn't meet his eye but shook his head. "She doesn't work for us any more, George. She's just Catherine Jones, the criminal psychologist. You're still in charge. And even if Shelly gets back early from the trial, she won't be taking over, OK?"

"OK. Good. Thanks, sir. Appreciate it." George took a sip of his coffee, but suddenly it tasted sour.

"One more thing, Beaumont."

"Sir?"

"I don't think I need to remind you of your history with Miss Jones. Nor do I need to remind you that Professional Standards almost got involved because of the recent accusations lodged against you." George nodded and held eye contact. He wouldn't let his boss down. Nor would he cheat on Isabella. "You're a young, single man, who definitely has his faults as he supports Leeds, but... how do I say this? Be careful. Don't fuck up a glittering career because of a young blonde. Alright?"

"I might be single, sir, but nobody will impede me in solving this crime. Nor will I screw up my career. I understand your concerns, sir, but please let me prove to you I can work with her. I don't want to, and it'd be better if I didn't have to. But I understand it's not your call."

"I'm sorry, George, but he's my boss. And I'm yours. Play ball, yeah?"

George sighed and nodded. His boss was right; even if he didn't like that, he was right.

***

As soon as George left Smith's office, he went outside for a breath of fresh air. It was pissing it down again. April was indeed the worst month of the year. It used to be January, but now he had his son's birthday to look forward to each year.

Catherine Amber Jones.

He didn't think he'd ever see her again. Though, thinking back, it wasn't that long ago, and she'd still be in her mid-twenties. It was quite the age gap when he thought about it. At the time, he'd been confused and, if he was honest, bitter at his girlfriend at the time who had broken up with him because of the demands his work placed on him. He'd been with Rachel for three years, getting with her when he became a DC and her ending it with him when he became a DS and transferred to Elland Road. Why was it that women liked the idea that he was a detective but then threw everything away when they realised it wasn't just a title but hard graft? It made no sense to him. It was during his promotion party that he'd bumped into Catherine, a five-foot-five athletic blonde bombshell with an easy, down-to-earth personality. To top it off, she'd also had the most amazing amber-coloured eyes and cute dimples. Despite knowing her by reputation, within hours of being at the party, she'd had him eating out of her palm. She left Elland Road not long after, and George assumed it was because of what they'd done. But now, it seemed, she was back.

"You OK, boss?" asked DC Terry Morton. "Case getting to you already?"

George shook his head and followed him inside. "You're in early today, Terry." They signed in and walked up the stairwell together.

CHAPTER SEVEN

"Er... Yeah, the wife has taken the kids to see her parents in London, so I've got the house to myself. Waking up alone meant I got up early. I hoped it would be the other way around."

George chuckled. "Aren't your kids my age, mate?" George asked.

"Aye, lad. Well, in their twenties, like. Gonna be a grandad soon, our kid. That's why our lass has taken them to London. They need the good news. To be honest with you, her parents are getting on a bit, and our lass is worried about them."

George nodded and thought about his mother. He hadn't seen her in nearly a year, and she hadn't come down from Scotland to visit her grandson yet. Their relationship was fractured because of George's father, the piece of shit who used to beat him black and blue.

"Sorry to hear about it, Terry." He said goodbye to Terry and made his way to his office. On his way, he spotted DS Cathy Hoskins, an experienced counsellor he'd been meaning to have a word with. Whenever he looked for her, it seemed she was busy on a case. She was laughing with another female officer, an officer he recognised but didn't know why. As he got closer, he realised it was Holly Hambleton, the DC from the Bone Saw Ripper case. Another victim of the criminal officer, Alexander Peterson. Cathy had a cup in her hand, and George thought that for someone who dealt with grief all the time, as she was an FLO, she was a remarkably upbeat woman. But then he guessed she had to be; otherwise, the horror of it all would drag her down.

"Hi, Cathy," he said. "Nice to see you."

She gave him a smile and a wave. "It's nice to see you too, George. How are you?"

DS Hoskins had worked with him, helping the relatives of the victims on the Miss Murderer case, and not only had he gotten to know her reasonably well, but he'd gotten to know just how good she was at her job. With her soft tone and matronly ways, she was the type of person anybody would listen to and open up to. She had a warm, inviting smile and sympathetic eyes, and he hoped Mia would benefit from any help Cathy could provide.

"Have you got a spare minute, Cathy?"

She nodded. "Your office?" He nodded and followed behind her.

With an encouraging smile, she said, "Are you OK, George?"

He took a deep breath. "It's Mia."

She smiled knowingly. "Is she still struggling?" Cathy not only knew what had happened after giving birth to Jack but knew she'd been a victim of the Miss Murderer—neither were secrets.

"Yeah. She's doing better, but I'm struggling, too. I really want to help her, but she tells me the only way I can help is by moving back in with her. I can't do that. It wouldn't be fair to either of them."

"It also wouldn't be fair to you, George. What are her symptoms at the moment? Does she have panic attacks? Flashbacks? Or is it more a mixture of highs and lows? Mia's been through a lot during the last year."

He ran a hand through his hair and stuck his tongue through his lips. "She's not being frank with anybody, and so I can only tell you what I've seen and what she's told me. Mia definitely has panic attacks, but I'm not sure about flashbacks. She's on a cocktail of drugs for post-partum psychosis and weekly CBT. I can see improvements, but she tells me she's struggling."

"It sounds like she might be struggling with PTSD, too,"

Cathy said. "How much help did she get after what she went through with Adam Harris?"

George wasn't confident because he was dealing with his own demons after Adam Harris. He'd been stabbed and was on strong pain meds for a while. He was also having nightmares and flashbacks himself and was using alcohol as a crutch. George knew Mia had sought help, but he hadn't been around for her as much as he should have been. Cathy must have mind-reading abilities because she said, "You can't blame yourself, George. She was the cause for the relationship to break down, and she's a grown woman who you aren't responsible for."

"Thanks, Cathy. Will you talk to her for me?"

Cathy raised her eyebrows in surprise. "Me? That wasn't what I was expecting, to be honest."

"Please, Cathy. DSU Smith knows she's struggling, and I can mention the trauma she suffered at the hands of Adam Harris. She met you after the case. She remembers you. I know this because she mentioned you in conversation, so I think she'll talk to you. You're also a trained trauma counsellor. Please, Cathy, you're the best option we've got. I don't know what else to do."

Cathy nodded slowly. "OK, get DSU Smith to clear it with my boss. If she says yes, I'll see her when I'm next available. How does that sound?"

He smiled and stood up, nodding. "Thank you, Cathy. I don't think you realise just how much this means to me."

She grinned and got up to leave. "You're a good man, George. You need to realise that Mia's trauma isn't, and never was, your fault. Take care, and I'll speak to you soon. Yeah?"

"Yeah," he replied and sat back down. As Cathy left his office, he felt as if a literal weight had been lifted from his shoulders.

He knew if anyone could get through to Mia, it was Cathy.

* * *

After Cathy had left, Yolanda had popped by to ask George to visit Incident Room Five when he got a moment so she could update him on the CCTV situation. George followed her immediately and learnt there were several CCTV cameras in the streets around the B&B where Rawlinson had been murdered, but annoyingly none that picked up any of the entrances in or out of the warren-like streets, nor the parking outside the B&B, or the front entrance to the B&B itself.

The pathologist had put the time of death between 7 pm and 9 pm on Sunday, and so the CCTV team, Yolanda and Tashan, were scrolling through footage they'd found of the surrounding area looking for anything suspicious within a six-hour window between five and eleven that night. So far, they'd come up with absolutely nothing.

DS Wood entered Incident Room Five and smiled at George. "The weekend girl, Cassandra Broadchurch, is here," Wood told him. "She's in Interview Room Two with an appropriate adult."

"Brilliant, Wood. Thanks. Shall we head down there now?"

She nodded, and they left the incident room. As they left the squad room, George felt a presence behind him. He turned.

"Can I come too, George?" a young, feminine voice with a Welsh accent said.

Chapter Eight

"Hello, Catherine," he said casually as if he were greeting a colleague he hadn't seen for a while, not a woman he'd slept with and, if he were being brutally honest with himself, fallen a little in love with. It was one of his flaws. Somehow, he'd always fallen in love just a little too quickly. He took her in. She still looked great—not exactly as he remembered; her hair now fell in waves down her back and was no longer blonde, but instead, an intense black. Her pale skin was practically devoid of make-up, apart from the smoky eyeshadow around her amber-coloured eyes. Overall, she pulled off a dark, seductive look.

DS Wood coughed, and with a start, he realised he was staring.

"Hey to you too. Can I come with you two and meet the weekend girl?"

He shrugged. "Sure, you can watch via video link."

Catherine hesitated. Once a detective, always a detective. She was clearly dying to sit in on the interview, but she'd only just arrived. He met her eyes, daring her to challenge him. This would set a precedent for their working agreement. She furrowed those dark, seductive eyes. She said nothing, clearly not wanting to muscle her way in. He knew that wasn't her style, anyway. Catherine Jones was the type that charmed her way in, and he knew that she'd charm the rest of his team before the day was out. He'd seen her at work before. The only question really was whether he was immune to those charms himself.

"OK, George. Whatever you want." She winked, yet those amber eyes lacked the sparkle they had just minutes before. Instead, she glared at him rather frostily as he smiled and nodded. The smile was petty, he knew that, but he didn't want Catherine, nor the DCS, to butt in on his investigation.

"Good. Shall we go, then?"

He led the way down the stairwell to the ground floor, conscious of Catherine's heels clicking on the steps behind him. Catherine was wearing white heels and blue skinny jeans, he noticed, and a white t-shirt exposing a small amount of cleavage, with a peach-coloured waterfall cardigan. Casual office attire. She looked good.

DS Wood had said nothing at all during the earlier exchange, and he wondered whether she'd been at Wakefield during the time of his fling with Catherine. He'd speak to her later and explain their history. It was the least he could do. They soon got to the ground floor, and as they walked past the office with the equipment for the video link, Wood spoke to a PC who pointed it out to Catherine. She pushed open the door and disappeared inside without glancing at either of them.

"Hello, Cassandra. I'm Detective Inspector Beaumont, and this is Detective Sergeant Wood. We're going to ask you a few questions about The Boundary where you're employed and about a guest who stayed there named Alec Rawlinson. We are recording this conversation."

The four adults—DI Beaumont, DS Wood, Cassandra's

solicitor, and Cassandra's father—identified themselves for the tape before Cassandra said, "I'm Cassandra Broadchurch. Call me Cassie."

"Hi, Cassie," George said.

"Am I in trouble?" She trembled as she spoke, her blue eyes showing fear.

"Have you done something wrong?" George asked her.

She shook her head. "No, detective."

"Then you're not in any trouble, Cassie." He smiled, and he saw her lips turned up ever so slightly at the corners; he saw the fear leave her eyes. Her shoulders dropped as she relaxed.

Her father squeezed her arm. "See. I told you," he said.

George couldn't believe how young she looked. From her date of birth, she was a week shy of eighteen, yet she looked no older than thirteen. Cassie had a pale complexion and dark shadows under her eyes. Either she worked too hard or had been up all night. Maybe both. Maybe she was guilty. But probably not. "How long have you been working for the Lancasters?" he asked.

She thought for a moment and blew a stray blonde strand from her face. "About a year and six months. Something like that."

"How did you find out about the job?"

"I live in Headingley. I go to college during the week, and at the weekend, I wanted to earn some money. The ad was on Facebook. I asked my mum and dad, and they said yes."

George glanced at his sergeant, who nodded. She was committing the details to memory, with not a pad and pen in sight.

"How are the Lancasters to work for? Are they nice men?"

Cassie hesitated for a split second. Her dad nor the solicitor noticed, but Wood did. She shot George a look. He shot one back. "I don't see James that much, as he's in the office a lot. Erm, as for Matthew, most of the time, he lets me get on with my job."

"Most of the time? Can you explain?"

She looked at her dad and shifted in her seat. Her dad smiled and nodded. "I think the Lancasters are having marital problems. Instead of being at the reception desk like he's supposed to be, sometimes he comes to the rooms and watches me work. I don't like it, but he says he wants to talk about his problems, and he has nobody else. They're close to a divorce, apparently."

George nodded. "James and Matthew Lancaster are close to a divorce?"

She looked at her solicitor, who nodded her head. "That's what it sounds like. I think—I think James is having an affair." She flicked her tongue out and in, then nibbled her lip. "He's always taking calls in the office. James is, I should clarify. I think he's got a dating app on his phone and meets people from there at the B&B."

"How do you know this and the fact he has a dating app on his phone?" Wood asked.

George nodded. They were excellent questions, ones he was about to ask himself.

From the look on her face, Cassie didn't want to answer. "Go on, love," her father, Justin Broadchurch, said.

"He—he paid me to nab his phone and check. It was—it was a few weeks ago. Maybe a month or so."

"He?" Wood asked.

"Matthew Lancaster. He paid me to steal James' phone. I did, and I checked his apps. I'm not gonna lose my job by telling you this, am I? I really need the money."

"Anything you say in here is being recorded, Cassandra," her solicitor said. "That means the detectives can, and will, use it if necessary. You can withdraw your cooperation at any point. You just let me know, OK?"

Cassie nodded, and a rush of anger ran through George. Whilst the solicitor was right, what Cassie was telling them made a lot of sense. It also put the Lancasters right in the frame, especially James Lancaster, if he'd arranged for Rawlinson to meet him there. But DSU Smith would need more than the words of a teenage girl to give them a warrant to search the Lancaster's devices. *Shit.*

"Did you work on Sunday?" George asked, attempting to shift the discussion away from the Lancasters for the moment and to the day of the murder. He'd come back to it later, hoping she was still cooperating.

"Yes. I work every Saturday and Sunday for Mr and Mr Lancaster."

"Was anybody else at work on Sunday?"

"Mrs Gordon."

"How many guests were staying at the B&B?"

She shrugged. "I don't know. That's not my job."

"I see," Wood said. "How many rooms did you clean on Sunday?"

She frowned, confused. Wood expanded on her question. "I have your statement here, taken by Detective Constable Blackburn." Wood smiled. "It states you clean the rooms of the people who check out Saturday morning and Sunday morning each week."

"Yes. Of course." Cassie smiled and nodded her head. "Two or three. I really can't remember."

"So two or three rooms were vacated on Sunday morning?"

"Something like that."

"Then what do you do?"

"You have my statement there?" She looked at her dad and solicitor.

"I do," Wood confirmed. "But I'd like to hear it from you in your own words. What do you do after cleaning vacant rooms?"

"I ran the reception."

George knew what Wood was getting at. Matthew Lancaster said he's been on reception all day Sunday. "Did you run reception on Sunday?"

She nodded. "In the afternoon until I left at 6 pm. I started at 10 am. I'm only allowed to work eight hours."

"Were you the one who got Mr Alec Rawlinson booked into his room?"

"Correct. At around 3 pm."

"And was he the only guest at the B&B that day?"

"He was the only guest I helped, but you'd have to ask the owners if there was anybody else."

"How did Mr Rawlinson seem to you when you dealt with him at reception?"

"Excited. Happy." She looked at her dad and her solicitor. They both nodded reassuringly. "He kept looking at me funny. It gave me chills. I find it hard to describe, but I felt like he was checking me out."

"Checking you out?" Wood asked. "I realise this must be difficult for you, but can you explain?"

"I was in leggings and a long t-shirt because I'd been cleaning this morning. When I turned around to get his key, I felt as if he was staring at me. When I took him up to his room, I felt the same. It was like he was trying to bore a hole into me as he followed closely behind me. It's a silly thing to say, but it's something the guys say at college. They're all dirty pervs trying to see underneath our clothes. It's fine, all flirty banter. But when you feel that an older adult is trying to do that to you, it feels wrong. Gross. I didn't like it."

"Did you report it?" Wood asked.

"No. He said thank you and tipped me. After that, I thought I was being paranoid."

"What did you do next?" George asked, moving the conversation along.

She thought for a moment. "I went back to reception."

"Did any other guests arrive until you left at 6 pm?"

She shook her head. "It was a bit of a boring day. Even Matthew, Mr Lancaster, was nowhere to be seen. I sat and read a book."

Matthew's statement didn't add up, and Wood realised it too, as she shot him a knowing look. He'd told them he'd been at reception all day. He'd told Tashan the same. They needed to get him in, and fast. He had the opportunity and means to kill Rawlinson. But what was his motive? He thought back to an earlier hypothesis that possibly Alec was a gay man. If so, maybe James Lancaster *had* arranged a meeting with him at the B&B, and if Matthew had found out about it, then that would give him a motive. Maybe Matthew killed his husband's lover out of jealous rage? It was one of the oldest motives in the book.

A thought struck him. "You mentioned Rawlinson watched you, and you felt gross. Did he ever..." He petered off, unsure how to phrase it. "Did he make an advance towards you?"

"What?" She didn't understand.

"Did he actually come on to you, try to touch you, anything

like that?"

She rocked her head, fear in her eyes. "No! I'm not like that. I don't do that..."

"Nobody is saying you did, Cassie," Wood said. "We have to ask the important questions. Has—has anybody older taken advantage of you before? Ever? A grown man or a woman? Have they tried to touch you or anything?"

She folded her hands in her lap and looked down at the table. "No." She began to shake. "Never." She looked at her dad, who smiled. "Trust me." George didn't. She took a deep breath. "Has something happened to Mr Rawlinson?"

A brief pause. He made eye contact with Justin Broadchurch, who nodded his consent. "Yes, Cassie. I'm sorry to tell you he was found dead in his room yesterday morning."

A shaking hand flew to her mouth, and a tear swelled from one eye.

"Are you OK, Cassandra?" her solicitor asked her. "Do you want a break? Some water, perhaps?"

She shook her head. "I'm OK. Thank you. I'm just shocked, alright?" She wiped away a fat tear and fought to regain her composure. George could see the questions were flying around her head.

"He was stabbed," he told her, observing Cassie's face for clues. He didn't think she was the killer, but after all, she was the last known person to have seen him alive.

Her shoulders flopped as if she had lost all her energy. Her face turned pale. "Stabbed by who?"

"That's what we're trying to find out," George said. "Anything you can tell us would be helpful."

"I—I don't know anything," she said as another fat tear welled up in the corner of her eye. "I did my shift and left at six like I always do. Dad picked me up like he always does." Her hand fluttered across her face to wipe away the tears. "I can't believe he's dead."

DS Wood bent over and whispered something in George's ear. He frowned. "Who picked you up from work on Sunday, Cassie?"

She looked confused. "My dad did. He always..." Then she clicked. "Sorry, detectives. He didn't pick me up this week. I live in Headingley, and I walked home."

"Where did you go after you left the B&B?" Wood asked.

She glanced away from George. "I went straight home."

"Do you have anybody who could confirm that?" Wood asked. George looked at her, wanting to know what she was getting at. The young girl wasn't a suspect. Was she?

She shook her head. "Mum was at work, and Dad couldn't pick me up because he was—"

"At Elland Road," her dad cut in. "Leeds were playing Newcastle."

George was pretty confident she wasn't the murderer, but Wood obviously wasn't. "You went back to an empty home?" Wood asked.

Cassie nodded. George looked at her. She barely looked thirteen, small-boned and slender. He couldn't imagine her attacking a man of Rawlinson's size. Cassie also had no motive. Killing Rawlinson made absolutely no sense.

"You said your mum was at work. I'm sorry, but—"

"She means her step-mum, of course," Justin Broadchurch cut in. "We're well aware you'll have done background checks on us. Cassie's mum died when Cassie was young. I've been with Marie for five or six years now."

Isabella Wood smiled, but only George knew she wasn't

actually smiling. She was onto something, something big.

"OK, Cassie. Thank you for your time today. If we think of anything else, we'll be in touch. If you think of anything, call me." George handed a card to both Cassie and her dad.

"I can go home now?" She glanced from him to her solicitor and back again.

"Yeah, you can go now. The officer at the front desk will sign you out."

They left a PC to help them sign out and headed back upstairs to discuss the interview. On the stairwell, George stopped her and stole a quick kiss.

"You ever thought they might be cameras in here?" She had a sultry grin on her face.

"Yep. I checked. We're safe," he said. "Tell me what you found out. I saw the way you looked at her. The way you started questioning. What do you know?"

"There's something dodgy about her father, something I don't like. Vibes. A feeling."

"Speak to Josh and see if he can dig up some dirt."

She nodded, and they both turned to the sound of the stairwell door opening below. "Someone's coming, George." He let go of her waist and stepped back. "But there's something about Justin Broadchurch I don't trust. You should have seen the fear in her eyes when you asked her if Rawlinson had tried to touch her."

Chapter Nine

Catherine Jones was the one who entered the stairwell and saw George and Wood walking up. "Did you forget about me?" The two detectives stopped and smiled. "I don't think she had anything to do with it, do you?"

It's just like her to cut straight to the chase, George thought. But he agreed with her. "Nope, but we'll check her movements via CCTV, just to be sure."

"George, I need to write these notes up and then speak with DC Blackburn. Come find me when you're done here?" DS Wood said, and without waiting for an answer, climbed the stairs to reach the squad room.

"She's nice," Catherine said. He nodded, and her eyes immediately scanned his face. "It really is good to see you again, George."

He hesitated. "Likewise. Shall we?" He started to walk, but Catherine didn't move.

She gave a wry smile. "I heard you got engaged. And you have a son?"

He wondered who she'd heard it from. "A son, yes. Jack."

"Congratulations. When's the wedding?" The sincerity in her voice surprised him, but then he remembered how easy she was to talk to. Even after they'd slept together and the entire station was taking the piss, there had never been any awkwardness between them.

"There is no wedding. Mia and I split up last year. We're co-parenting Jack. I'm seeing him tonight, actually."

She raised her brows. "That's nice, some father and son bonding time. Are you single?"

George nodded his head upstairs. "Shall we?"

Catherine stepped forward, and they took the steps up to the squad room together. "You never answered my question. You look good, anyway. That's all I wanted to say."

"Thank you," he said, relaxing a little. "And to answer your question, yes. I'm single."

She laughed, and he realised he'd forgotten how nice her laugh was. "George Beaumont, the eligible bachelor, is single? Now there's a surprise. Does that mean I finally have a shot?"

She had her shot and broke his heart. His smile faded, and he changed the subject. "Have you profiled the killer yet?"

"Tell me about Rawlinson."

"Haven't you read the case files?"

"Yes. I have access to HOLMES via the DCS, but I want to hear it from *you*."

He shrugged. "I thought *you* were sent here to help *us*, especially with info on Rawlinson. Apparently, he's the Detective Chief Superintendent's best mate. We don't really know anything yet, considering we aren't even twenty-four hours in. So, in my opinion, you know a lot more about him than we do."

She fluttered those enormous amber eyes of hers, but her face remained neutral. "Fair enough, George. I'll tell you everything I know about Alec Rawlinson. OK? Get your team together, as I'd rather say this once, and move on to more important things." He didn't miss the sarcasm in her voice nor the harsh tone. It was clear she'd wanted to sit down and discuss the case with him personally, but he'd thought it was best to keep things official, keep his entire team in the loop. It saved repetition. And to be honest, it saved being alone with her.

George called his team together, and they all filed into the large incident room. Everybody was there, with George and Wood at the front, the sergeants behind him, and the constables behind them. Even the Detective Superintendent squeezed in at the back.

"Before Catherine speaks, Lindsey Yardley, the Crime Scene Co-ordinator, has agreed to share with us her working theory of how Alec Rawlinson was killed and to answer any questions you may have."

His team nodded, and Lindsey stood up at the front. She cleared her throat before she said, "Alec Rawlinson wasn't attacked at the door. He was attacked whilst he lay on the bed after being cuffed. There was no blood spatter in the room other than what was on and around the bed. We used luminol, a chemical used to detect trace amounts of blood at crime scenes, as it reacts with the iron in haemoglobin. Even if blood is washed away, we can still see it using this technique. It also proves your suspect entered the bathroom to wash, as tiny globules of blood were found. Like a trail of breadcrumbs. There were no drops identified on the way out of the room, suggesting a change of clothes."

"That rules out a surprise attack at the door, then?" DC Scott asked.

"Correct. Any questions?" she asked.

Nobody volunteered, and so Yardley and Jones switched

places.

"This information has come straight from Detective Chief Superintendent Mohammed Sadiq," Catherine began, standing at the head of the room. She had a kind of aura about her, a charm and charisma that made you lower your guard. "Alec Rawlinson was a local entrepreneur with great standing in the Leeds community. He was a success story, a man born into poverty who built a successful property business from nothing. He was a good friend and beneficiary of our force. Just this Friday, DCS Sadiq attended a dinner event to celebrate Rawlinson's business success this year. As you can imagine, he's personally affected by this terrible news."

She paused to let this sink in. George's team all had their eyes on Catherine, and all were silent. "His untimely demise," she added, "means it's in our interests to investigate Mr Rawlinson's unexpected death thoroughly, even if, as members of the police, you have to remain impartial. DI Beaumont suspects foul play, and given the high-profile nature of this incident, I have been asked to assist you all, but I need full disclosure. I thank you in advance."

"You'll have everything you need, Catherine. Won't she?" DSU Smith's voice boomed from the doorway. The detective constables in front of him shit themselves. "Also, we must be sensitive to the volume of press interest this case will generate. No leaks. Is that understood?"

George's entire team nodded, to which Catherine smiled.

"As you may have already heard, I'm a criminal profiler and a criminal psychologist. I have a lot of experience in those areas, and it's my job to come up with a profile of the sort of person *we're* looking for, to help *us* narrow down a pool of suspects." George noticed the way she used the words, we, and us. Catherine was invested.

"OK, Catherine," Terrence Morton said. "What *sort* of *person* are *we* looking for?" His words sounded edgy, and after speaking, he took a deep breath and smiled. "A white male, aged between eighteen and sixty. Am I right?" George saw him turn in his seat, looking at his colleagues. Most of them gave him a raised eyebrow, as did Lindsey.

She smiled, which lit up her face. George recognised Terry's tone and turned around to throw daggers at him. "What you must understand, DC Morton is that killers are just like you and me. Though, probably more you than me. I'm not a white male aged between eighteen and sixty like you said."

As George predicted, Catherine knew how to ruffle a few feathers and produce a few laughs. He held up a hand, calling for order at the giggling detectives.

She continued. "What I mean is, the killer is a hunter, just like you and me. A killer hunts its prey, and then we hunt them. The key to hunting them is to understand their motivations so we can arrest them and bring them to justice. A killer does the same. But instead, they try to understand their victims' lives, so they can come up with the best way to kill them."

There were murmurs of approval around the room. Catherine held up her hand. "I bet you're wondering how this relates to Rawlinson. Well, he was picked for a reason."

"In other words, motive," DC Morton shouted out. "They also have means and opportunity. This is nothing we don't already know."

Catherine shot Terry an irritated look. George noticed Lindsey did, too. *Morton better be careful,* George thought. Lindsey and Catherine didn't come across as women you could mess with.

"You're right, of course. Alec ticked the right boxes for the killer," Catherine replied. "There was something about the B&B that made the killer relax, so they could move freely without being rushed. And in a way, Alec was vulnerable; whoever did this cuffed him to the bed and mutilated him. He was a big man. Tall and muscular. Yet vulnerable."

"Yeah, exactly. You're not making sense, *girl*!" Morton called out. The room was deadly silent. He'd obviously expected his comment to send a ripple of laughter around the room. It hadn't.

On making eye contact with Morton, George noticed Lindsey. Her cheeks had turned red, and her eyebrows had narrowed.

"Stop it, Terry!" George commanded. "Miss Jones is here as our guest and at the request of the DCS."

Catherine flashed a quick smile at George and continued. "Alec didn't put up a fight. Why?"

"So, he likes victims who don't put up a fight," Morton said. "How does that help us find him?"

"A killer's behaviour mirrors their personality," she said. "From what we know, Alec paid for the room and, according to the weekend girl, seemed rather excited by the prospect of being there. Whoever killed him must have lured him there. Yet, the location was risky, being a B&B. This tells me the killer is calculated and not averse to risk. Think about the nature of the crime and the ultra-violence, and you begin to build up a picture of a killer who's violent, calculated, and not averse to risk. That's one hell of a terrifying killer."

George agreed with her. Whoever killed Alec Rawlinson was still out there. And that terrified him.

"So, tell us why he did it?" Morton asked.

"When killers kill, they've usually reached a stage where

their real life and their fantasy life have merged into one. In their real life, they're the opposite of what I've described; albeit to compensate for lack of power in their personal life, they may have sought a position of power in their professional one. This isn't uncommon and is often developed in childhood."

"The killing of animals and such?" Morton said. It wasn't a question.

"Precisely. How does a killer deal with that? Well, they build up a powerful fantasy in which they imagined things being extremely different."

"And then, killers can no longer distinguish between the two," George added.

She smiled at him. "Correct."

"From what I've seen of the scene and from the notes, the killer didn't dominate their victim sexually. That's interesting, considering he was cuffed naked to the bed," Morton said.

She shrugged. "Whoever killed Alec maybe didn't dominate him sexually, in a literal sense, but the fact he was naked and cuffed to the bed is suggestive, is it not? My initial theory was that a woman had cuffed him up with the promise of sex, and then when he was vulnerable, the violence started."

"A crime like this is very unlikely to be committed by a woman," DS Brewer said.

"The textbooks would agree with you, DS Brewer. I'm still on the fence," Catherine said.

"And there was no sign of sexual activity," Elaine continued. "Must be a man."

Catherine shrugged. "We don't have enough information yet. What's important, DS Brewer is that we look at the posing of the body. We have a killer who wants to be powerful, to dominate. We have a killer who wants to demean their victim.

That alone makes them powerful. It shows their dominance. Theory and experience tell me Alec Rawlinson was picked because of his size, his stature, and his wealth."

"And so, you think they killed Alec because they were jealous of him?" Elaine asked. "Well, that, or spite?"

Catherine nodded. "That's what I believe, yes. It's somebody so repressed in their private reality they felt the compulsion to divulge in their fantasy reality."

There were more murmurs around the room as George's team tried to wrap their heads around the idea of a person being capable of having separate, and even merging, realities.

"So why was Alec killed now?" DS Wood asked. An excellent question.

"Motive, opportunity and means most likely triggered by a recent traumatic event. It could be that the killer has killed before, and it's slipped through the net. Whatever it is, the killer is escalating." George thought back to Shelly Arnold's cold case. He hadn't shared that with Catherine yet.

"So? Who is it?" Morton said, his tone cocky.

"You know I can't do that, DC Morton. All I can do is help you narrow the pool of potential suspects. Look, I won't tell you the profiling system is perfect because it isn't. It's an educated guess, but I need you to try to do the best you can with it. To do that, I'll need your help."

"How can we assist?" DSU Smith asked from the back.

Catherine's gaze landed on George. "I need to be involved in the murder investigation at all levels. I need full disclosure so that I can help."

There was a soft murmur from his team. George hadn't expected any less from her.

She smiled. "But to answer your question, DC Morton.

CHAPTER NINE

Whoever killed Alec was known to him in some way. You don't let strangers into B&B rooms, and you certainly don't allow them to cuff you to a bed. There were no defensive marks on his body and no drugs in his system. He allowed his killer to cuff him to the bed."

Morton wolf-whistled. George was losing his temper with the man, and it seemed he wasn't the only one. Lindsey Yardley stood up with a clenched fist, suddenly slammed a hand on the table and said with a raised voice, "I think that's highly disrespectful of you, DC Morton."

"Yes!" George added, turning to face his detective. "Lindsey's right. If you have nothing good to add, then shut up!"

The middle-aged man nodded sheepishly.

"Maybe it was an escort? Or somebody he was meeting from a dating app? What about an old flame?" said DS Wood, diffusing the awkward atmosphere. "Perhaps he was cheating on his wife? His ring finger was found in a rather unusual place."

"I was getting to the ring finger. Thank you, DS Wood." Catherine pulled a stray strand of black hair away from her face. "And you're right. It's significant, if not symbolic. I'm hoping any leads you dig up will help narrow the suspect pool."

"We'll do everything in our power to assist you and the DCS, Catherine," cut in DSU Smith from the back.

Catherine beamed at him. "Thank you, sir. Your cooperation is very much appreciated."

George had to give it to her. She certainly knew how to get people on her side. Morton hadn't fallen for it, though. He wondered why as the meeting broke up, and his team all went back to their desks. But first, he went and asked Morton to meet him in his office. Once they were there, George gave him a right bollocking.

* * *

Lab reports with evidence from the crime scene were coming in dribs and drabs, but they provided no new leads. The search of the bins and skips in the area hadn't turned up any knives or bloodied clothing, and as yet, nothing of interest had been seen on the CCTV footage. Cassie had gone straight home as she'd said.

"The problem," George said when Catherine had come to his office for an update, "is we don't know who we're looking for yet." She smiled and perched on the corner of his desk. She seemed completely at ease with him whilst he felt nervous and was conscious of her every movement. "I know it's why you're here, but it could be anybody—man, woman, black, white, Hispanic, Asian. We've no idea. The majority of the lab reports have come in, and there's not a strand of DNA evidence at the crime scene. And as for CCTV, we've picked up even less. Headingley is like a labyrinth." He ran a hand through his thick, blond hair. He'd managed to cut down on the whisky drinking, but God, he'd kill for one right now. Maybe when he got home, he'd have a quick one.

"Have you spoken to Rawlinson's wife?" Catherine asked.

"No, not yet. She's coming down with Alec's mother this afternoon to identify his body. I said I'd meet her there so I could take a statement." He glanced at the time on his computer. It was just after half two. The afternoon was running away with itself.

"Do you mind if I come?" She winked and flashed him a dimpled smile.

He thought back to what the Detective Superintendent had said. It meant being alone with her on the way over, but he didn't have a good enough reason to refuse.

"Sure." He kept his tone jovial and added a smile. "Let me grab a sarnie from the canteen, and then we can head out."

"OK, I'll meet you in the car park in fifteen minutes."

His phone rang. He glanced down and saw that it was Mia.

"Make that twenty," he said.

Chapter Ten

After speaking with Mia and telling her he couldn't come and see Jack tonight due to a new murder investigation, George and Catherine set off in good time.

George wanted to know everything Catherine knew about Alec Rawlinson, and she obliged, explaining that as a boy, Alec lived in a flat in Beeston. His mother was a single mother who worked at a care home around the corner from the flat. His father left when Alec was very young, and because of the depression caused by the separation, his mother was soon sacked from the care home. Catherine told her all about Mrs Rawlinson's struggles with alcohol and drugs.

"How do you know all this?" George asked. He knew most of it himself but had only found out this morning when DS Josh Fry handed him a manilla folder full of details.

She winked and carried on with Alec's life story. His father, Alec Rawlinson Sr., drifted in and out of his life for the first five years of his life, apparently always drunk. The last time Alec or his mother saw Alec Rawlinson Sr. was the day he beat her up. The police had been called, and Alec had been sent to stay with his paternal grandmother for a couple of weeks. She'd been his salvation.

George agreed. When he'd looked through the printouts this morning, her name and signature had been on every school admissions form and every school meeting. In fact, if you named every positive action a parent could take for their child, his grandmother Eunice was the one responsible for it.

Despite having to navigate the nightmare traffic through the centre of Leeds, the pair arrived about twenty minutes before Christie Cauldwell Rawlinson was due to arrive, their patience wearing thin. They made their way through the corridors of the empty building, their footsteps echoing loudly until they reached the visitors' waiting room.

The area was sensitively furnished, the sofas and armchairs light grey and pastel green like the walls. There were tables within easy reach of the furniture, each displaying plants, magazines, and boxes of tissues. Mrs Rawlinson, Alec's mother, was sitting in a lonely armchair whilst Christie Cauldwell Rawlinson, Alec's wife, was sitting on a sofa between her two young children, holding their hands. Both kids had dark hair like their father and grandmother, but Christie was an attractive redhead about thirty, wearing a black, slim-fit mock neck t-shirt, charcoal skinny jeans and candy-red heels. The group's intense nervousness was obvious. He couldn't help but notice Christie Cauldwell Rawlinson was much, much younger than her husband.

George and Catherine introduced themselves to Mrs Rawlinson, Christie Cauldwell Rawlinson, and her children.

"You don't have to do this," Mrs Rawlinson said to Christie when George offered to take them to see Alec's body. "I can go. You can stay here with the children if you want to."

On their way over, George had received a text confirming the body was Alec's. They'd used his dental records, and because of that, they didn't need a person to identify the body positively. He understood why people would want to do it still; however, as though highly unusual and tiny by comparison, bodies had been wrongly identified by dental records before.

"No, no, I want to see Alec," Christie replied in a voice that was barely louder than a whisper. She looked terribly upset. He wondered what reason she would give him, why Alec was in the B&B without her.

When George had last seen Alec's body, it had been full of holes and covered in blood. Observing the corpse after it had been cleaned up, George could distinguish the stitches used to close the wounds to Alec's neck. But he was relieved most of the stabs had been to the chest and abdomen because his face was virtually undamaged.

Christie Cauldwell Rawlinson let out a faint yelp that sounded like a cry of pain. George was trained to watch for signs of guilt. Often, it was the one closest to you who killed you. But not today. He didn't suspect Christie Cauldwell Rawlinson at all. He watched as tears slid unchecked, ruining her make-up. It was strange, but George thought that at that moment, he'd never seen a woman as beautiful as the crying Christie Cauldwell Rawlinson. He assumed it was something to do with his morbid fascination with death. George believed that when someone you loved dies, a part of you dies too.

He'd seen enough, and in this case, there was no need for words. "Is that Alec?" he asked.

"Yes, that's him," she eventually said as they made their way back to the waiting room. "That's Alec." Her voice cracked as she spoke Alec's name, and as though that was her cue, Mrs Rawlinson wept. He stood with Catherine and waited for their initial shock to dwindle.

CHAPTER TEN

"I'm so sorry this has happened," George said, sweeping his gaze between the two adult women. "Trust me when I say we're doing everything we can to find out who did this, and I promise you we will find the person responsible. Now, we can do this another time if you prefer, but Detective Chief Superintendent Sadiq explained you'd be happy to answer a few questions."

Christie nodded and blinked the tears from her eyes. If she was lying, she deserved an Oscar. "If it helps you find whoever did that to our Alec, then fire away," Christie said, her eyes bright with emotion.

It was clear she was a strong woman. He looked at the children, a boy, and a girl about five and seven, respectively. Parents had to be strong for their children. Yet, Mrs Rawlinson had collapsed on a sofa, weeping silently. George spoke to her.

"Could you please take the children out of the room whilst we speak to Christie, Mrs Rawlinson?" He looked over at Christie to make sure she was OK with it. She nodded, and her mother-in-law took the children out of the room. "Do you mind if I record this, Christie?"

"No problem," she said.

He placed his Dictaphone down on the table and pressed the button to begin recording. He sat down on the sofa, and Catherine sat down next to him, their knees touching. "Do you have any idea if anybody would have wanted to hurt Alec?"

She shook her head but hesitated to explain. He let the silence speak. She soon spoke. "I doubt it. Alec was well-liked by his subordinates and strangely popular with his peers. He was a business executive who was good at what he did. He made many people a lot of money. Legally. He—"

George waited, thinking it wise not to hurry her. Let her

speak when she wants to talk—the oldest trick in the book.

"He was an arsehole. Who am I kidding? Whilst I'm terribly upset about his death, we weren't in a good place. I don't even know why he was in Headingley in the first place. I'm sorry to say."

The shock must have been clear on George's face because Christie shrugged and continued. "I can't think of one person who would want the man dead."

Apart from you, George thought. She had a motive, but did she have the means and opportunity? He wondered how the DCS would react if he asked for a warrant to check Christie's phone.

"We haven't been in a romantic relationship for a while," she continued awkwardly. "We were sleeping in separate rooms back at the house in Wetherby." She drew in a deep breath. "The papers hadn't been signed yet, but we'd agreed to a fifty-fifty split. I'd keep the house in Wetherby and have custody of the children, but he'd help co-parent." She paused. "Now that I'm saying these things to you, I'm aware it sounds as if I have a motive. I don't. I have an alibi for Sunday night."

George smiled. "Go on."

"I was with Juozapas. Joe. He's a beautiful man from Lithuania who loves me and loves my children. As I said, Alec and I were no longer in a romantic relationship and were co-parenting our children. He will confirm I was with him all day. And of course, I'll confirm I was with him all day. If necessary." She pulled a business card and pen from her purse and scribbled something down. It was his name and mobile number.

"Where were you, and at what times?"

Her face flushed, and she didn't answer for a minute. Was

she trying to come up with a story, or was she simply embarrassed? "We were at Goldsborough Hall, in Knaresborough. We checked in at 12 noon, and we didn't—" Her face flushed again, and she gave George a nervous smile. "We didn't leave until the following morning."

He frowned and fired off a text to DS Wood to ring Goldsborough Hall and ask them to provide both CCTV and statements from whoever checked them in and out. "Thank you, Christie. Where were the children?"

"With their grandmother, of course. Gloria is aware of our separation, even if other people are not."

Fair enough.

"So, you know of nobody who would want to see Alec come to harm? Was he seeing anybody new? Was there somebody from his past? He was married before you, right?"

She shook her head. "Right, but you'll have to ask his mother about that. Sorry. As far as I know, there isn't a single person who would want to harm him." She dropped her head in her hands, and her shoulders shook whilst she sobbed. "You may not believe me, but his death has saddened me. My children love their father. Very much. It was heartbreaking for them. And for me. We still have Gloria, Alec's mother, of course. But to lose him is terrible." A fat tear dropped from her eye once more.

"And you're sure you don't know why he was in a B&B in Headingley?"

"I'm sure. Check his phone. His diary is on there."

"It's missing. Can you provide us with his mobile number? We've found what we believe to be his by speaking with different providers, but it'd be helpful if you could confirm it." She nodded and scribbled it on the back of the business card. She had an excellent memory. He barely remembered Isabella's number and always had to double check he hadn't got the last two digits the wrong way round. He texted Josh Alec's number and asked him to work with Jason to get as much information as they could. "Did he only have the one mobile, or did he have a business one, too?"

"Just the one," she said. "Alec mixed business and pleasure. Having two phones would have made that difficult for him."

"Thank you, Christie," George said, looking around at Catherine. "Is there anything you need to ask, Christie, Catherine?"

She spoke for the first time in a while, but only to say, "Nope."

"I'm going to get the train back with the children, but Gloria is staying at a hotel. The InterContinental, on Crown Point Road, not to be confused by IHG luxury resorts." *This woman, he* thought. *All she cared about was wealth and class.* "She used to live in Beeston and has family there who she wants to notify of Alec's death. If you need me, call me."

Christie Cauldwell Rawlinson bent down and picked up the business card from the table, passing it to DI Beaumont before leaving the waiting room. Two minutes later, Mrs Gloria Rawlinson entered.

Chapter Eleven

"Would—" There was a long silence. Gloria Rawlinson blinked many times in quick succession, but her eyes remained tearless. Then she whispered, "Would it have been painful for my Alec? You know how he died?"

Murdered, George thought. *Your son was murdered with no way of defending himself.*

"I have it under good authority the first wound would have killed him instantly," he lied. "I'm so very sorry for your loss," George said and watched the expression on Gloria's face. There was a flicker of pain mixed with sadness and regret, a wide range of emotions. But then her expression changed, replaced by the calm façade she'd erected earlier.

Mrs Rawlinson nodded. "Thank you. Is that all you wanted to talk to me about?"

"Actually, no. Because of the nature of his death, I wanted to ask you a few questions on the record," he said, pointing to his Dictaphone down on the table. "Is that OK?"

She nodded her consent, and he pressed the button to begin recording.

"Thank you." George composed his thoughts. "When was the last time you saw your son?"

She paused. "Friday night. It was his night with the children, but he had a work dinner he needed to attend. Christie went with him. He didn't come home, so." She left the word hanging in the air.

"Weren't you two close?"

Another pause. Her sharp eyes regarded him defensively. "No. We used to be."

"What happened?" he asked.

Gloria glanced towards the door to the viewing room, her voice tight. "His dad left. I struggled with depression. He formed a relationship with his dad's mum. His grandma, Eunice. I barely saw him growing up."

"How would you describe your relationship?" asked George.

"He asks me to have the children, and I say yes. I can't say no. He lets me live in one of his houses, rent and bill-free."

"So, like a business transaction?" George wanted to know.

Her mouth curled up at the edges, and for the first time, George saw a hint of genuine emotion, a flash of anger mixed with a dark gaze. "Almost certainly. We had a business relationship. For the company. For the children. But don't let that fool you. I've mourned the loss of my son. I loved him powerfully, but not in the way he wanted."

George felt sorry for her. Did she have a motive to kill? Probably not. And why would he let his mother cuff him to the bed naked? He wouldn't. "Where were you between the hours of 2 pm and 10 pm on Sunday the thirteenth?"

"At my son's house in Wetherby, watching the children. Both parents were out. It was Christie who asked."

George nodded. She seemed to be telling the truth.

"Tell me about Christie."

Her sharp eyes furrowed. "What about her?"

"Can you confirm Christie's whereabouts between the hours of 2 pm and 10 pm on Sunday the thirteenth?" he asked.

The older woman shook her head. "She left between 10 am, and 10.30 am. Took her car." She paused.

George nodded. "We know about the separation, Gloria. Christie has given us her alibi. You can be truthful with us."

"You know about Joe?"

"Yes."

"Christie left about 10 am, and 10.30 am. She took her car and, as far as I know, went to Knaresborough. She got back to the house the following morning around eleven. I took the children to school. It's a common occurrence. Christie's only young. Why she married a man nearly twice her age, I'll never know." The look on Gloria's face told George everything. *Money.*

"Is there anything else you can tell us, Gloria? Anything at all?"

"What about his daughter, Caroline?" Gloria said, looking around the room uninterested. "Have you notified her?"

George caught Catherine's eye, who shrugged. "Caroline? Who's Caroline?"

"From his first marriage. Caroline's mother took her away as a young girl to Grimsby, though last I heard, Caroline was living in Cleethorpes. You know it?"

George knew it. He knew it well.

"The girl must be about twenty or twenty-one now."

"Do you keep in contact with her?" She shook her head. There was sadness in her eyes. "OK, Gloria. Do you know how we can get in touch with her?"

The older woman sighed, then began rummaging around her purse. "Yes." She produced a photograph of a slender,

85

raven-haired teenager. She handed it to George. "Her mum's contact details are on the back."

George flipped it over. On the back was the name Florence Burns, and beneath the name, an address for Grimsby and a mobile telephone number.

"What did you think of that then?" George asked once they'd got back into his Honda. He wasn't relishing the journey back to the station.

"Both Christie and Gloria both have motives. Did they have the means and the opportunity? Christie certainly did, though unless something comes to light, or she's lying about her alibi, I doubt Gloria did. Do you think Caroline was involved in his death?"

"I doubt it," he said. "I'll call her and see if she's available to meet." Then he glanced at the dashboard and realised the time. Grimsby was ninety minutes there and ninety minutes back. At least.

"Don't you have to get home?" Catherine asked. "I thought you were seeing your son tonight?"

George hesitated. He hadn't told Catherine he'd cancelled his plans to see Jack and was torn. Mia would be happy to see him, but now they knew about Caroline. They couldn't exactly wait until tomorrow to tell her that her father was dead. This was his job, his career, his life. Was Caroline more important than Jack? No, definitely not. But Jack was only months old and wouldn't even remember his visit. It was unfair to Caroline.

'...are you sure you're able to commit a hundred per cent to this case?' DSU Smith's words echoed in his mind.

He made his decision.

"Fancy a trip to the seaside?" he asked.

"Do I ever," she said with a grin.

CHAPTER ELEVEN

* * *

Isabella Wood frantically threw herself into George's arms the moment he walked through the door to his flat. "I've been trying to reach you. I thought something awful had happened."

He held her tightly, then gently disentangled himself. "Even Mia called the station. She told me you cancelled on her and Jack. That's so unlike you."

He wondered when Mia and Isabella started chatting without his knowledge. "Sorry. I was following up on a lead. I didn't expect it to take me as long."

"Why didn't you tell me? I'm supposed to be your deputy." She was right. And even if she wasn't his deputy, she was his girlfriend.

"I'm sorry. You're right. I should have told you. It took me ages to drive there and back, and we only stayed a short while."

"We?"

Shit!

He scratched his head and looked at his feet. "Catherine. We went to see Caroline Burns, Alec Rawlinson's daughter. We knew he was married before Christie." Wood nodded. "What we didn't know was they had a child together. She lives in Cleethorpes."

"So, you went to see her in Cleethorpes. With Catherine Jones?"

George walked through the kitchen to get a drink from the fridge. "That's right. I didn't think to tell you. I'm sorry."

Isabella wrapped her cardigan around her seductive figure and took a few steps toward him. "You don't need to be sorry for doing your job, Inspector Beaumont. But as your deputy, no, your girlfriend, I think you should have told me."

He smiled at her. "You're right. And that's my exact reason for being sorry."

Isabella laughed. It was a beautiful laugh. "Oh, I see. So, you're not sorry for spending the entire afternoon with a raven-haired vixen?"

"We're colleagues. Should I be?"

"We're colleagues, too." She winked and draped her arms around him from behind. She smelled of vanilla and coffee.

"I love you," he said.

"And I love you," she replied.

"I need to tell you something." He disentangled himself from her arms, took her by the hand and led her into the living room. "Catherine and I have history. A few years ago, I was in a relationship with a woman named Rachel. We'd been together three years when she broke up with me. It was because I was promoted to DS and transferred to Elland Road." Isabella said nothing, letting him finish. "Anyway, I was bitter about being dumped. My mates threw me a promotion party, and that was where I met Catherine. Though, she used her middle name, Amber, then. We had a great time, and we slept together. We started seeing each other. Then she left the station. DSU Smith reprimanded me for it. Then I met Mia."

"I already knew all of that, George," she said with a loving smile and the squeeze of his hand. "But thanks for telling me."

He was glad she was OK about it all. He knew he had to tell her at some point, especially if the three of them were going to continue working so closely together.

She snuggled up into his arms. "I was scared something had happened to you." He kissed her lips, and she wrapped her arms around his neck, not answering her. When they opened their eyes, she threw him a mischievous look. "Take me to the bedroom," she whispered in his ear.

Making love to Isabella that night had been different. Frantic, rather than the usual slow and sensuous. Whenever they made love before, he'd felt wanted and enjoyed. It was profound and significant. Not that it hadn't felt or been that way this time, it was just different. He felt windswept and a little edgy afterwards.

Because of that, he left her to sleep and went downstairs. He was hungry and languid and realised he'd been running on coffee all day. George made himself a couple of slices of toast and sat in the living room with the television on mute. He was just about dozing off when his phone sprung to life.

"Hi, it's Catherine. I'm sorry if it's late. I actually didn't realise it was that time. Sorry."

"No, it's fine. I was just about to head to bed, but I can spare five minutes." He turned off the television. "What's up?"

"Something's bugging me about Caroline Burns. Yeah, she was a lot more upset than Rawlinson's mother and wife was, but it didn't seem genuine."

"I agree. It's almost impossible to show genuine emotion over somebody who you haven't seen for over a decade."

"I did some digging, and I think she lied to us."

George waited, knowing she'd continue without his prompt.

"It seems she wanted to be part of the family business. She came to Leeds and stayed at the Wetherby home for a couple of months last year. Apparently, Alec made it clear that if she wanted in, she had to be a Rawlinson and not a Burns. It's all a bit complicated. Anyway, she refused, and Alec told her she was going to be removed from his will once his divorce from Christie went through."

"Jesus, that's one hell of a motive. How do you know all

this?"

"Christie Cauldwell Rawlinson. It felt as if she was hiding something earlier. I spoke with Mohammed, and he rang her. Then she rang me."

"Why you?" he asked. "I'm SIO on her husband's case."

"It's not like that, George. She wants you to send a detective over, and she'll make an official statement. Tomorrow."

He ground his teeth and took a deep breath. He was worried this would happen. And calling the Detective Chief Superintendent by his first name—she'd obviously charmed him like everybody else. "OK, fine. I'll send DS Brewer and DC Morton over in the morning." He hesitated. "Thanks, Catherine. We asked for her whereabouts on Sunday, and she gave us a pretty decent alibi."

"That she did, but she could by lying."

"Caroline said her boyfriend could confirm it. Are we still asking the local police to question him and be present via a video link?"

"That's right. Why do you think she's lying?" he asked.

"A feeling. She has the most to gain by killing him. We didn't know about her until Gloria mentioned her. She was being written out of the will. If you think about the current suspects, we have Matthew and James Lancaster, Gloria, Christie, and Caroline. The Lancasters have no motive, not really. Gloria was living freely, and Christie was getting the house, the kids, and half of his wealth. Caroline was being written out of the will. She stands to gain the most by killing him."

It made sense, too much sense, and sometimes sense blinded you. It had blinded him late last year when he was sure Tony Shaw was the Bone Saw Ripper when it was, in fact, his DCI, Alexander Peterson.

"Maybe you're right, Catherine. Maybe you're not. She could have been involved in the business and continued being in his will. You're suggesting murder over a surname change—"

"People have killed for less," she interrupted.

"Fine. When I speak with the South Humberside detectives in the morning, I'll ask them to put pressure on him. She said they'd only been together a few months. There's no way he'd go to prison for her. I just don't see it."

"I agree, and so if she wasn't with him, we can spin our webs and ensnare her. I really think you'll get something tomorrow. Speaking of which, can I be there with you and DS Wood?"

George hesitated. Isabella shouldn't have an issue with it. "Yes, of course."

There was a slight pause. "Oh, and George. Mohammed told me he'd approved the warrants for Rawlinson's phone and bank records, both personal and business. He agrees with me that the Lancasters aren't really suspects, and neither is Christie, so he won't be providing warrants for access to their mobiles."

George still suspected Christie, despite the information she'd shared. "That's great, Catherine. Send it over to DS Fry for me, will you?" He wasn't surprised by the sway she had. "He's working with DC Scott. I'll email him now and copy you in?"

"That's great, George. I'll email over the records once I have them in the morning."

"I'm only interested in calls made in the days leading up to Rawlinson's death. I especially want to focus on who he contacted on the day of his death. Someone cuffed him to that bed. He was separated from his wife, and if he knew about Juozapas Petrauskas, Christie's new partner, then maybe he was seeing somebody, too. That, or he hired an escort." He didn't share with Catherine his theory that Alec could be a gay man; that James Lancaster may have arranged a meeting with him at the B&B; that if Matthew Lancaster knew, it would give him a motive.

"Hey, listen, I think it'd be easier if we spoke about the case in person. I'm dying my hair, but you're welcome to come over. Or if you wanted, I could come over to yours when I'm done. You don't sound tired. Maybe we could do some extra hours?"

"Thanks, Catherine. I appreciate the call, but as I told you, I was just on my way to bed."

She said good night and hung up, and he spent a long time sitting in his chair, staring at the darkened screen of the TV.

Chapter Twelve

By the time George arrived at the station that Wednesday morning, all the work on Alec's phone number had been completed, and various other reports had filtered through. Nothing stood out from the reports other than Juozapas Petrauskas' statement. DC Scott had taken it, and Joe confirmed both he and Christie had checked into Goldsborough Hall at noon and didn't check out until the following morning. A report from Yolanda, with stills attached, confirmed the check-in and check-out times the pair had provided via CCTV footage. They decided they didn't need an official interview as their alibis were watertight.

From work on Alec's phone, only one number had caught their eye. Josh had found out it was a Tesco Mobile pay-as-you-go SIM used in what they assumed was a burner phone as it had been switched off since Sunday. They were untraceable. Whoever contacted Alec had been careful.

"There needs to be a law passed that dictates ID should be shown when you purchase a pay-as-you-go SIM," DS Josh Fry complained, staring at the spreadsheet of Alec's call history on his computer screen. "We could then at least link the numbers with the names."

"Agreed." George scratched his beard. It was getting long

and itchy. Isabella liked it, and George found himself keeping it longer for her.

"A proper criminal would use a fake ID anyway, so the names we'd get would be of innocents and only waste more time," Catherine said. He couldn't help but notice she was wearing a skirt suit which showed off her toned, shapely legs. She smiled and met George's eyes. Was she asking for his agreement or daring him to challenge her?

He did neither, and she moved on.

"They arranged to meet for five at the B&B, right?" Catherine asked. She bent down next to Josh, looking at the spreadsheet on his screen.

Josh looked uncomfortable with how close the beautiful woman was to him, her considerable cleavage right next to his cheek.

George didn't want to embarrass him but needed Josh to clarify.

"Is that right, Josh?"

He looked up at his boss and smiled. "That's right. A meeting time of 5 pm at the B&B."

"What's the progress on the profile?" George asked. DS Brewer and DS Williams had come over to DS Fry's desk, the five of them having an impromptu meeting. It was half-past nine, and everybody was in, except for DS Wood and DC Morton, who'd gone into the city to interview the Lancasters again.

"I've had a few ideas, though it isn't complete yet."

"Right?" He felt as if she was hiding something.

"It's complicated," she said. "Fancy grabbing a coffee, and I'll fill you in?"

There was a split-second hesitation. "Sure. Downstairs?"

There was a look of disappointment in her eyes.

Yolanda told him she was going to finish the work on the CCTV with Tashan, and Elaine had some reports she needed to type up on HOLMES 2. George smiled and nodded his head.

As soon as they were alone, she smiled at George. "Downstairs. In the canteen?" He nodded. "Sure. Why not? It's drinkable, I suppose."

The canteen didn't do a bad latte. It wasn't as good as drinking out, but it was cheaper and provided the caffeine required. George, who hadn't had breakfast, grabbed a banana. Catherine chose a table in the corner, away from everyone else.

Catherine handed him a stack of papers. "This is research, so read it when you get a minute."

George glanced down as she explained who she thought they were looking for.

When she'd finished, he looked up at her and spoke. "Interesting, Catherine. I must admit, I thought the same."

"What was it that drew you to the same conclusion, George?" Her eye contact was intense.

"The cuffs, the bleach in his mouth, and the removal of the ring finger inserted up his anus. Whilst the culprit left no evidence behind for us to prove this was a lust murder, I believe it was."

She was nodding and smiling at him. "Exactly, George. As you know, a lust murder is a killing in which the culprit searches for sexual satisfaction. As I said during the briefing, whoever killed Alec blurred the lines between their real and fantasy selves. We call this erotophonophilia, a rare and sadistic paraphilia, in which I quote, 'sexuoeroticism hinges on staging and murdering an unsuspecting sexual partner, or the re-staging of it in fantasy'," she said, looking down at her notes. "In other words, people suffering from it get sexual arousal or gratification from the death of a human being."

"And the blurred lines. The fantasy? You're saying whoever did this could have fantasised about it or indulged in it before?"

"That's right. I've read HOLMES, and you've attached DCI Arnold's cold case notes. They could be related, though I'm unsure at the moment. There are too many dissimilarities."

George nodded. He was disappointed, but he knew that himself. Still, the killer could have escalated, or improved, his MO.

"Now, commonly, a lust murder is expressed either by murder *during* sexual activity, which we know isn't the case here or by mutilating sexual organs or areas of the victim's body. Again, our culprit left Alec's sexual organs alone but eviscerated and mutilated him. Evidence on the condition suggests the mutilation usually takes place post-mortem. From Lindsey Yardley's report, this appears to be the case."

"Definitely a lust murder, then?"

"Yep. I'd agree with you, George. Now I can see the look on your face. You're thinking about sexual intercourse. Right?" She winked at him, and he blushed. "In these types of killings, sexual intercourse does not always occur, and other types of sexual acts may be part of the murder."

"Like what?"

"He was cuffed to the bed. His mouth was bleached. As I said during my report, I believe the victim had oral sex with the culprit. You know from previous experience that stomach acid breaks down sperm and semen. There was no trace in his mouth because of the bleach."

George thought back to his earlier thoughts. Was Rawlinson really a gay or bisexual man? From what the weekend girl told them, she certainly felt as if he was watching her. He was married. He had children, though it wasn't unusual for people to change their sexuality. George's great cousin's brother-in-law had been happily married with two kids before leaving his wife for a man. If so, maybe one of the Lancasters *had* arranged a meeting with Alec at the B&B. It was certainly then possible that the other Lancaster had found out about it, giving them the motive to kill out of jealous rage. Or, using Catherine's suggestions, maybe one of the Lancasters had committed a lust murder, satiating a fantasy.

He called DS Wood and asked her to bring both Lancasters down to the station in separate vehicles.

Chapter Thirteen

"How's the investigation going, George?" DSU Smith asked.

"I've just ordered DS Wood to caution the Lancasters and bring them in for questioning, sir." He shared with Jim Smith Catherine Jones' profile and the notes they'd discussed over coffee.

"I don't want you to lose sight of our aim, which is to see Alec Rawlinson's killer prosecuted," DSU Smith said. "The DCS is putting pressure on me now, too."

"We only found out about the murder on Monday, sir. Did he really expect a conviction by now?" George asked incredulously. "It's only Wednesday. We've had just over forty-eight hours on this."

"I understand, George, but Alec was a close, personal friend," Smith hastened to explain. "As is his wife, Christie. Apparently, Christie met Alec through Mohammed Sadiq. This business about him being a gay or bisexual man worries me. The press has wind of the theory, and I want to set up a press conference tomorrow to update everyone. Let the people of Leeds know we are in control. You think one of the Lancasters did it?"

George was silent for a moment. "It fits, sir. Catherine's

profile suggests a male killer." He went into detail on the pathology report, explaining Alec had been aroused before his death and had his mouth bleached. Because of the time that had elapsed between death and post-mortem, any sperm or semen would have been broken down by the acid, and as such, Lindsey suggested absence didn't mean it wasn't once there. He explained the lust murder theory again, going into detail about the cuffs, the theory about oral sex, linking it to the bleach in Alec's mouth, and how the culprit left Alec's finger in his anus.

Smith nodded his understanding. "This press conference needs to happen, George. I can't hold off until you have the proof you need."

George felt like he needed a drink. He definitely needed more time. "That's fine, sir. I'll email Juliette Thompson and make time to meet with her."

Smith regarded him seriously. "Well, OK. The press will put two and two together as well. We need to be prepared. Which family liaison officer has been assigned? I can't find the details?"

George shook his head. "Christie and Gloria both declined one." Smith grimaced. "Speaking of family liaisons, sir, did you clear an appointment for Mia with Cathy's boss?"

"I did, and I think you should assign Cathy to Christie and Gloria Rawlinson. We need someone like her who can provide a two-way flow of information. You should have insisted, Beaumont. Cathy's skills would have been invaluable to your investigation. She'd have spoken with the Rawlinsons and would've been able to sensitively and compassionately investigate whether they knew if he was a gay or bisexual man. It's what FLOs are there for. Do you know how many cases I solved with help from an FLO? As you damn well know, Beaumont, many murders are committed by the people most close to them. Is Christie cleared from the investigation?"

"No, sir. She has motive, means and opportunity. But she also has an alibi."

"Yeah, from her boyfriend?" George nodded. "Wouldn't be the first time, nor the last time, a partner gave a false alibi. My suggestion is not to exclude anybody just yet."

"We have CCTV evidence that corroborates their stories, sir."

"Of course you do. Well done. Keep me informed, yeah?"

"Sir."

As George left the office, he spotted Catherine heading out of the squad room, phone glued to her ear. The look on her face told him it was serious. He followed her. Having worked at Elland Road before, she must have known the reception in the elevator was dodgy at best, and so she entered the stairwell and took the stairs. That was lucky. For him, at least. He stalked after her, hoping to overhear what she was saying.

He listened intently as he closed the door quietly. Catherine hovered in the stairwell one floor down, her voice resonating clearly in the confined space. She must have assumed she was alone, as he could hear every word.

"You don't agree with my opinion, sir?"

A pause as she listened to the person on the other end.

"That doesn't mean it's a woman?"

A woman? Were they discussing the killer?

"All signs point to Alec being a bisexual male."

Another pause.

"Well, that doesn't mean he wasn't. Just because he had a wife and kids doesn't mean he didn't fancy men. You know him best, sir. I remember, yes. Womanisers can still fancy

CHAPTER THIRTEEN

men."

A womaniser? George assumed she was talking to DCS Sadiq by the way she kept calling him sir. Why were Sadiq and Catherine having secret conversations?

"What do you mean, don't quote me on it? It's what you said, sir."

The person on the other end spoke for a long time. Eventually, Catherine said, "The SIO, DI Beaumont, thinks the same as I do. It's clear from the cuffs, the evisceration, the mutilation. It seems rather obvious from the bleach he gave somebody a blowjob. You can't give a woman a blowjob. Well, not unless she's a trans woman."

Another pause. "No, sir. I've read the report too, but Yardley even admitted she couldn't be sure. Absence didn't mean it wasn't there initially." He heard her sigh. "I've not fucked him to get him to agree to my opinion, sir, no. Who do you think you're talking to?"

Catherine's heels clicked on the stairs as she walked down another flight. "Well, that's because you're different." The tone in her voice had changed. It sounded almost flirty. "Absolutely. Tonight? Sure." George followed her down, slowly and silently.

"I'll think about it, sir. The evidence very much suggests a male, yes. I'm aware the wife won't like it, but I can only follow the evidence. Yes, sir. Thank you, sir." She hung up.

George, who'd been hanging over the handrail to listen to her, straightened up. He didn't bother to go back upstairs and into the squad room. He needed to confront her now. Catherine's heels got louder as she climbed the stairs, and she stopped short when she saw him standing there, waiting for her.

"You OK, George?" she asked.

"What was that all about?" he asked.

"Resorted to eavesdropping now, have we?" She raised an eyebrow and pursed her lips.

"Remember that word you kept throwing around? Disclosure. I thought we were a team. I've let you in on everything during this investigation. We even went to Grimsby together instead of me asking another detective from my team. I've shared everything with you, Catherine, but for some reason, you don't see fit to do the same."

She sighed. "It's complicated, George."

He said nothing and didn't move. He was blocking her exit. It was an intimidating stance, and he knew it. "What's complicated about disclosing everything? Aren't we out to get the same thing?"

"For fuck's sake, George. I'm not beholden to you or your team. I've got a job to do. And a boss who wants results."

"So, it was DCS Sadiq you were talking to?"

She blushed at his name and didn't meet George's gaze. "How much did you hear?"

He considered his options. Tell the truth or manipulate her as she'd done to him? He chose the former, hoping she'd see the error of her ways. "Everything. Including how he thought you'd fucked me, so I'd agree to your opinion."

She hesitated. "I'm sorry about that."

"Why?"

"He knows our history. I had to beg him to let me on the case."

He glared at her. "Why were you so interested in the case?"

She sighed. "Because it's not very often that you get to make a name for yourself."

CHAPTER THIRTEEN

George stepped back, closed his eyes and rubbed the bridge of his nose. A headache was brewing. "You want me to believe this is all, so you can what, get a promotion?"

"Yes. Cases like these make-or-break profilers like me. We get it right, and we're the next best thing since sliced bread. We get it wrong, and well—we're fucked. It's why I was talking to Mohammed alone. He disagrees with me and wants me to re-write my report before submitting it."

George's heart sank, and he gazed at her, fire in his eyes. "You can't do that, Catherine."

"I know, and I won't. Please, George. Trust me." She smiled and stepped closer to him, so they were on the same level. She put a hand on his arm. "I'm doing my best, and I will not change my mind because of somebody else's opinion. Alright?"

"Alright, Catherine. Fine."

Her cheeks flushed a bright pink. From what little he knew of her, he should have known better than to question her integrity. One of the things that had interested him initially had been the reputation she had for being dogged in her pursuit of the truth. She was exactly like him. "This is a major investigation, George. I'm here to help, not to hinder you by suggesting the wrong paths. Remember that."

George was silent. He nodded at Catherine, who still had her hand on his arm. She smelled of roses and honey and was a bit too close to him for his liking. He tried to move back, but there wasn't much room to manoeuvre. "So, now what?"

She smiled. "We keep doing what we're doing. You've got the Lancasters to interview, right?"

He shook his head. "DS Wood and DS Fry are doing it. DSU Smith's idea. If I want that promotion to DCI, I need to prove to him I can delegate more. Be more of a manager."

She kept a hold of his arm but moved closer, her face inches away from his. He could see the red lipstick on her lips as he looked deep into her amber-coloured eyes. "I think you'll make an incredible DCI, George. Who knows, maybe this case will make it for the two of us?"

He could feel the warmth from her body, see the beating of her heart by the tiny flickers in her throat. George had hidden the feelings he had for her instead of ridding them as he'd thought. Suddenly, he was hit with an overpowering urge to kiss those cherry-coloured lips. His pulse quickened. It had always been like this with her. It took him back to his party when they'd first officially met. The urge to be with her had been so strong back then he'd been unable to resist.

But he was stronger now. He had Isabella. He stepped back towards the door to the floor where the FLOs were. She looked disappointed but removed her hand from his arm. "I'll see you later, George?"

"I'll keep you informed," he murmured, his softened gaze drawing another blush.

"I hope so." She smiled as she walked past him, up the stairs, and back into the squad room.

Chapter Fourteen

Her inebriation seemed to have hastened in the cold air, and Edward Kennings supported the young, leggy blonde as he walked them back to the hotel. There was nobody covering reception. In fact, it was all dark as he led her inside and up to his room.

He was glad she'd eventually met with him at the bar, and getting her back to his room had been more straightforward than he'd believed possible. The wine had helped—she hadn't kept her hands off him as he'd helped her into the bedroom and locked the door behind him. She was young. Very young. The younger, the better. When they were young, they did anything to please you. And once she'd found out he was an actor, she'd told him she was up for anything.

The blonde was a great kisser, but he wanted more and manoeuvred her towards the bed, removing garments one at a time, leaving a trail on the floor behind them. He took in her beauty once more. Her blonde hair fell in curls over pale shoulders, barely long enough to hide pink nipples and perfectly pert breasts. He desperately wanted to lie beneath them, desperately wanted to pluck at her nipples, to taste them with his tongue like ripe fruit. Her eyes were wide and intelligent. She had the cheekbones of a model.

But the arousal had taken him, and he pushed her onto the bed, where she fell in a giggling heap. He stood up for a moment, his penis erect, ready, taking in her lithe, naked form. It tempted him to take her right there and then, yet a young, fit girl like that deserved exploring. She was undoubtedly tempting, her blonde curls spreading out like a fan, contrasted against the dark duvet.

"Come over here," she breathed, wagging her left index finger at him.

"If that's what you want," he whispered, an intoxicated grin on his face.

But as he took a step towards her, she rolled over. "If there's one thing you need to know about me, Eddy, it's that I like to be in control. OK?"

He wasn't sure she could see him nodding because of the dark, so he said, "Yes."

"Good. Lay down on the bed on your back, and close your eyes." She licked her cherry-coloured lips and tossed some curls back over her shoulder. Her breasts really were like ripe fruit, but it was the fruit between her legs he so desperately craved. "Now, Eddie!"

After all the effort he'd spent getting her into bed, he didn't want to be spent straight away, and so he did as he was ordered and closed his eyes tight.

Being tied up by a young blonde was one of his fantasies, one he'd shared with her during their messages. Edward was glad she'd paid attention. It meant he didn't try to open his eyes once, not until she'd finished tying all four of his limbs to each bedpost.

"There. All done." She licked those cherry-coloured lips once more, and it sent him wild.

CHAPTER FOURTEEN

"You are legal, right?" Edward asked.

"I thought you liked young girls?"

I do, but—"

She straddled him, interrupting his sentence. She smelled good. Edward thought it smelled sweet and fruity. "I may not look it, but yes. I guess I'm not quite the forbidden fruit you had in mind?"

"You'll do for tonight. Stop teasing me and let me inside you," came his reply.

"How about you let me inside you?"

Suddenly, he felt a sharp jab to the stomach. "Hey!" He glanced down, and his eyes widened in disbelief. A knife was sticking out of his abdomen. "What did you do?"

Confusion descended. A slow, burning heat erupted into excruciating pain. Tears fell from Edward's eyes, and he clutched his stomach to pull out the knife. It was already gone. The next stab was to the chest, piercing a lung. Suddenly, it was hard to breathe.

He could barely speak as he begged for her to stop. He gazed at his attacker with terrified eyes. "Stop. Please. What are you doing?" Edward tried to use both hands to try and stop the bleeding from both wounds. It was then he remembered his hands were bound to the bed. It was already too late.

The beautiful blonde struck again, thrusting her knife through his neck, his liver, and his bowel. From above, the knife fell, again and again, raining the blows down upon him as the blood gushed from his wounds. His breath came in loud gasps as he fought to keep from blacking out. Again and again, the knife was thrust into his abdomen. He coughed, spurting frothy red foam over her.

She stopped for a moment and smiled; her eyes were fury

personified. Her porcelain skin was awash with crimson. It was only then that he realised she wasn't done with him. He tried to cry out, but this time, he only managed a wet gurgle. The knife fell again and again until Edward couldn't hold on any more. His lungs were filling with blood, and his vision was blurring at the edges. Soon, all would go black.

Why are you doing this to me? he wanted to ask, but nothing but a wet gurgle came from his mouth. Darkness surrounded him on all sides. It was too late. His vision went red, and all he could feel was pain.

Edward knew then that he was dying. He wished for it all to end quickly. Yet, for him, there was no respite. He lay there as the sharp thrusts kept on coming.

Chapter Fifteen

It was around 2 pm the following day when George found out about the second body. DS Wood, who'd been in a meeting with DSU Smith, rushed into George's office panting. "George, I think you're going to want to hear this."

George finished typing and looked up at her. "What's up?"

"We've just received a treble nine call. A body's been found at a hotel in Yeadon, with multiple stab wounds."

George stared at her for a moment. "Like Alec Rawlinson?"

"Yeah, the same. The first responder counted at least sixteen puncture wounds, but there are possibly more. Whoever he was didn't stand a chance. The first responder said it's a bloodbath."

George stood up. "Right, OK. We'd better get down there."

"I'm coming too," Catherine cut in. He didn't know where she'd come from, but obviously, she'd overheard the conversation.

George frowned. "We don't know if this is related to Alec Rawlinson. You're not a detective any more. You're not even on the Contamination Elimination Database."

Catherine fixed her amber eyes on him. "It's the same MO, right? And I can be on it if you want me to be on it. OK?"

George nodded and relented. She was right. It was the same

MO, and he didn't have time to argue. "OK, fine, but we're leaving now, Catherine."

"I'm already ready." She showed him her bag and put on her jacket. She followed the two detectives out of the room.

"Where was the body found?" she enquired as they took the stairwell downstairs, out through reception and into the car park.

"Yeadon," Wood told her. "At the Tall Oak Cottage Hotel, near Tarnfield park. I've googled it, and it's apparently popular with people travelling from Leeds Bradford Airport. We know little more than that."

"Tall Oak Cottage, Yeadon?" She wrinkled her forehead. "Never heard of it."

"I hadn't until I googled it."

Traffic was light, and the drive took them less than half an hour via Armley Gyratory. As they parked, DS Wood glanced at the 4-star hotel. "This is a lot nicer than the B&B in Headingley," she said.

The metallic plaque on the white wall beside the door read Old Oak Cottage, and beneath it was a more prominent, enjoyEngland sign proudly declaring the hotel's 4-star status.

The entrance had been taped off, and a police officer armed with a clipboard was stationed outside. "I see Lindsey and her team of SOCOs are already here." George nodded to the CSI van parked outside the building.

After the trio had donned their protective kits, the two detectives showed their warrant cards to the guard and explained who Catherine was before being permitted entry.

The hotel was quite lovely inside, with walls immaculately upholstered in fabric. The inky blue carpet was clean and looked new. Up above, emitting warm, welcoming light were rose-coloured French chandeliers.

"I can see somebody booking a room at the Headingley B&B for a sex session, but this place doesn't have the right feel," George said to Wood.

"Maybe we have a copycat?"

George thought about it. The press release had gone out that morning. "Nah. Not enough time. Maybe the victim chooses the place and not the culprit?" George said as they reached the third floor. Another officer, who looked as if he'd chucked up his guts already, directed them to room fourteen.

"That would make it harder for the culprit to plan the murder, though, right?"

"Right." George, heart pounding, entered the room, followed by Isabella Wood and Catherine. Despite seeing his fair share of bodies, he still mentally prepared himself for the worst. There was something about a dead body that still seemed to turn his blood cold. And the shock never lessened. George didn't think he'd ever get used to death.

The first thing George did was pinch his nose. The coppery odour of blood was present, a thick, pungent smell that stayed with you for days. As before, the victim was laid on the bed. A crime scene photographer was clicking away. "Would you mind giving us a minute, please?" George asked. The charcoal grey room was too small for all four of them at the same time. The photographer nodded and entered the en-suite.

Careful not to disturb anything, the two detectives crowded around the body whilst Catherine watched from the door. The sheets were drenched with blood, and, as with Rawlinson, it had pooled beneath his body in a sticky puddle. The puncture wounds looked to be the same size as those inflicted on Rawlinson. It was probably the same weapon.

Catherine looked at George. "Is this crime scene similar to the other?" she whispered.

"Yeah, similar," he replied. "The only difference is that this guy isn't cuffed. Rawlinson was cuffed to the bed. This guy has been cabled tied."

"Any other differences?" George thought he could hear a slight twinge of disappointment in her voice. She wanted to advance her career off the Rawlinson case, and more bodies would only help in that regard. Catherine must have been hoping for a connection.

Wood was to the right of the bed, the victim's left. "The ring finger isn't missing. Though, there's no ring on it, either. No evidence of one having been there, anyway."

"I need some more light," said George. He called in the photographer and asked her. She left the room, and a minute later, she and a young male SOCO set up a portable spotlight. He switched it on. Immediately, a bright light illuminated the dead man. Where his penis should have been was a mess of skin and coagulated blood. "I think I know what Dr Ross will end up finding in this guy's arse," he said to Wood.

Isabella looked in his direction and immediately understood. She knew it was significant, but why? Was this a lust murder, too?

At that moment, Lindsey Yardley strode into the room carrying her metal case. "Hello, George. We must stop meeting like this."

"Lindsey." He gave her a small smile. "Or is it Dr Yardley?"

She raised a brow but said nothing. She looked down at the body. "Have we finished taking the photos in situ?" she asked. The young female photographer popped her head through the en-suite door and shook her head.

"That's my fault. I asked her to wait," said George.

Lindsey nodded and then glanced at the young lady. "OK, come in now and take the rest of your pictures, please, Michaela."

The photographer got back to work. George took the now vacant place in the en-suite doorway and watched. She seemed to take a lot of photos before she left the room, more than what he thought was necessary. *Probably wanted to impress her boss,* he thought.

"Do you think you could tell us how many wounds he has?" George said and crouched down beside her, looking up to meet her eyes. His back was hurting him. The wound the Miss Murder had given him still gave him a lot of gyp even a year on. Wood and Catherine backed out of the room, too, to provide them with more space.

"I can if you give me a minute," she said, looking away from him. "I've just got here, remember?"

Patience wasn't one of his virtues, and George's sigh was audible. "Thanks, Lindsey. And also, his penis is missing. It could be up his arse." She gave him a mischievous look, and he stood up to survey the hotel room. He trudged around it, making every attempt to avoid disturbing any potential evidence. It was clean, and there were no clothes sprawled on the floor. A black suitcase stood near the wardrobe. He didn't have to lift it up to know it was empty.

George inspected the ivory bedside cabinet, a French-inspired design with ornate floral detailing. There was a notepad and a pen alongside the hotel telephone but no phone, no wallet, no keys. He looked around the room. Where were the victim's clothes? "There's no sign of a fight," he said. Just like with Rawlinson, it looked like this guy had invited his murderer in and didn't put up any fight.

"No defensive wounds on the hands," Lindsey said.

"Do we know who he is?" Wood asked from the doorway.

"He's naked, and I can't find any clothes," said George.

"Not even a mobile phone?" asked Wood.

He shook his head.

George opened the wardrobe next to the wardrobe and looked inside. Two suits and two pressed shirts hung from hangers, all Armani. He bet each suit cost more than his monthly wage. Two pairs of shoes sat on the wardrobe floor.

"There's a safe inside the wardrobe, sir. I've taken photos of it," the young female photographer said through the door.

The safe was open. George put his hand in and pulled out a leather wallet. "I've found a wallet with an ID."

Both Wood and Catherine turned to him eagerly.

George found a driver's licence and read out the name and address. "Edward Kennings. From Horsforth."

"Horsforth?" said Wood. "Not that far away then? Why rent a hotel room?"

George pulled a business card from the wallet and showed it to them.

Edward Kennings. Actor.

"An actor?" said Catherine. "Never heard of him."

"Not much else in his wallet. No worn photograph of a partner of kids. Just cash, debit cards and credit cards. They're all in his name."

George slipped the ID and business card back into the wallet and handed it to Wood, who turned to find a young blond SOCO watching her. Hayden Wyatt took it from her and put it in an evidence bag, sealing it up and making a record on his clipboard. Every item had to be logged and recorded

CHAPTER FIFTEEN

before being taken into evidence. There, the items would be photographed and inspected, and then a detailed report would be sent to the senior investigating officer. George had no experience when it came to mistrials, but he knew from speaking to the DCIs that failure to follow this protocol could have disastrous results for them, especially if that piece of evidence were something the prosecution relied upon in court.

"Any sign of a laptop or a script? You sure there's no mobile phone?" asked Wood, who was still standing outside the door.

George rummaged through the wardrobe but felt nothing. Nothing at the bottom. "Guy lives in Leeds. I doubt this was a business trip. And there's definitely no mobile phone," said George.

"Who doesn't have their mobile phone with them?" asked Wood.

George tensed his jaw. "Clearly, the murderer's taken it. As an actor, Edward Kennings would have had one. Luckily for us, his number's on the business card." George remembered the number as it wasn't too dissimilar to his own. He texted DS Josh Fry, who should be back at Elland Road HQ, to speak to the provider and speak to Smith for a warrant, if necessary. He needed to know who Edward had been talking with recently.

"It was the same situation with Rawlinson, right?" said Lindsey. "Personal mobile missing?"

George tightened his lips. A headache was brewing, and his back was killing him. "Yeah, the same as before. I think the killer contacted him to arrange a meeting and so the killer's number must be on the phone. It's the only logical reason why he takes them. It's to slow us down."

"I agree, but I also think they might be trophies. Think about the fantasy and real life being blurred together. The reason I think that is because he must know we'd access the records eventually," said Catherine.

"Yeah, but I think it's a burner like the other. It wouldn't surprise me at all if it's another supermarket Mobile SIM."

DS Wood leaned against the door frame. "So, what's our working hypothesis?"

Catherine smiled and said, "The killer contacts the victim by phone, or vice versa. They arrange to meet at a hotel or B&B, which the victim books and pays for. Then he comes over, probably with a bag of some kind to conceal his weapon and stuff like cuffs or cable ties. He ties his victim up and then attacks them, eventually killing them and receiving sexual satisfaction from the act. Then the culprit calmly washes themselves and the murder weapon in the bathroom before taking off."

"Was there blood in the sink?" George asked Hayden Wyatt.

"A small amount, sir," he said. "There's not as much as there was at the Rawlinson crime scene; I had to use the UV light to find it. I've taken samples, and Michaela photographed it—"

"You'll get the report tomorrow," Lindsey Yardley cut in.

George felt his pulse rate speed up. He hoped this time the killer wasn't careful enough to avoid cutting themselves. "It's the same person, I'm sure." He went into the small bathroom to look for himself, but as Wyatt had said, the blood wasn't visible to the naked eye. The killer was more careful this time.

"Any signs of sexual activity this time?" asked Catherine.

Lindsey shook her head. "There's bleach in his mouth, but as his penis has been removed, I can't advise whether it's been used sexually. You'll have to wait for the post-mortem."

George nodded. He hated waiting, but there was nothing he

CHAPTER FIFTEEN

could do.

Lindsey leaned forward with a ruler and inspected Edward's torso. He left her for a minute to measure. After two agonising minutes, she said, "The entry wounds are smooth and measure thirty-eight millimetres across. The murder weapon had a sharp tip and was non-serrated. They appear to be the same size and shape as your last victim."

George nodded sternly. "Same killer." It wasn't a question.

Lindsey nodded. "I'd say so, yeah. Dr Ross will have the specifics for you after the post-mortem."

Catherine and Wood stared at George. Now they had confirmation. They weren't quite sure what to make of it. Two wealthy men dead in less than a week.

Shit!

"Can you give me the time of death?" asked George.

Lindsey hesitated. "I'd guess about twelve hours ago because rigor mortis has peaked. Dr Ross will measure his temperature. I don't know whether you noticed, but the air-conditioning was left on. That means his body would not only have lost the temperature quicker but would have a lower room temperature. He was definitely dead at least two hours before he was found."

"How do you know that?"

"Livor mortis. You may know it as hypostasis. It's more pronounced twelve hours after death, which is the case here. It makes sense as rigor mortis has peaked."

"So, twelve hours at least?" She nodded. "Our guy seems to enjoy playing these kinds of games to slow us down, eh?" George said to nobody in particular. He glanced at his watch. "That means he was killed between 2 am, and 4 am?" Lindsey nodded again. "Where's the owner or receptionist? There must have been a night manager. I didn't see anyone downstairs when we came in."

DS Wood nodded her head towards the stairs. "Let's go find out."

"Let's bag up the Do Not Disturb sign and, like the other murder, check it for prints and DNA, yeah?" George asked.

Hayden Wyatt nodded. "Already bagged for you, sir." Last year, George thought Wyatt had been the Bone Saw Ripper because of his blond hair and forensic awareness. He always seemed to be in the right place at the right time, with a smirk on his face. George was glad he wasn't, as he was an efficient, if not an overbearing, hard young worker.

DS Wood led George and Catherine downstairs, leaving the crime scene under the control of Lindsey Yardley. Downstairs, next to the check-in desk, was an empty lounge. As with the B&B, all guests had been asked to leave for the day. Wood found the receptionist in the back office, crying. It had been her who had discovered the body. She was a pixie of a woman in her mid-thirties with red-rimmed eyes and shoulder-length ginger hair. He couldn't tell her ethnicity from her accent, not wanting to label her as Polish if she was, say, Ukrainian.

"I'm Detective Inspector Beaumont, and this is DS Wood. Sitting there is Catherine Jones, a criminal profiler. May we take your name for the recording?" George had received permission to record the conversation with his Dictaphone.

"I'm Dana, Dana Szymańska."

"Tell us about Edward Kennings, please Dana."

"Mr Kennings was supposed to check out at noon," she told them in a quivering voice. "He's a regular, and so we always allow him a couple or a few extra hours. When he didn't come down, I gave him some more time and went up to check that

CHAPTER FIFTEEN

he was OK. He sleeps late and forgets he must check out. But as I said, he's a regular. Or he was." She started crying again.

"So tell us how you found him, please," DS Wood said.

"I—I went up around 1 pm and called to him through the door. When there was no answer, I was worried about him, so I opened the door with my key card and—" She gave a whimper—" It was the smell I noticed first. The metallic smell of blood." She closed her eyes in an attempt to stop them from filling with tears again. It didn't work. "I entered a couple of steps, and I saw him lying on the bed covered in blood."

Catherine leaned forward and smiled at her. "It's OK, Dana. I know it isn't nice what you saw, believe me. What did you do next? Did you go over and touch the body at all? Did you check for a pulse?"

The red-headed woman flushed red, embarrassed. "Oh, no. Should I have?" Catherine smiled. "I just ran out of the room and came downstairs to call the police."

"Good," Catherine said, the smile still plastered on her face. "You did the right thing, Dana."

She sniffed and rubbed her nose on her sleeve. "I thought nothing like this would ever happen."

George nodded, but he needed information. He asked, "Who was the night manager?"

"It was me last night. I finished at 2 am, and I've been on days for five days now. I started at 1 pm this afternoon. That's why I know what time it was I found Mr Kennings."

George leaned forward in his chair and gazed directly at her. "OK, so to be clear, you worked until 2 am this morning, left work, and returned at 1 pm this afternoon?"

"That's right."

"Did you go home?" She nodded. "Can anybody confirm

that?"

"Yes, my partner. Would you like her details?" She furrowed her red-rimmed eyes.

"Please." He slid over his pocket notebook and pen. She began writing as he asked, "Who took over from you at 2 am?"

"Amari. Amari Ibrahim."

"Who's Amari?" DS Wood asked.

She turned to DS Wood and said, "He's the other night manager. We both share the job, and when not on nights, we're on during the day. It's a small team."

"OK. When you left this morning, did you see anybody suspicious?"

"Suspicious. You mean like a guest?"

"Yeah, anyone. A guest or a visitor of a guest, maybe even a stranger. Maybe not even a stranger, but somebody who wasn't supposed to be on shift?" Wood asked.

She thought for a moment, nibbling at the edge of her lip. "No. I saw nobody last night other than Amari."

"Were you at your post the entire time?" George asked.

She nodded but didn't meet his eye.

George thought about pushing her because he believed she'd left her post. He gazed at her once more before deciding against it. The poor woman had been through enough, and there was no proof she'd left the front desk. There was no CCTV, and if she got caught leaving her station, she'd lose her job.

"OK, Dana. You've been great." He saw DS Wood glance at him in surprise. "Can we have a copy of Mr Kennings' ID documents? The ones from when he checked in?"

She straightened her back and took a deep breath. "Of course, detective. I can give you his credit card details, too."

CHAPTER FIFTEEN

They had his wallet bagged up, but having those copies would tie Edward to the hotel room. "Thanks," said George. It didn't hurt to be thorough. "I noticed there was a phone in his hotel room. Can you check to see if he made any calls for me, please?"

"He doesn't usually, but I can check for you."

"Please."

She got up and walked around the corner to the front desk, then disappeared into the back office again. After five or six minutes, she was back. "This is everything we have." It was a printout of the guest register, complete with Kennings' driver's licence and credit card details. "Also, he didn't make any phone calls from his room."

"Perfect, Dana." George nodded at the door, indicating to the others to leave. "Thanks again."

Chapter Sixteen

On the way back to George's Honda, Isabella stopped him and asked for a word. Catherine continued towards the car park.

"It's obvious to me Dana Szymańska left her post, George. Why didn't you ask her why?" she asked.

"Because I knew she'd deny it," he said. "Her admitting she left her post could mean her job. That's why I didn't push it. She probably went outside for a smoke. I could see the nicotine on her fingers."

"Or a toilet break, I suppose," she said. "That or she killed him. She was the only one on duty."

True. "Or, the killer could have waited for her to leave the desk and then have slipped in." Whilst it was a modern hotel, there was no buzzer or automatic locking system on the front door. Because it was so close to the airport, the front door was always left unlocked, with a sign asking all visitors to report to reception.

"Wood, contact the owner when we get back and ask if there's any CCTV on or around the premises," said George. "I didn't see any."

"Already in my notes, George," she said, tapping her temple with a smile. "But you're right; I didn't see any either. If I get

CHAPTER SIXTEEN

some, I'll give it to Yolanda."

"Good. Speak to Leeds City Council, too. A nice area like this is bound to be a CCTV treasure trove. Yeadon is riddled with them."

When the pair made it back to the car, Catherine was shivering. "Shall we grab a coffee?" Catherine pointed to a place on the opposite side of the road. It had a wooden sign and a pun for a name. They nodded. The coffee shop was next to a barber shop by a hectic road, and the smell of dense exhaust fumes was in the air. Once inside, it was soon replaced by the soothing aroma of roasted coffee beans. The trio ordered and took a table by the window.

George thought the warm, inviting coffee shop was a welcome change after the grisly crime scene at the hotel. Catherine cradled her breakfast tea, complaining they had no Yorkshire tea, whilst the two detectives nursed strong coffees.

DS Wood got straight to the point. "Are we assuming that the person who killed Alec Rawlinson also killed Edward Kennings?"

There was a pause.

"Yes," said George. "Lindsey said the entry wounds were the same size and shape as found on Alec. There was also bleach in his mouth. And the killer removed Edward's penis, which I know is different, but probably an escalation."

"I'd agree with that," Catherine said. "It's hard not to see the connection."

"What about the victims?" George blew on his caramel latte to help it cool down. "How are they connected?"

"They're a similar age and build," suggested Wood. "Until we know more, it's difficult to say for sure. But, from seeing both scenes, the victims were remarkably similar."

"Differing jobs, though," George said.

Catherine sipped her tea. "Fancy being in Yorkshire and drinking this rubbish," she muttered. "But yeah, one was a property tycoon, the other an actor. Victim selection must be something to do with their age and physique."

George thought she was right and nodded his agreement. She smiled at him. The guy obviously had a type. They just needed to find out how he was selecting them and why. Wood had called Josh on the walk over, asking for a background check on Edward. George was getting texts every ten minutes or so with snippets of info.

"It says here that Edward was quite rich. Worth three million quid apparently," George said, looking up from his phone.

Catherine perked up. "Alec was rich, too. Could it be financially motivated? About thirty per cent of killers kill for money."

"I'll get Josh on his accounts," said George, firing back a text message. "We found nothing in Alec's accounts, though. Nothing dodgy at all."

"OK." Catherine drummed her left index finger on the edge of her mug. "Maybe the killer did it for enjoyment purposes? That's also just short of a third of murderers. It certainly fits with the lust murder theory."

George fell silent for a moment. His phone pinged. Edward Kennings had been married. "Edward was a rich, single man. As of now, there's only one person who can inherit that."

"Who?" Catherine asked.

"His ex-wife, Lorraine Cox. Get her details from Josh and arrange an interview," George said. "She has a motive."

"OK," Wood said with a nod of her head. "Why does Lorraine inherit if she's his ex?"

"Good question. It's a common misconception that a divorce means you can't claim part of an estate. If a person hasn't remarried, then their ex-spouse is entitled to make an inheritance claim."

Wood nodded her understanding. "How do the Lancasters fit into this?"

Both Catherine and George stared at her.

"That's a good question," he said.

"In my opinion, they don't," Wood said. "Neither one of them could have killed Kennings. They were asleep at Elland Road. Stewing."

"Call the station," George said. "Get them released. You don't think Cassie Broadchurch was involved, do you?"

Wood's face darkened. "She's so young. Does she have the means and the opportunity?" Wood spread out her hands and shrugged. "Does she even have a motive?"

George studied Isabella intently. "I doubt it. But we need to be thorough. Send Yolanda and Elaine around, and make sure Cassie's Father's in, too. We need an appropriate adult there. Ask her where she was."

She sighed. "OK. Will do."

"I'm convinced it's a man, George," Catherine said. "I think you're wasting your time and resources."

"We have to keep an open mind," Wood explained.

Another Silence filled the air as the trio thought about this. Eventually, George said, "It's no use speculating so early on. Let's see what Lindsey and her team come up with, yeah? Maybe the killer was careless and left a sample of his DNA on the body?"

"If only things were so simple," Wood said. "I guess it's feasible Lindsey might pick up something when they dust for prints?"

"Exactly," George said with a smile.

"Forensically speaking, hotel rooms are a disaster," Catherine pointed out. "A ton of people go in and out, most staying for one or two nights. They might look as though they'd had a decent clean when you arrive, but you'd be wrong—disgusting places. I had to stay in one myself recently. A B&B in Headingley. Bloody awful."

"Christ." Wood shuddered. George met her eyes. They'd stayed in a hotel themselves not that long ago, too, a nice one on Denby Dale Road in Wakefield. It had been just the two of them that entire weekend. Bliss! "We can hope, anyway." She tilted her head and smiled at George. He hoped she was thinking about their memories together, too.

"Every contact leaves a trace, remember?" he said. "Somebody murdered him, and so that means they should have left a piece of themselves behind."

"Right, so we wait for Lindsey Yardley to get back to us. In the meantime, I'll get Kennings' phone records," Wood suggested. "His number was on the business card, so I'll get Josh on it asap."

George chugged down his latte. "Already messaged him, Wood." She smiled. "Hopefully, there will be evidence on his phone leading us to his killer. He wouldn't have taken it otherwise."

"Agreed," said Wood. "But what sort of person is called to a hotel room?"

"Lots of people. He could have been a loan shark, though doubtful because of the money in his bank. Otherwise, a prostitute, an escort, or even a masseuse," said Catherine. "And I know what you're thinking, but research shows that in the LGBTQ+ society, male prostitution is common and more accepted than female prostitution."

"There's no sign of sexual activity, though," said George.

"I disagree," Catherine interjected. "The bleach in the mouth? If not for the large amount of time elapsed, I'm convinced you'd find semen during his autopsy."

George raised an eyebrow. "Who knows? We might find it this time."

"I can't see it." Wood argued. "I can't see a man committing this type of murder. In fact, I know it isn't a man."

"How do you know?" Catherine asked.

Wood was about to answer when George sighed and said, "Look, we're chasing tails here. We need to wait for the evidence before speculating. Hopefully, Lindsey found something that will be able to shed some light on why Edward was murdered."

* * *

"Please, George, speak to Mark Finch and ask him to take a look at the two murders," Isabella asked him once they were safely in his office back at Elland Road. She was sitting on his desk facing him. If they were in a film, it would have been the kind of situation where George drew the blinds and laid her down gently on the desk before carefully removing each garment and exploring every inch of her body.

"George, are you listening to me?"

"We have Catherine. Why do we need Mark?"

She pouted her lips, and George thought she looked incredibly sexy. He was about to tell her as much when DC Morton barged his way in.

"Can I help you, Terry?"

"Oh, shit. Sorry, sir. I'll come back, yeah?" Terry said.

"Go on?"

"I've got you an interview with Ms Cox. Mr Kennings' ex-wife. Saturday morning."

"Cheers, Terry." Morton slammed the door shut. He was glad he hadn't said the words he'd wanted to say. There was still a rotten seed he needed to weed out, and he still wasn't sure who it was. He looked at Isabella. "Why do we need Mark?"

"I thought he might offer some useful insights, as he's well-respected. He could help us link the two murders?"

"We have Catherine, though. The DCS put her in place. I don't have the authority."

"You don't have to do it officially. Just speak to him. Please?"

"Tell me why."

"Because I don't—" She paused. "I don't trust Catherine. She's blinded by her profile. I'm convinced she's leading us down the wrong path."

"Fine. I'll speak with him. For you."

She nodded. "Thank you, George. Catherine thinks a man is responsible for both murders. I don't."

"OK, Isabella. I'll speak with him."

"Thanks. Just make sure he doesn't know that I think it's a woman, and Catherine thinks it's a man. I want him to give his opinion without any influence. OK?"

George sighed. "OK, gorgeous. OK."

* * *

CHAPTER SIXTEEN

After the second press conference, George had been answering calls from reporters sniffing around to find out if there was anything more to the story than the diluted statement he had issued.

Later that evening, Edward Kennings appeared in various brief articles that stated the Yorkshire actor had been found stabbed to death in a hotel in Yeadon. DI George Beaumont had been named as Senior Investigating Officer, and anyone with any information was asked to contact the Homicide and Major Enquiry Team. It had been Juliette Thompson, the HMET's reliable press officer, who had quietly released the statement once they'd known his identity. As of yet, nobody had linked it to Rawlinson's death, which, George thought, was miraculous considering he was SIO on both cases.

As George was about to leave the station to head to Mia's to see his baby son, Jack, his phone rang. It was Samantha Fields, the office manager. "I have Mr Duke on the other line. He wants to speak with you. It's urgent, apparently."

He said thanks and waited, his stomach churning. Duke never came with good news. Suddenly, Johnathan Duke's American accent echoed out from the speaker. "Ah, Inspector Beaumont, nice to hear your voice. How are you, my friend?"

George sighed. The way Duke spoke was far too regular for it to be an act. It was as if he lived every second like an actor on the stage, and every person he spoke with was the audience. George found it annoying, yet he knew Duke was the best-connected person in the city. It also meant he probably knew Edward Kennings. "Forgive my manners, Mr Duke, but I was on my way home. How can I help you?"

Chapter Seventeen

After dealing with Johnathan Duke last night, the DCS had stopped by, making sure George asked his team to arrive early for a briefing. It was 7 am, and most of his team should have been at home in bed. George would get them to claim overtime, whether the DCS liked it or not. Smith had told him to claim whatever he needed.

"All right, let's go, detectives. Incident Room Four. Now!" Detective Chief Superintendent Mohammed Sadiq said.

As he walked towards the incident room, he thought about Duke. He, of course, had found out about the murder of his old friend Edward Kennings and explained Paige McGuiness had made the connection between the two murders. Like before, she would delay her article if George gave her an exclusive. He promised to see her later that evening.

When most of George's team was inside and sat down, Sadiq started reading from his notes. "Twenty stab wounds to the chest, lower abdomen, and neck. Dr Yardley compared them to the wounds from Alec Rawlinson's body. They're the same. The SOCOs found no usable prints or DNA. His mouth was bleached. Sounding familiar yet? There were no signs of forced entry, and nothing was missing. What does this tell you?"

In other words, thought George, *it means we have nothing.*

CHAPTER SEVENTEEN

"When was the confirmed time of death?"

"Dr Yardley advised between 12 midnight and 3 am," Mohammed Sadiq said after looking down at his notes. "It's an educated guess based on the data she had, as the body had been there for hours with the air-conditioning turned on."

DS Wood entered with a cup of coffee for him. Strong but milky, with two sweeteners, just the way George liked it.

"So, we have nothing then, sir?" DC Terry Morton said. "Again?"

"I wouldn't say that, Terrence," Sadiq said, his tone hard and firm. "We have some hairs that were found at the scene. DNA results, if we can extract some, should be back tomorrow. We could get a lead."

It wasn't like the DCS to take a leading role in a case. "Where's DSU Smith, sir?" George asked. He picked up the coffee Wood had put down and sipped it. It was good.

"He's ill, Beaumont. All the DCIs are busy with other things. Shelly should be back early next week, and you will report to her if Jim isn't back." He sighed. "Back to business. There was no murder weapon found at the scene," said Sadiq. "But there were signs of a clean-up in the en-suite."

"The same as the other murder?" DS Fry asked.

"Correct, Josh. We've had all the other DNA results back. There was, as you can imagine, a lot. We isolated all DNA that didn't belong to Edward or the staff. No matches on the DNA database. No match on the CED, either." The CED is the Contamination Eliminated Database, a database of DNA from officers and detectives who visit crime scenes.

"Whoever did this was a forensically aware piece of shit," Morton added. "But at least when we find them, we can place them at the hotel."

"Did we find any DNA that matched the DNA found in Headingley?"

Sadiq thought for a moment and looked down at his notes. "Good question. It's not in my notes, George. Follow up on that for me."

George nodded, making a note.

"The killer used cable ties this time. You can buy them in a thousand shops, anywhere in the country. We'll never trace them, so I won't be putting uniform on it. It's a waste of time and resources," Sadiq said.

George knew Sadiq meant money.

"Anything else, sir?" asked George.

"A single gold hoop earring. No prints or DNA. Expensive. Glamira—the set goes for just shy of seven hundred pounds." Sadiq said and shook his head in astonishment.

There was an audible whistle.

"Seven hundred quid for a pair of earrings? Who has the dosh for that?" Josh added.

"Rich people," Morton said.

"I pity the woman who gets with you then, tight-arse," Elaine Brewer added with a laugh. She winked at Josh, who had turned scarlet.

"Seven hundred quid for a pair of earrings, though? Even if I got rich, I wouldn't spend that much," Josh said.

Sadiq was standing there at the front with a look on his face that suggested they all shut up at once. They weren't used to their bosses' boss being upfront.

"I got DS Fry to check with Glamira—the closest shop is on Vicar Lane, Bradford. Then it's Meadow Hall, Sheffield. The Arndale in Manchester. Then there are two down in London. There are eighteen shops in the UK that sell seven to ten pairs a week on average. More at Christmas and Valentine's Day. Apparently, they sell ten-thousand pairs a year in the UK alone."

"Christ!"

"We could concentrate on sales in Bradford, Sheffield and Manchester first," said Josh.

"We could, but we're not, Josh. We don't have a chance of tracing the earring. He could have stolen it, bought it at a pawnshop, or even been given it by a family member. And even if we find the other one, the stamp would be the same as a thousand others as they're mass-produced. It's a waste of time and resources."

A waste of money.

"He?" asked Wood. "How do you know our culprit was a he?" Isabella still wasn't sure their culprit was male.

"Lack of sexual activity. No long hairs. I also value our profiler's opinion. So it's the same culprit as whoever killed Alec."

"It was a he, DS Wood," Catherine said. "The frenzy and the violence."

"So are we just ignoring all the signs that point to this being a lust murder like the previous murder?" said Wood. "I've had a look at both bios, and neither suggests a sexual interest in men. There was no sperm or semen inside Rawlinson's stomach. Did Lindsey find any inside Edward Kennings'?"

"No, DS Wood. But as Dr Yardley already mentioned, absence doesn't mean it wasn't once there. Both bodies were left for long periods of time. Also, his penis was cut off post-mortem. Everything fits."

"Edward's penis wasn't used sexually, though, so this idea of a lust murder seems ridiculous," Wood added.

"You don't need to have sex to fulfil a lust murder fantasy," Catherine explained. She was beginning to lose her patience with DS Wood. It was evident to everybody in the room.

"You've read Edward's bio, I assume?" said Sadiq, in an attempt to move the conversation along. She nodded. "Tell us about him then."

"Edward was a rich, single man who had about three million pounds in his bank with no one but an ex-wife to inherit. He didn't have a criminal record, and all we have on file is a complaint brought against him when he was twenty-one. His landlord took him to court because he trashed the flat whilst he was at university. He received a caution and paid a fine. He even paid damages."

"His bank accounts look fine, too. I looked through them last night," Josh added.

"OK," said Sadiq. "Somebody needs to question the ex-wife. If she was the only one able to inherit, she stands to gain from his death."

"We've arranged an interview already, sir," George said. "She's called Lorraine Cox."

"Good. Is Dana Szymańska still a suspect?"

"No, sir," DC Tashan Blackburn said. "I spoke with her partner, who gave her an alibi. We've cleared Amari Ibrahim, the other night manager, too."

"Thanks, Tashan," Sadiq said, smiling. He turned back to the entire room and said, "What's this about a young girl? From the Alec Rawlinson murder?"

"I sent Yolanda and Elaine around to Cassie Broadchurch's house. With her father present, they asked her for an alibi. Cassie was at home together with her father and stepmother."

"Right, OK. What's this I hear about a young blonde on

CHAPTER SEVENTEEN

CCTV?" Mohammed looked at Yolanda.

"A statement from the hotel owner. She told us Kennings went out drinking in the local area last night. We looked at the CCTV, and we can see him talking to a young blonde woman."

"According to the owners of the bar, her name's Emily Sanderson. She's a regular."

Sadiq nodded. "We need to find out who Sanderson is. Is she a suspect?"

When nobody answered, he turned to the SIO. "George?"

George shrugged and sipped his coffee. "Sorry, sir. I was thinking about the earring. I thought we were looking for a man. That's what Catherine says." He turned to his team and met DS Wood's pleading eyes. "I think we should bring her in, anyway. She may know something.

Sadiq nodded again. "DS Wood?"

"Well," said Wood, "in my opinion, she's a suspect. Sanderson is the last person we know to have seen Edward Kennings alive."

A few of George's team looked at their deputy SIO with surprise, but Morton jumped and turned around to her as if he had just been given an electric shock. "You what? We're looking for a man, DS Wood. Unless you think the two cases aren't related?"

"I think they are related, Terrence. I think the culprit is a woman."

Josh raised his hand, and Sadiq nodded at him. "Background check on Sanderson has just come in. Emily Sanderson aged nineteen. No cautions, no nothing. She's squeaky clean. She works at OnlyFans, apparently. That's according to her social media pages. Daughter of Geoff and Denise Sanderson."

"They own the gambling company, right?" said Tashan.

"Right. But she's at university. Leeds Beckett. Creative writing."

"Does that give her means, motive, or opportunity?" Sadiq asked.

"Not really. She has no motive. If Edward was a fan or even a customer, if that's where we're heading with this, keeping him alive is to her advantage. I still think it's a man. I trust Catherine's opinion." George didn't look at Wood as he said it.

"Anything else, Josh?" Sadiq asked.

"Just that I don't think she has a motive, either. I think if we look at her bank accounts, her parents probably pay for everything. I've seen it before with rich parents. They give their children an allowance. From her bio, she isn't the killer. I'm waiting for more information."

Sadiq turned back to his notes. "Right—"

"Whoa!" said Morton.

The silence after the shout lingered in the room for a moment.

"Geoff and Denise Sanderson died abroad last year," Morton said. "It says here her uncle, Alistair Sanderson, bought Emily out. She's worth fifteen million quid."

George shook his head to try to clear it. "Shit. Are you kidding me? How on earth is a kid of nineteen worth that much money? Why the OnlyFans then?"

"It doesn't say," said Morton.

"Take that with a pinch of salt," said Josh. "Wait for the official information."

"She definitely has no motive then," said Elaine Brewer.

"I agree," Yolanda said. "There's nothing we have that suggests she had any reason to want Edward dead."

"Bring her in, anyway," Sadiq said. "We need to know everything we can about Edward Kennings. Ask her to cooperate. But don't arrest her or place her under caution. OK?"

Chapter Eighteen

Sitting in front of George was a beautiful young blonde. She had blue eyes that were wide and knowing, with the cheekbones of a model. She wore a white long-sleeved crop top, her toned stomach showing, with tight high waist black polyurethane leather leggings and white Adidas trainers. There was a sweet, fruity smell in the air. He thought he recognised it.

George looked at Josh, who couldn't take his eyes off the young woman. Clearly, his DS had a type.

"What do you want? Why am I here?" Emily Sanderson asked.

DI Beaumont ignored the questions, turned on the DIR instead, and said, "Let's make it clear, Emily. You haven't been arrested. You're here simply to help with our inquiries. I've been advised you've not requested the attendance of a solicitor. You're free to leave whenever you want—"

"Well, I've done nothing wrong," she said. "I don't need one."

Good. It certainly made it easier to get what you wanted with no solicitors around. "You've also said you're quite happy with Detective Sergeant Fry sitting in." Catherine Jones was watching via video link. "I'm Detective Inspector Beaumont, and this is Detective Sergeant Wood. We are investigating the death of a man named Alec Rawlinson."

"Alec, who?" She ran her manicured nails through her hair before tossing it over one delicate shoulder. George saw nothing on her face to indicate she knew him.

"What about a man named Edward Kennings? When was the last time you saw him?"

"Is he dead?" she asked.

George had not taken his eyes off her face since he'd entered the room. He saw no hint of any guilt. If she was guilty, then she was an excellent actress. "Dead? Why would you think he was dead?"

"I wouldn't be here otherwise. You said you were investigating the death of a man named Alec. You're also detectives."

A sharp young woman. Fair enough.

"You were with him last night, right?"

She didn't answer immediately but locked eyes with George. He could see the cogs in her head turning, calculating how to answer the question. Was she figuring a way out?

"It'd be better for you if you told us the truth, Emily," Wood explained. "Don't make things harder for yourself."

Emily hesitated a moment longer, then said, "Yes. I was with Eddie last night."

"See, that wasn't so hard, was it?" Wood asked, a smile on her face.

"How did he die?" Emily asked.

"He was murdered," Josh explained.

"Duh. How?"

"With a knife," Wood said. "He was stabbed. Twenty times."

Emily closed her eyes as if she imagined the bloodbath. Then, she met eyes with George and smiled, her lips thin, her eyes dark. It was a cruel smile, one that made her look guilty. George didn't like it.

"How long were you seeing Eddie for?" DS Wood asked.

"I wasn't," Emily explained. "We fucked a few times, that's all. Met on a dating app."

"Did you have sex with him last night?" Wood asked.

"No."

"But you were with him last night?" George asked.

"Yes."

"And you left the bar with him?"

"No."

"No? Are you sure?"

"Yes."

"Yes, you're sure, or yes, you left the bar with him." George clenched his fists tightly. The young blonde was making him angry.

"Yes." She smiled and winked.

"Which is it?" Wood cut in.

"You know, you're cute, Detective Sergeant Wood. I don't just fuck boys; I fuck girls, too."

"Edward Kennings was hardly a boy. He was old enough to be your father," Wood said.

Emily shrugged. "So, I have daddy issues. You know mine's dead, right? And anyway, that doesn't mean I killed him."

"You left the bar with him. Yes or no? Which is it?" DS Wood's tone was insistent.

Emily sighed and said, "You're no fun, sweetheart. I already told you, didn't I?" She drew her tongue across her crimson-coloured lips.

"Explain it to me in detail," George said. He took a deep breath to calm himself but kept his hands under the table where they couldn't be seen. He was sure his nails had drawn blood from his palms.

"This is boring me. We set up a date via the app, met in the bar, and had a few drinks. I left because he'd apparently bumped into somebody he knew, and I don't play second fiddle. I don't know whether he stayed or left. It was none of my business."

"What app did you use to contact Edward on?" DS Wood asked.

She told her the name and then said, "Can I go now?"

"You're free to leave whenever you want, Miss Sanderson," Josh said. "But we want to eliminate you from our inquiries. We have some more questions if you're happy?"

"Now, this boy is a nice boy, a cute, polite boy. I like you. You go ahead and ask me all the questions you want, alright?"

George's anger grew. She was younger than Josh at only nineteen, yet acted as if she were older than him. How condescending.

"What time did you leave the bar?" DS Wood asked.

"11 pm, I think." She thought for a moment in silence. "Yes, 11 pm."

Yolanda and Tashan were checking the CCTV in minute detail. He texted Yolanda the time. "How do you feel about Edward now that you know he's dead?" George asked. If he asked questions, then he could keep his heart-rate level.

Emily looked at him, her blue, wide eyes sweeping over him, looking him up and down. "I don't know how I feel yet. I've only just found out."

Josh said, "That doesn't really answer the question—"

Emily Sanderson cut the young DS off, holding up her hand like a traffic officer stopping traffic. "I said I don't know. OK?"

George could see the interview slipping from his grasp. "Tell us about OnlyFans. You're worth millions. Why—"

"Why not," Emily interrupted. "There's something about showing off my body that turns me on, you know? I'm appreciated by thousands. It's not about the money. As you say, I'm worth millions."

George wondered what Catherine was thinking. He was thinking about fantasy and real life. Blurred lines. Lust murder. "I'm told you're a student at Leeds Beckett University?"

"Correct."

"A student of what?" Wood asked.

"Creative writing."

Though more detailed, the information Josh received half an hour after the briefing ended matched that found by Morton's search of Sanderson.

"I believe you published a novel last year under a pen name. Is that true?"

"Under Emily Anderson, yes. What of it?"

"The plot's interesting." George paused dramatically. "I haven't read it myself, well, not yet. I'm told it's about a young, nineteen-year-old blonde millionaire who does OnlyFans and murders her customers in hotel rooms. Sound familiar?"

The tension could have been cut with a knife.

"I'm done," Emily said. "I withdraw my cooperation."

She got up to leave, a smile on her face. It took Isabella Wood a lot to lose her temper, but Sanderson's attitude was beginning to affect her like it had affected George. "Listen, Miss, we can continue doing this the easy way, or we can start and make things difficult for you if that's how you want to play?"

Emily laughed. What Wood had said hadn't ruffled her.

CHAPTER EIGHTEEN

"Fine. Arrest me. Tell me my rights."

"Where were you between the hours of 11 pm Wednesday and 4 am Thursday, Emily?" George asked.

"No comment."

Josh tried to calm the situation. "Miss Sanderson, we really don't want to—"

"Go on, arrest me. Tell me my rights, hold me in a custody cell and then question me with my solicitor, or else—"

"Or else what, Miss Sanderson?" Wood cut in.

"Or else I'm leaving. I'm sure the press would like to know why I was asked to come down here to Elland Road."

They had nothing on Emily Sanderson. Nothing physical or circumstantial. No evidence at all. She didn't seem to have a motive, means, or opportunity. Yolanda and Tashan were syphoning through the bar's CCTV at that very minute. "OK," George said. "DS Fry will see you out."

It was ten or so minutes before either detective spoke. "Nice girl," Isabella said. There was a frown on her face.

"Yeah, a nice girl without an alibi," George retorted.

* * *

The trio met in George's office after the interview with Emily. "What did you think of Emily Sanderson, then?" George asked Catherine Jones.

"She's interesting," was all she said. Nobody spoke, so Catherine continued. "I need to do more research. She might be the killer, but I still think it's a man."

"So, you keep saying," DS Wood said, venom in her tone. She looked at George for backup. She knew he had arranged a call with his profiler friend, Mark Finch, for later that afternoon and was glad George was listening to her opinions.

"I'll explain, DS Wood. Most killers have experimented with violence in other, smaller ways," she said. "We've had two kills in quick succession, and so, I believe a recent traumatic event must have triggered the change in violence, and now they're escalating."

"So, the usual serial killer stuff? The whole children who are abusive toward animals are serial killers in the making, spiel?" Wood enquired.

"Yes, that's what I meant by smaller ways of violence. Another reason I believe they're escalating is because of the two locations of the murders. Usually, a first murder is committed away from where a killer is based so that they don't come under suspicion."

"They usually still do that in a comfort zone, though, right?" George added.

"Yes, a gold star for you, George. To be frank, they know the area, but they don't want to shit on their own doorstep." She grinned, and George mirrored it. "The first murder was committed in Headingley, and the next in Yeadon."

"So, if he's moving closer to home, then he lives in North Leeds?" George asked.

"It's possible. However, you need to remember that I'm talking about what usually is the case; that doesn't mean it's accurate here. I can't lead you to the killer with my profile, but I can help to narrow down any suspects. Anyway, the reason a killer moves closer to home is that they grow in confidence and look for targets a little closer to where they live. This is because they're more familiar with the area, and any other locals who may see them won't think that they're suspicious. Think about witness statements. We always ask about suspicious people.

CHAPTER EIGHTEEN

Local people aren't suspicious, right?"

"Right." He met Catherine's eyes.

"It allows them to slip in and out more regularly."

"And that will increase their confidence even more?" he asked.

"Yes. That, and the threat of the HMET investigation, hasn't deterred him. He's killed again, and more boldly and more violently this time, even knowing you're after him. He's escalating and taking more risks. This means he's enjoying the taste of power, and from what I know from my research, George, power can be very addictive."

"So, you're saying he's going to kill again?" Wood asked.

"Of course he is. Did you not take in my lecture about lust murders and blurred lines?"

"Anyway," George said, moving the conversation along. "DS Fry and DS Brewer have compiled a list of people known to Alec Rawlinson who have no alibi for the time he was killed, no matter how small the connection. We've come up with a short list of names."

Catherine nodded. It was what she expected from George and his team: good, solid police work and precisely what they needed.

George added, "Josh and Elaine are doing the same for Edward Kennings so that we can see if there's any crossover between the two lists."

Catherine smiled because, for the first time, she thought George and his team were taking positive steps in their investigation. It was also because George Beaumont bore the look of a man in command of the situation and himself.

And that self-confidence and authority, mixed with a chiselled physique and a handsome face, really fucking turned her on.

Chapter Nineteen

"It's been a year, George. Don't tell me you're only calling because you need help on a case again, eh?" Mark Finch said, his Scottish brogue flowing out from the speaker.

Mark was an experienced and well-respected criminal profiler who only last year secured tenure at the University of Leeds as a Professor of Criminology. His time was expensive and minimal. But for George, he'd give him all the time he needed. And for free.

George grinned down the phone at his old friend. "Hiya, Mark. Nice to hear your voice, mate. You got me. I need your help."

"Before I ask what I can do for you, I hear congratulations are in order?"

It took George a moment to realise he was talking about his son, Jack. "Thanks, mate. He's such an incredible boy. Did you get my card?"

"We did. Thanks. You'll have to let us know when the christening or baptism is. Florence and I would love to see you. Also, have you received your invite to Freya's christening yet?"

Neither he nor Mia was religious, so they weren't getting Jack baptised or christened. Freya was Mark and Florence's little girl, who was born a month before Jack.

"Sorry to disappoint you, but there won't be a religious service. We decided if Jack wanted to join a religion when he was older, then that would be up to him."

"That's a good choice to make. Good for you. To be honest, I wasn't too bothered getting Freya christened, but Florence insisted."

"I haven't received the invite yet, but yeah, I'll come. Can I bring Jack?"

"Course you can, bud. Bring him to the wedding, too. You never said whether you were bringing a plus one."

George thought about Isabella. He couldn't exactly take her, not when she was his subordinate. But at the mention of Jack, he was relieved. He knew Mark would have put pressure on him to bring a plus one if not for his son.

"Sounds good to me, mate. Hope Florence and Freya are well."

"Florence's still on maternity leave, and both are doing incredible. Thanks." George felt as if he could see the smile in Mark's voice. "She hasn't decided whether to go back to the academy in Roundhay yet. We'll see. We can survive on my salary."

George chucked. "I'm proud of you, mate. You know?"

"Thanks, bud. We can talk next month, anyway. Let's get back to business, eh?"

As much as he enjoyed speaking with his childhood friend, he needed Mark's opinion. Isabella was worried that Catherine's profile was wrong, and whilst George didn't have an opinion on it, either way, he wanted Isabella to know he took her view seriously. With a lack of DNA and other hard evidence, he was willing to go to whatever length it took to find the killer.

"So let me get this straight," Mark said. "There were multiple stabbings?"

"Yeah, for both victims. Pretty much the same MO."

"I've got the images on my computer, and I must say, they look like vicious attacks."

George remembered the scenes and shivered. "Yeah. Frenzied. There was a lot of blood. Thirteen and twenty stab wounds, respectively."

"Tell me about the removal of the finger and the penis?" Mark said. "Ring finger, right?"

"Right. According to pathology, the removals were postmortem. As were some of the stabbings." Lindsey Yardley had told him they could tell which wounds were made postmortem because of the way some had bled more than others.

"At first glance, you'd assume lust murders."

So Catherine was right, he thought. He said nothing and let Mark continue.

"However, because of the nature of the attacks, the rage and the frenzy, I'd suggest a revenge killing."

That's what Isabella thought.

"Reason I say that is because there must have been a lot of blood spatter," Mark said. "Have you found anything? Discarded garments covered in blood? I can't see anything if you have."

"No," George said. The disappointment could be heard in his tone.

"Yeah, I thought so. It's hard to get away without being seen when you're covered in blood."

"On page two of the report I sent you, it states the killer cleaned the murder weapon, and possibly himself, before leaving the crime scene."

"Yeah, I noticed that. I also noticed you using the pronoun, him. Any reason for that?"

Isabella Wood's words appeared in his mind. 'Just make sure he doesn't know that I think it's a woman, and Catherine thinks it's a man. I want him to give his opinion without any influence.'

"Because we don't know the killer's gender yet. It's my fault. We should have used 'they'." George moved on quickly, explaining the tiny traces of blood in the sink at both crime scenes. "No DNA yet. We found some hairs, though. Hopefully, they will tell us something."

"So, it's clear your killer is forensically aware as they leave little, if nothing, behind. They're cleaning the blood before leaving the scene. Do you think these were planned?"

George nodded, despite his friend being on the other end of the phone. "Premeditated for sure. And we believe the victims booked the rooms themselves. Whoever did it planned it and adapted accordingly."

"So very intelligent, then. And meticulous. Any CCTV?"

"No, nothing we've found yet. Kennings, the second victim, was seen with a young woman before his death. We've had her in for questioning, and I'm unsure it's her. There's no link between locations, either. Rawlinson was killed in Headingley, while Kennings was killed in Yeadon."

"Do you think the murderer had a vehicle?"

"Got to have. Think about the blood," George said.

"Sure. Guessing you've got ANPR data?"

"Aye," George said. "We're working on narrowing down the vehicles in both Headingley and Yeadon. The volume of traffic is large and has been difficult to sift through. We're cross-referencing both lists, hoping to get a lead."

CHAPTER NINETEEN

"Be careful. Your boss probably thinks it's a waste of time and resources. I know I would. Sorry, mate."

"I get it. We're struggling, though."

"I bet. I've just looked through the forensic reports you have. As I mentioned earlier, your culprit is a careful, meticulous individual who is a planner, too. They were in and out, unseen and unheard. My guess is the murders were set up perfectly. No sign of forced entry means the victims granted the killer access. They even got undressed for them."

"You're thinking male prostitute or male escort?" George asked.

"Was either man gay? Bisexual?" He didn't wait for George to reply. "I can see why you thought of an escort or a prostitute. It's the nudity, right? Could be a partner, an ex-lover, or even a stalker if you take that into account."

"We had a theory that Alec was gay, and one of the B&B owners killed him. It was ridiculous, to be honest. We were desperate. It's because the killer sent messages to the victim's phone about their meeting arrangements."

"Makes sense. But to be honest, if all of your checks have turned up that he's a heterosexual, then from everything you've told me, I'd suggest the killer is a woman, George."

"What?" George thought for a long moment. Because of Catherine, he'd dismissed the killer as being a female. Not only that, but he also knew from his own research that it was more likely the culprit was male. Isabella wasn't convinced, though. Never had been. Suddenly, he felt guilty.

Shit!

George could hear Mark clacking away at his keys. "Both murders were well planned, with meetings set up in advance. The murderer makes sure the victims are alone, and there's nobody else around. Any evidence is removed. It says here their mobile phones are missing. They attempted to remove all traces of DNA. Even in the second crime scene, the traces of blood in the sink were negligible."

George was convinced, but he wanted more. "I've read all the reports, Mark. Could a woman really inflict this level of slaughter?"

"Of course, they can. Don't be one of those who underestimate the fairer sex, George. Whilst statistics suggest it's unusual for a woman to go for such a violent method of murder, it's not unheard of. It's everything we discussed, as well as the subterfuge. She's covering her tracks and is making you believe these are lust murders. She's making you chase men. Meanwhile, she's probably setting up another kill."

"Convince me, Mark. Please. I need you to convince me so I can convince everybody else."

"Fine. The images of the crime scenes are not showy. If this were a man out for revenge, there would be blood-written signatures on the walls, insults aimed at the police, dismemberment far more than what you have, which tells me this is a woman, an efficient woman who killed these men for one reason, and one reason only."

George stuttered. "O—OK."

"She's out for revenge, George. Think about the level of control. The pathology report suggests the wounds are all the same size. She was cool-headed when she killed. Yes, it may look frenzied and bloodthirsty. There's none of her DNA, and we both know from the Miss Murderer case that frenzied attacks normally cause accidents. It's prevalent for people to hurt themselves when they're frenzied. The wounds would all be different sizes, too, because if she weren't thinking, then the entry wounds would measure at different depths."

George said nothing, and an awkward silence filled his office.

"Come on, George, think about it. She's so cool-headed that she even remembers to clean off the knife and even herself before leaving the crime scene. And that's not even the 'silver tuna', to quote my favourite film. She bleached their mouths. Did you assume something sexual because of the Bone Saw Ripper?"

"Right?" George said. That theory was written in the reports he'd sent over.

"She must know. So not only is she forensically aware, but she's aware of previous cases. Could she be a copper? Or a detective? Maybe she's a pathologist or a criminal psychologist? It could even be a SOCO or somebody higher in that chain of command. It could even be an author or a reporter, George. Police procedure is straightforward to research. There are enough TV shows about it, too."

George hadn't thought about that at all. "That means she could be a member of the public who loves true crime."

"Scary, isn't it? It could be anyone. But it's not a man; I'm sure about that."

Shit!

"As for how she fled the scene unnoticed, I don't know. Maybe she's naked and wears a trench coat after? Then she showers at home? Even that shows a level of control, George. And though I'm generalising, women are far better at that level of control than their counterparts."

What Mark was saying made sense, but it was still just an educated guess. And with the DCS hiring Catherine and keeping her on a short leash, how was he supposed to broach this new theory with his team? "Both men were tall and strong.

They went to the gym, ate well, and had expensive lifestyles. Would a woman be strong enough to attack men of their size?"

Mark chuckled. "You're thinking about this all wrong, Beaumont. Your killer was trusted enough to be let into their rooms. They were tied up, naked. Think kinky sex games gone wrong. Then add to it that the murder was planned. Your victims couldn't fight back, George, so yes, a woman could easily kill men of their size."

George tapped his desk, struggling to get to grips with this new theory.

Mark gave him a moment to think before saying, "Society has made it difficult to picture a woman as a violent killer. They're normally viewed as mothers, nurturers, carers and homemakers. But, George, women can be as violent as men. They just usually slip under the radar. Have you ever heard of the Damsel of Death?"

"Aileen Wuornos," George said, "right?"

"Right. Women often kill as black widows, killing husbands or partners. They're also angels of death, killing people under their care. Sometimes they kill for greed, usually for financial gain. And other times, they're sexual predators, which you clearly had thought of. But there's no sign at all of any sexual activity. These are decoys because your killer is nothing like that. She's exactly like Aileen Wuornos. She doesn't fit the mould."

"But why Alec and Edward?"

"It might be they represent a person, or persons, your killer hates," Mark said.

"What, like a proxy?"

"Yes, well done you. Or she knows them as men who were abusive towards women or men who neglected their wives or partners. The ring finger being dismembered could represent a cheating husband, for example. As could the removal of Edward's penis."

George exhaled slowly. "So to be clear—are you saying that the murderer is A, going after men who are proxies for somebody else, or B, is going after a type of man for revenge?"

"Could be either, could be both," Mark said.

"Oh shit, she only needs one more before she's a serial killer. Detective Superintendent Smith is going to love this."

George could hear the sound of Mark flipping pages out of the speaker. "Look, you don't have too much to go on yet, and so it's too early to say. But from what we've discussed, and from what I've read, I think you already have a serial killer on your hands."

An icy feeling dropped down George's throat and into his stomach like he'd swallowed a ball of ice. "So I need to look at cold cases?" He thought about Nate Patterson once again.

Mark's tone changed. "That's right. A serial killer who is obviously escalating."

Chapter Twenty

"I'm sorry to bother you whilst you're off sick," said George. He was sitting in his office, glad he wasn't sitting across the desk from his stony-faced boss.

"This better be good, Beaumont."

George told Jim Smith everything his profiler friend told him.

"Is Mark sure about this?" Smith growled.

Mark wasn't sure, of course. Criminal profiling was an educated but calculated guess using a mixture of statistics and common sense. But, Mark had been right many times before. "With everything I've given him, yeah. He's about as sure as he can be. As you know, it's not an exact science."

George heard an audible sigh. "Jesus Christ. I can't say I like it, George, especially as we already have Catherine Jones."

"Always good to have another opinion, right sir?"

"Suppose. So, we're looking for a female knife-wielding killer who may or may not be a serial killer already?"

"Yes, someone who's out for revenge," George said.

"Revenge?" the super asked. "I thought Catherine said these were lust murders?"

George thought back to his conversation with Mark, where they'd analysed every aspect of the case. Despite trusting

CHAPTER TWENTY

Catherine, by the end of their discussion, Mark had convinced him they were looking for a woman. Whoever had killed Alec and Edward had quickly gained their trust and had taken them by surprise. Not only that, but the perpetrator had meticulously planned everything and had even cleaned their weapon and left no trace. Everything spoke of a shrewd, female mind. That was, apart from the act of murder itself. Stabbing was messy and violent, and statistics showed female killers preferred to poison, shoot, bludgeon and strangle their victims. Only about eleven per cent killed by stabbing. Whoever she was, she must have had a powerful, personal motive for yielding to that level of anger and for causing that much pain.

He explained this to Smith and elaborated. "It's got to be revenge because of the ferocity of the attacks. Mark also feels as if the killer is aware they are killing for revenge, and so the lust murder mutilations were done to slow us down. Mark is adamant revenge is the only thing that can generate that level of rage."

"Did he give you an indication of who this person is?" Smith asked.

George wasn't sure what to say and hesitated. "Not really. He tells me the data over the years reveals that one in ten murders is committed by a woman. As such, the data is scarce, not giving us much in terms of the age and race of female killers. He believes she's aged between seventeen and forty-four, and as she's killed two IC1 males, Mark believes she's also white."

"Bearing in mind what he said, do we have any leads?"

George hesitated again. "We're looking at a young woman named Emily Sanderson, but I'm not convinced. There's also Alec's wife and Edward's ex-wife. Both have motives, but

Alec's wife has an alibi." George paused. "DS Wood and I are going to see Lorraine Cox, Edward's ex-wife, in the morning. We're looking at vehicles that turned into the B&B where Rawlinson was murdered, and we're narrowing it down slowly. We're doing the same for Edward Kennings and the hotel in Yeadon, but it's going to take time. I've asked Yolanda and Tashan to cross-reference the lists to come up with a list of suspected vehicles. That also takes time." He thought about the conversation with DCS Sadiq. "We're waiting on lab results from the second crime scene, and hopefully, we'll find something. I'm hoping we find DNA that matches the DNA found in Headingley."

"OK, Beaumont. Keep me posted."

George hung up his phone and looked at the clock. He was due to meet with Paige McGuiness soon. He didn't relish speaking with the press, but he knew it was necessary.

* * *

Later that night, George sat alone in his flat, reading The Blonde Delilah by Emily Anderson. George had checked out the back flap where there was an author picture and a brief biography: Emily Anderson lives in Leeds, in the UK, where she is working on her follow-up novel.

At first, he'd struggled to get into the novel, his thoughts on Paige McGuiness, and their talk earlier. Paige had made a lot of money from the exclusives he'd given her about his time in Alexander Peterson's basement and so wanted to keep him sweet. She'd made the connection between both murders and wanted his blessing to publish the story. As such, he'd asked her to keep the story until Monday, which should give them enough time to make the progress they needed.

With a cider in his hand, George consumed page after page, barely noticing as the clock crawled past midnight when he suddenly stopped reading. He put down the book and grabbed his mobile. Quickly, he found Catherine's contact and pressed the green call button.

Before she could complain about how early it was, George said, "Catherine. Read page sixty-nine. She kills her second victim on a bed in Yeadon with a knife, his hands tied with cable ties to the bed."

After discussing Emily's novel and how she could be the killer, George hung up the phone to stunned silence.

It was then that he realised his first reaction was to call Catherine instead of Isabella.

Chapter Twenty-one

The next morning, George's entire team met in Incident Room Four. As they entered, he handed each one who didn't have a copy, The Blonde Delilah by Emily Anderson. George had read the entire book and wasn't sure what he thought of it. Crime thrillers weren't his thing, not really. Because of his job, he enjoyed leaving the real world behind and reading a Harry Potter novel or a horror novel by the master, Stephen King. Not that he had much time to read the novels he wanted to. Recently, he hardly ever read anything beyond police reports and the national newspapers. Regardless, George could sense the skill of the writing and the surprising accuracy of the murder sequence. Emily knew what she was talking about.

As George continued to read the novel throughout the night, he must have, over a dozen times, flipped to the beginning of the book. There, in black and white, was the hard truth: the book had been published way before Edward Kennings' murder last year, in fact. It seemed, in this case, life—or, more correctly, the taking of life—was imitating art.

"Before Catherine speaks," George said. "I just wanted to let you know Dr Lindsey Yardley, the Crime Scene Co-ordinator and pathologist, who carried out both post-mortems, has

CHAPTER TWENTY-ONE

agreed to attend this briefing and will answer any questions you may have about the crime scene after Catherine has shared her thoughts with us."

"Thank you, DI Beaumont," Lindsey said, not standing up.

Catherine Jones stood up at the front of the room, and George introduced her once more.

"After reading the book and watching the interview with Emily, I can tell you it's really simple," said Catherine. "There are two options. One, the person who wrote this book is your murderer and acted out the killings described."

"Why would a person do that?" queried Morton.

Catherine smiled. "Think back to the last time we spoke, Terrence. The author has created a fantasy and acted it out. Fantasies are a crucial component in lust murders, ones that can never be completely fulfilled. As such, the lust killer's fantasy will continue to develop, and it—and they—become increasingly violent as they struggle to fulfil said fantasy."

"Hence the escalation?" George asked.

"Precisely, George. Our killer cut off Edward Kennings' penis and inserted it inside him. Plus, they stabbed Edward more times."

George nodded. They were going over old ground, and he was keen to move on. "The second option, Catherine?" he asked.

"Well, it's also very simple—and with us thinking our culprit is a man, this is the one I believe is our option—someone was affected by reading Emily's novel—"

"Affected? Affected how?" Morton interrupted.

"Well, if you let me finish, Terrence, then I'll tell you. Our guy could have read the book and wished to act out the events described by Emily. I'd suggest the act of tying up a man and stabbing him in a frenzied way is an innate desire or a fantasy he needs to fulfil."

"But if we're linking Rawlinson's murder and Kennings' murder, why wasn't our culprit's fantasy fulfilled, to begin with?" Josh asked.

George thought it was a good question and so smiled at him.

Catherine explained. "Fantasies can never be completely fulfilled; sometimes, the experience of violent murder can generate a new fantasy. The MO changed slightly."

"So, you're suggesting our killer is going to kill again?" George asked.

"Almost definitely, George. You need to catch him, as he's stuck in a repetitive cycle. Each murder creates a new fantasy."

Morton stood up and shook his head. George watched Catherine closely. "So, what about Rawlinson and Kennings?" he asked. "Either option suggests you're saying they were nothing more than the means to an end."

Catherine shrugged. "It's true, and with either option, we're dealing with a deeply disturbed person."

"An evil person, you mean!" Morton shouted.

She shook her head. "No. A deeply disturbed, *sick* person. With psychopathic disorders, we don't call people evil, Terrence, nor do we gauge how evil they are by their MO."

"That's bullshit, and you know it." From a stern look from George, Morton sat back down. He'd need to have words with the man after. Again. George accidentally met eyes with Lindsey Yardley. He saw a flicker of irritation on her face. Was it Morton who was annoying her? If it was, he certainly understood.

"What I will say, Terrence, is I hope it's not option one," Catherine said. "If the killer is Emily Sanderson, then you're dealing with a devious, disturbed young woman. This book was published last year and must have been written months, if not a year before it was published. If she did it, then her crime was committed with words ages before the initial murder."

"So," George said. "If her crime was committed with words ages ago, then why bother to commit murder now?"

"Because we're talking about a lust murder. Initially, the victims in the novel would have been proxies, probably resulting from childhood trauma."

Elaine Brewer raised her hand and asked, "Excuse me, Catherine, but what's a proxy? I'm sorry if everybody else knows."

Catherine smiled and shook her head. "I bet there are a few people in here with the same question, and by asking, I think you're brave, Elaine. Never be sorry. Think of a proxy as a replacement or substitution."

"So, you're saying our culprit is murdering these men as stand-ins for other men?"

"Exactly. Or another man."

"So we have another Co-ed Killer situation on our hands?" Morton asked. He was referring to the infamous American serial killer, Ed Kemper. "You said earlier you didn't think our killer would stop unless we capture him."

Despite being extremely annoying, Morton's knowledge of killers was unmatched. He turned to smile at him, hoping his minute of being the teacher's pet would get him to shut up. What he saw worried him. Lindsey Yardley looked as though she was almost choking on her rage. He could see her clenching her fist, breathless with anger. "Are you OK?" he mouthed. She didn't see him.

"Very good, Terrence." She winked at him, and he turned

scarlet. "Kemper killed several women as proxies for his own mother before killing her and one of her friends. Then he handed himself into the police."

"So, you're saying our guy will stop once he kills his intended victim?" asked DC Blackburn.

"I can't answer that, I'm afraid. If the abuser is still alive, then possibly. If not, then their fantasy of killing them will continue in that loop I described earlier. It also depends on whether the killer is the author or the reader. I believe it's the latter."

"Why?" DS Wood asked. "Why are you so sure? From what you've told us, it makes sense that Emily Sanderson is the killer."

"I agree, but only because of what it says in the novel," said George. "In the novel, where the killer turns out to be a novelist writing a crime novel, a criminal psychologist suggests the killer intended her book to be an alibi."

"Very, very clever," Morton said, a tinge of admiration in his voice. "As if I'd kill somebody in the exact same way I got my killer to do it in my book."

"Yeah, exactly," said George. "Are you sure you haven't read the book?" He'd taken a copy from George earlier, so he assumed not.

"Well, it's refreshing to know we're looking at a female killer instead of assuming it's a man for once," said Wood. She was the kind of detective who was always considering all the angles. "What if it's not Emily? What if it's a woman who just happened to read the book and thinks it's a great idea?"

"And this is why I agree with it being option two, DS Wood," said Catherine. "We're dealing with someone who is so obsessed that he—"

"Or she," interrupted Wood.

"No," said Catherine with a shake of her head. "It's a he, and what worries me is he's so completely obsessed with his fantasy that he is willing to kill innocent people in such a way as to place the blame on the author."

"I'm with DS Wood on this," Lindsey Yardley said. "When I think about my experiences, whilst I agree it's rare women kill with knives, it's too meticulous, too planned. It's got to be a woman. Think about the men. They were tied up. There's no evidence they were gay or bisexual."

"I wish you two would shut up about it being a woman," Morton said. George was boiling inside. He was furious, and the DC would get it later, away from the team. George looked at Lindsey Yardley once again, noticing her face and body had contorted as if anger stirred within her.

Catherine smiled at him and continued, "You're right, Dr Yardley; there's no evidence, not yet."

"Why would somebody want to place blame on the author?" Josh asked.

"Revenge?" suggested Elaine.

Catherine nodded but said, "I don't know. Not yet, anyway. Whoever it is has no respect for human life and—thinking about what you just said, Elaine—has an obsessional, deep-seated hatred for the author."

"So, we're dealing with somebody who is very dangerous and extremely ill?" George said. "Somebody who is killing in such a way to bring the author of the novel to our attention?"

"That, or it is the author?" added Wood.

"Yes," said Catherine. "Though I tend to incline towards DI Beaumont's idea, rather than yours, DS Wood." The women's eyes met. It was clear they didn't like each other.

"Me too, Catherine," Morton said. Lindsey Yardley stood up, and George expected her to say something. Instead, after noticing George watching, she shook her head frantically, and George swore he could see the resentment blossoming within her.

"OK, thank you, Catherine." George stood up and turned to his team. "DS Wood and I are going to see Lorraine Cox, Edward Kennings' ex-wife. DS Brewer and DS Fry, I want you two to bring Emily Sanderson back in."

"You think we need to ask her some questions about her novel and whether she thinks anybody has a grudge?" Elaine asked.

"Yeah," he said with a nod. He also wanted to make sure she wasn't next. And if she was the killer, he wanted to make sure she couldn't kill again.

"Do we have any questions for Dr Yardley?" George asked.

His team shook their heads, which was a good job, as she had left the room without him noticing.

Chapter Twenty-two

Outside, April rain still battered the city of Leeds, a stark contrast to inside the Alwoodley mansion with the heating had been on full.

Lorraine Cox was a forty-something who wore too much make-up and a lot of gold jewellery. Her blue eyes were ice-cold. There was a diamante choker around her skinny neck, attracting his eye to the ample cleavage she displayed. Ms Cox was precisely what George had initially assumed: a common as muck, gold digger. His only compliment was that she carried her age well.

Lorraine didn't give them much that they didn't already know. Though she did give them a motive. *Money.* The DCS had been clear when he'd said, 'If she was the only one able to inherit, she stands to gain from his death.' But Lorraine had an alibi for the night of Edward's murder. She was with a man named Timothy Hill.

She also confirmed that Edward was a bisexual man, adding strength to Catherine's theory that the killer was male.

* * *

DI Beaumont's phone buzzed whilst he was buckling himself

into his car. It was DS Brewer.

"Hi, Elaine. DS Wood and I are on our way back. You're on speaker."

"Sir, you're not going to believe this."

He was desperate for some good news. "What?"

"I was conducting further door-to-door inquiries around the hotel in Yeadon this afternoon, and one of the residents, Mrs Shawcross, saw a woman in a trench coat and red high heels leave the hotel just before two o'clock Thursday morning."

George shared a glance with DS Wood, who said, "Is she sure the woman left the hotel?"

"She's sure. Normally it's hotel staff having a cigarette break, but she knows both night managers. She swears she'd never seen her before."

"Did she give a description, Elaine?" George asked. He fired off some more questions, his heart racing.

"Slim and of medium height, with blonde hair," Elaine replied. "That's all she could say because she couldn't see her very well. It was pretty dark, and the woman kept her head down. She thinks the lady wore red."

They'd checked the back of the hotel, and he'd noticed the lack of lighting. "Was Mrs Shawcross outside her property, then?"

"No. She was in her conservatory having a drink of tea. She lives further down." George remembered the alleyway rose to a steep incline, and the houses followed suit. If Mrs Shawcross lived at the crest of the hill, she'd have seen the woman in the trench coat easily. "Apparently, she was curious because she knew all the staff at the hotel. Mrs Shawcross waited until the woman had gone. She turned left—"

CHAPTER TWENTY-TWO

"Back towards the main road?" guessed George.

"Yeah, exactly. She headed back towards the main road before Mrs Shawcross lost sight of her."

"OK, great work, Elaine." A gigantic grin spread across his face, and he could barely speak. "Get all CCTV footage sent over to Yolanda. We need to identify this woman as soon as possible."

"Yes, sir."

She hung up, and George shared another grin with DS Wood. Finally, they had a lead.

* * *

Kennings' phone records had arrived whilst George and DS Wood were interviewing Lorraine Cox and had already been analysed by the time they arrived back at the station.

As before, only one number had caught their eye. Josh found out that number belonged to an ASDA Mobile pay-as-you-go SIM used in what they imagined was another burner phone. It had been switched off since Wednesday night.

There was a single text message sent to the SIM from Edward's number that read: 'I'm in Bar Ten, where are you?'

There was a single reply: 'I'm behind you.'

Suddenly, there was a knock at the door.

Yolanda came in, looking flushed. "Sir, we've found something. Do you have a minute to come and look?"

George followed her into the warren where Tashan was sitting in front of a large screen showing colour CCTV images of the street to the back of the hotel in Yeadon.

"We've found this woman leaving the hotel at 1.49 am the night Kennings was murdered." Yolanda pointed to a blonde figure walking down the alleyway. She was wearing a short skirt, high heels, and a burgundy trench coat, which she tried to wrap around herself tightly. The wind kept blowing it open, revealing her outfit underneath. George couldn't see any blood spatter, but then her skirt *was* black, and her top *was* red. She was looking down, so the camera picked up only shadows and not her face.

"That's got to be her, right?" said Tashan, slightly out of breath because of how excited he was.

George nodded. "Got to be. A shame we can't see her face. Do you have anything clearer? If you did, we could run it through facial rec."

Once they had a suspect, they could use images, and the computer would search for them. The more images, the better, but it was useless without a clear CCTV image. They'd used facial recognition during the Miss Murderer case, and it had worked wonders.

Yolanda grimaced and moved the video on a bit. It showed her walking down the alley, away from the hotel. "Not really, no. If you look here, she looks to the side, and we can see her blonde curls near her cheek. The rest of her face is still in darkness, though."

They were so close, and George knew it. They had the woman on camera, but it was impossible to confirm her identity. All they knew was she was slender and of medium height, blonde-haired and looked good in a pair of heels. At least it confirmed what the resident had said during their door-to-door inquiries.

"That's not all, sir. Look at this CCTV image of Emily Sanderson. On the night she was with Edward Kennings—"

"Shit! She's wearing the same outfit as the girl on the CCTV."

He immediately went to DSU Jim Smith with the information.

CHAPTER TWENTY-TWO

"Find her, George," Smith said. "Find her, now!"

***

DC Terry Morton sighed deeply, his fingers twitching around his coffee cup.

"Problem, Terry?" Wood asked. The confusion on her face was unmistakable.

"Why would there be a problem, *Wood*?" He gestured to Incident Room Four with his drink. "It's like the sun shines right out of your arse."

"Excuse me? Where'd that come from? I was just—I was just making sure you were OK." She folded her arms and moved away from her desk. "And how dare you speak to me that way, Terry?"

"Oh, sorry. It's like the sun shines right out of your arse, ma'am?"

"Why the hell, Terry?"

DC Morton masked a scowl with a smirk as he took a sip of coffee. "Because you're wrong about it being a woman and, for some reason, George Beaumont only seems to listen to you. He even has that Catherine eating out of the palm of his hand. It's sickening."

"Why are you bringing George into this?" she asked. "This is obviously *your* problem, Terry. So, leave him out of it."

"Always so protective of each other, aren't you, *Wood*? I wonder why?"

Wood gritted her teeth, then raised a cup of her own coffee to her lips. When she was finished, she said, "I don't know what issue you have, but whatever it is, take it up with the Super. George has worked hard to be where he is. He's a brilliant detective. And I'm his deputy for a reason."

"Yes, I can't imagine why." He rolled his eyes.

"What? Just what are you suggesting?"

He shot her a look.

"Tell me, Terry. What are you suggesting?"

"Well, it's common knowledge that DSU Smith pulled DI Beaumont to one side before Professional Standards got involved last year. DS Fry replaced you on the case. It doesn't take a genius to—"

"Terry!"

Members of the team turned in their direction. Terry gave them all brief smiles and tried to ignore how their smiles wavered before they got back to work. He'd never felt part of the team, and the way George had spoken with him a few days ago when they had all been together had touched a nerve.

"You need to stop with the accusations," she said. "One minute, your issue is that I'm wrong, and you're right, and next, you're making baseless accusations." She held out her hands, palms up.

He raised a brow and whispered, "It's not an accusation if it's true, right, *Isabella*?"

"But you don't know the truth, do you, Terry?"

He pretended to consider what she'd said, then shrugged, a broad smile on his face. "You've no idea what I know. Believe you me."

"Go on then. Share this wisdom with me."

George made his way out of Smith's office and into the squad room and immediately noticed the tension in the air. DC Terry Morton stood up, shaking, his face red, practically foaming at the mouth, champing at the bit. About ten metres away was DS Isabella Wood, Terry's senior, her arms folded across her

CHAPTER TWENTY-TWO

chest. The rest of his team was busily trying to ignore them.

"I know all about the Holmfield Arms Hotel, *Wood*," Morton whispered. He could see the look of shock on her face. "And *Isabella*, if you don't start respecting me, everybody will know all *about* the Holmfield Arms. Alright?"

Wood ground her teeth. "Fuck you."

"Oh. How petty. Kiss your mother with that mouth, *girl*?" Spittle flew from his mouth.

"Just tell me what the problem is, Morton?"

"With you, or—"

"Tell me what your problem is!"

As he got closer, George heard Morton say, "Just stop going on about the killer being a woman, for God's sake. It's getting boring."

"Excuse me?" Wood replied. "How dare you speak to me that way?"

"You heard me, *girl*," Morton said menacingly. "It's getting boring."

George was conflicted. Morton was a DC and shouldn't have spoken to a senior detective that way. Yet he knew DS Wood could handle herself. It was why he stood there, watching, waiting.

"It's a guy, DS Wood," Morton continued. "He's using these victims as a proxy. That poor Emily Sanderson is being framed."

"How are you so sure, Terry? Are you the killer?"

He smiled a toothy grin. "Who me?" There was a slight hint of desperation in his tone. "No, not me. I'm not a homosexual."

"Nobody ever said you were," she said and wolf-whistled. A grin threatened to spread across her face. What she'd said had shocked him. "No sign of sexual activity. Maybe you simply pretended to be gay?"

"Not me." His hands balled into fists.

"Then who?" DS Wood said, her words sounding edgy. After speaking, she took a deep breath and smiled. "What *sort* of *person* are *we* looking for? A white male aged between eighteen and sixty. Am I right?"

"Probably, yeah." His eyes narrowed.

"So? Who is it then?" Wood said, her tone cocky. "You fit that category."

"We don't know who it is because you're constantly trying to delay the investigation, *girl*. Let us do our job and find the man responsible. Stop getting in the fucking way!"

"I'm not getting in the way, Terrence. Believe me. It's detective work like yours that delays investigations. You have a one-track mind."

"A one-track mind? I'm not the one fucking the boss, though, am I? I bet all you can think about at work is your next fuck," Morton said as his lips twisted into a snarl.

"What? I'm not—"

"Speak to a superior or fellow officer like that again, Terry, and I'll personally make sure you're logging evidence for the rest of this case." George paused for effect. "Understood?"

"Yeah."

"Yeah?"

"Understood."

"No apology?"

"What the fuck, Beaumont?" Morton asked. "On her side, really? Shouldn't have been surprised."

"Take some time, Terry. Go home. When you come back in tomorrow, I expect an apology. You certainly owe her one!"

As he slammed the door to exit the squad room, he shouted, "You're going to get what's coming to you, Isabella Wood. You too, George Beaumont. Mark my fucking words!"

Chapter Twenty-three

Already, the office had started to clear; the atmosphere created by the argument dissipated.

The first email George saw in his inbox was an email from DC Jason Scott, explaining he had taken a statement from one of Edward Kenning's friends. George read it and learnt Garry Clarke knew nothing. He'd been expecting it but was still disappointed. His team were speaking with Edward's other friends and taking statements, so he didn't really know the kind of person Edward was. But what he did know was that people usually had two lives, their private one and their public one, though Catherine had explained some people also had a fantasy one, too. All that meant was you had to be involved in a person's private life to claim you really knew them.

There was an email from Josh stating he'd found no dodgy transactions when looking through Edward Kenning's bank accounts.

Lindsey Yardley had also emailed her reports, including the toxicology report. There was nothing much to go on, really, only that Edward Kennings' blood alcohol level was sixty-nine milligrams of alcohol per one hundred millilitres of blood. The limit when driving in England was eighty, so he wasn't particularly drunk.

George clicked through the attachments. The blood in the hotel sink they'd had to use UV light to find belonged to the victim. The bleach in his mouth had destroyed any evidence that could have potentially been in there. His dismembered penis showed no signs it was used sexually, which he knew already. The DNA they'd found at the scene didn't match any of the DNA they'd found at the crime scene in Headingley. As before, he was disappointed.

Then, he clicked the last attachment and threw his hand up in the air. *Yes!* The hairs they'd found belonged to two different people, one that was on the CED, the Contamination Elimination Database, and one that appeared on zero databases. Emily's DNA profile hadn't come back yet, but when it did, he'd cross-reference it immediately.

* * *

George had one more task to complete before going home, and that was calling Paige McGuiness for help before anybody could change his mind.

"Hello, George," said the journalist, as if she hadn't seen him recently.

"Paige, have you seen YappApp?"

The line went quiet, but he knew better than thinking she had hung up on him. "Yep. It was obvious a connection was going to be made."

"Perhaps I can offer you something by way of an apology?"

"Go on, George."

"I have images I need circulating. CCTV stills from Yeadon. We think it's the culprit, but the images are too low-res to be of any help. Maybe the images will refresh the minds of people in the area. You've got time to circulate and get an issue out, right?"

There was a fumbling sound. She had put George on speaker. "Email the images over to me now."

"Already sent. Thanks."

"No, George. Thank you. Again. For the exclusive. I really appreciate this. We'll send this out. These images will be all over social media within the next hour. Facebook, Twitter, Instagram, you name it. I'll make sure it makes the news, too. Local and national."

"Thanks. We're also looking for a woman named Emily Sanderson. We need to speak with her in connection to the murders. I've sent her picture over to you, too."

"I don't know about you, George, but this Emily sure looks like the woman on the CCTV."

George said nothing.

"Thanks again," she said, her understanding clear. "I'll make sure everything is out within the next half an hour."

He knew she'd follow through. After all, she'd get all the credit. George hung up, wondering whether he had made a mistake. She'd no doubt come up with a silly name for their killer, as the press usually did.

A moment later, DS Wood knocked on his door and entered. "Let me send this email to Juliette and our internal PR department, please." An APB had already been put out for Emily Sanderson, and images taken of her during questioning had been posted on their various social media sites. Juliette Thompson, their reliable press officer, would soon release a statement. They'd even set up a dedicated phone line where members of the public could call in any sightings.

Sanderson's picture would be everywhere. She couldn't

escape.

He tapped at his keyboard for a minute before looking up. "Are you OK, Isabella?"

"No, I'm not."

"From what I heard, you handled yourself great. He was the one being unprofessional." He grabbed her hand and kissed it.

"It's not that, George. He knows all about our stay at the Holmfield Arms Hotel."

Shit! Was Morton the bad seed in his team? Was Morton really the bad seed Adam Peterson had warned him he needed to weed out?

* * *

DC Terry Morton lived in East Leeds. It wasn't the most affluent, but by living in Colton, he'd bought a home in a pleasant area of the city where the house prices were reasonable for his salary.

Born and bred in Leeds, he'd worked his ass off over the years on several major crimes, though nothing was as disturbing as this bout of brutal murders. Even the Bone Saw Ripper's murders weren't as distressing as the sheer frenzied nature of the ones they were currently dealing with. The only solace was that the killer who had committed them seemed to be after fit, good-looking men with money. At twenty stone, five foot seven, and crippled with debt, he was safe.

At a few minutes after ten, Morton finally got home to his three-bed home. He'd spent the night driving around Leeds, thinking about the situation he'd caused back at the station. He shouldn't have had the argument with Isabella Wood. It had been pointless. He knew he'd have to apologise. DSU Jim

Smith didn't believe him last year when he took his concerns about Wood and Beaumont having a sexual relationship. And other than seeing them together at the Holmfield Arms Hotel in Wakefield, he had no evidence. Maybe he'd ask for a transfer. Yes. A transfer. Perhaps Wakefield HMET would suit him?

He wondered what his wife would think about a transfer. His wife was down in London with their children. He'd lied to his superior recently, saying his wife was down there because his daughter was pregnant. His daughter was pregnant, but that wasn't the reason why they were down in London. His wife was down there because they were getting a divorce.

It had been a hell of a day, and he was sad there was nobody there to greet him. The drive had convinced him Emily Sanderson was the killer and that stupid criminal psychologist had got it wrong. It was why he should never have argued with DS Wood. He didn't exactly respect Catherine Jones, and the cherry on the cake was that everything she'd told him, and everything she'd led him to believe, had been proven wrong.

His house was at the end of a cul-de-sac on Elm Tree Close. The street was deserted. From his view in his rear-view mirror, he could see security lights that glowed like twinkling stars down the street.

His vision was obscured when bright lights flashed in the rear-view mirror of Morton's white Peugeot 108.

Its headlights shining, a blue Ford Ka stopped at the bottom of his driveway.

A person got out and waved a hand that was clutching a mobile phone. The figure was wearing a hat and a red coat.

"DC Terry Morton? I'm Paige McGuiness, from South Leeds Live," she said as she strolled up the driveway. The figure flashed her ID lanyard quickly.

CHAPTER TWENTY-THREE

Morton thought she had a young, sultry voice, almost as if she was putting it on. He wasn't the kind of guy to be seduced. His wife may have wanted a divorce, but he still loved her. The journalist took her hat off and held it under an armpit. He'd never met Paige before, nor had he seen her before, but he knew her reputation. She wore a tailored business suit and heels, had long blonde hair, and was very young. *She's pretty cute,* Morton thought. He liked a woman wearing glasses. And she had the look of somebody he knew. Who it was she reminded him of, though, he wasn't sure.

Terry hated journalists with a passion, and Paige McGuiness wasn't exactly screaming professional visiting him at his private residence at a ridiculous hour.

"It's a bit late, isn't it, love? Whatever you're 'ere for, you've wasted your time. Anything you ask me will be returned with a no comment, Miss McGuiness. I'm sorry that you've come all this way for that. Drop by the station tomorrow, and I'll see if I can get George to speak with you. Alright?"

He was being polite when he didn't want to be and was aware his words sounded insincere. He thought his boss, DI George Beaumont, had already spoken with Paige, and if he had, she obviously wanted more. And the last thing Terry needed was the press snooping around his own life. "Sorry, I realise my words sounded insincere. But I meant them. Detective Inspector Beaumont, SIO, is fielding all questions from the press. Call him tomorrow?"

Terry didn't wait for a reply and headed towards his front door.

"That's OK, Detective," she said, following him up the drive. He got a waft of her perfume. Something sweet and fruity. "That's fair, but only if you promise to answer one question for me. Pretty please?" She batted her eyes at him. "One question. I understand that you have the right not to say anything, but this is important. It's why I'm here so late. It couldn't wait."

Morton unlocked his door and stood facing her, folding his arms across his chest, blocking the threshold. The young journalist closed the distance, and she took out her phone. Terry assumed it was acting as a Dictaphone. "OK, one question. But I might not answer it, alright?" He pressed the button on his fob to lock the car and invited her into his hallway.

She followed him, and as he turned right to head into the living room, she said, "Is it just you at the police station who's fucking stupid or are all of you idiots?" She put her phone back in her pocket, and Morton realised it wasn't even switched on. He hadn't even entirely understood what the girl had said until it was too late. The hat she had been carrying fell slowly to the floor, and a knife was glinting in her hand.

Morton had frozen. His bladder let go, and he felt a hot liquid flood down his legs.

A quick thrust of the knife punctured Morton's heart, and a gush of blood erupted from his mouth, spraying the assailant.

The murderer thrust again, laughing as she did so, piercing Morton's neck as he fell. Another gush of blood erupted from the wound.

The killer waited for a second before removing her prosthetic nose with her free hand. Next, she removed her glasses. Then, she said something Terry had heard before, in a voice he was familiar with.

With a look of understanding, Terry Morton knew who his killer was.

The killer dropped to her knee and continued in her frenzied attack. There had been no time for Morton to react, and not a single scream had interrupted the fragile silence of the night. A large thump signalled that Terrence Morton had fallen dead in his hallway. Still, she continued. She'd stabbed that prick Eddie twenty times. Terrence Morton deserved more.

"Thank you, Terrence, and fuck you!" the killer said. "I always knew you were a fucking idiot!" Then, the killer bent down and whispered, "Why would a journalist come out at this time of night and to your private residence? You were only a DC, you fucking idiot."

Her words fell on deaf ears.

Then the executioner drove away from the murder scene. The death of Detective Constable Morton wasn't a big deal, really, not even a cog in the plan's wheel. But it would cause a panic, the killer knew; it would wake everybody the fuck up.

She looked down at Morton's phone she'd placed on the passenger seat. The news article showed a picture of her police clearly found on CCTV. The headline stated they'd named her the Blonde Delilah, and the article suggested they were looking for a young author named Emily Sanderson, who they needed to speak to in connection with the murders.

Chapter Twenty-four

George's mobile phone buzzed on his bedside table. He groaned and reached for it. The time on the screen said 01.57 am, and the caller ID showed it was Mia. "Mia? Hello?"

When she said nothing, George sat up in a panic. "Is Jack OK?"

Nothing.

"Mia?"

Nothing.

"Hello?"

He cancelled the call and rang her back. When she said hello, he felt flushed with relief and gratitude—he was worried something had happened to her, or worse, Jack. Each day without living with his son was getting longer and becoming harder on him.

She said, "I miss you, George. I love you. I need you." That was all it took to erase any positive feelings. Calling to tell him she missed him, loved him, and needed him? She knew they weren't getting back together, and he couldn't understand why she was so incapable of maintaining a life without them being romantically involved.

She made a few cutting remarks when he didn't reply and

CHAPTER TWENTY-FOUR

threw in a jab about his work and how he always prioritised it instead of Jack. She was guiding him toward an early hang-up as if he were a sheep and she was a collie.

He didn't bite but asked about his son.

"He's—He's with Melissa at home." Her words were slurred. Melissa was her aunt.

"At home. Then where are you?"

"Out. I'm allowed to go out, aren't I, George? I'm not a child. I can do whatever I want, and *whoever* I want."

George rolled his eyes at her attempt to make him jealous. "I'll see you Monday night, alright?"

He hung up before she could protest and got out of bed. He'd only been asleep for an hour. If that. Isabella's argument with Terry was on his mind. It was unlike him, and George desperately wanted to know why he'd started a fight.

After finding Morton's number in his contacts, he dialled it. It rang through and went to voicemail. He hung up, not wanting to leave a message. When he called again, he was advised the phone was switched off. *Guess Terry doesn't want to talk,* he thought.

Shaking his head, George went back to bed. He struggled, tossing and turning for an hour or two until sleep took him.

It didn't take him very long.

George's mobile phone buzzed on his bedside table. He grunted and reached for it once again. The time on the screen said 03.12 am, and the caller ID showed as unknown. "Hello?"

A male voice said, "Sir, this is DC Zhang from DCI Arnold's team. I've been called to an incident that I think you might be interested in."

"What incident?" Shelly's team were on call by the look of it, so why were they calling him?

"A homicide, sir. An IC1 male in his late fifties with multiple stab wounds."

George sat up straight in bed. *Another one?*

"How many stab wounds?"

"Oh—" He sounded flustered. "I'm not sure, sir. I didn't want to contaminate the scene."

"Good job on that, DC Zhang. Can I have the address?"

"Elm Tree Close in Colton. End of the cul-de-sac," Zhang said. "You can't miss it."

The address sounded familiar. He didn't know why. "One minute," he said to Zhang and typed the address into Google Maps. "I'll be there in twenty minutes."

* * *

As George took a right from Yew Tree Lane onto Elm Tree Close, flashing lights were visible to his right. He followed them to the start of the cul-de-sac, which he could see had been cordoned off. Two police vehicles were parked in a V shape, blocking access, along with a CSI van and an ambulance waiting to take the body away.

George parked his Honda in the centre of the two police cars and glanced up at the surrounding houses. All he could see were lines and lines of glass windows, some lit and some in darkness. Curtains were twitching. His eyes moved from the first floors to the ground floors. A few people were standing in their doorways, watching. Some were speaking to uniformed officers, and others were filming on their phones. George walked down to the house at the end, where the homicide had clearly taken place. Before the cul-de-sac swallowed him, he noticed the sky had turned deep indigo. Soon it would be sunrise.

"DI George Beaumont," he said to the policewoman guarding the cordon. She shone a torch on his warrant card and then supplied him with a protective coverall, blue latex gloves, and shoe covers. Once he was suited and booted, she nodded him through the cordon, signing him in. Despite it being nearly May, an icy blast whipped at his face as he got closer to the house.

Several police officers stood by the front door, their faces blotched by the cold. George saw an inner cordon, which he ducked under to find DC Zhang.

The first thing George noticed was the smell. A mix of pungent piss, stale takeaways, and coppery blood filled the air. He shuddered and walked into the hallway, putting on his mask.

"The body is over here," called a voice. George recognised it as belonging to DC Zhang, who he'd spoken to on the phone. "DC Zhang?"

"Yes, sir. DI Beaumont?"

George nodded.

"It's over there, in the doorway to the living room." He shuffled down the hallway towards what George assumed was a kitchen. "Victim's name is Terrence Morton according to his driver's licence. Whoever killed him, well, it was frenzied."

Time seemed to stand still. The throbbing in his ears drowned out all sounds. George stared past him towards the kitchen. "Repeat his name?"

"Are you—Are you OK, sir?" Zhang stepped closer to George. "Sir, you've turned white."

"What was his name, again?" George didn't want to look at the body, and he began to shake as if there were ice in his veins.

"It's—It's Terrence Morton," Zhang said. "DI Beaumont?"

George gave him a vacant nod. "Are you sure?" he said. His mouth was dry. *It must be a mistake.*

"I'm sure," Zhang said. "It's bagged up for evidence, but you can look if you like?"

A chill shot down George's spine. He turned and ducked under the cordon, searching for Morton's Peugeot 108. There it was, in all its glory. He hadn't noticed it on the way in.

Before George rushed back inside, he called the only person he knew could console him. Isabella Wood.

She didn't answer her phone.

Shit! Shit! Shit!

After taking a deep breath and calming himself down, he composed himself and went to see Morton's body. He was on his back, and there was blood everywhere—on the skirting, spread out on the wooden floor, on the corner of the leather sofa. His white shirt was drenched with it.

This wasn't the same as Alec Rawlinson and Edward Kennings. There was nothing sexual about this; it was simply a cold-blooded murder. "Fucking hell," he muttered, taking the scene in.

"Brutal, isn't it?" a female voice said.

George turned around to find the blonde bombshell that was Lindsey Yardley dressed up in full protective gear. He missed Stuart Kent but rather enjoyed working with Dr Yardley. However, he still found it suspicious that despite how highly qualified she was, she only wanted a Crime Scene Co-ordinator job. She certainly oozed ambition.

"I don't think I should be here," George said.

"I didn't either at first. However, I've measured the entry

wounds. They're smooth and measure thirty-eight millimetres across. The murder weapon had a sharp tip and was non-serrated. I suspect during the post-mortem, we will find the murder weapon had been recently sharpened." Dr Yardley was referring to the previous murders. During each post-mortem, she'd found microscopic fragments of metal in the victims' throats, indicating that the weapon had been recently sharpened. "Morton still fits the victim selection criteria of an IC1 male in his fifties. And in my opinion, it's the same weapon. If anybody should be here, George, it's you." She closed the distance and put a consoling hand on his shoulder. "Are you OK?"

"Yeah. It's a shock, that's all," George said. "The last time I spoke with him, I bollocked him."

"It's not your fault. You didn't know he was going to die."

He puffed out air. "Any signs of sexual assault?"

She didn't answer but shook her head. "My working theory is he let the culprit in, as there's no forced entry. They got to the living room, and he turned to face his attacker, who stabbed him in the heart. If you look at the wall over there, you can see blood spatter. My guess is it sprayed the assailant. Morton's carotid was breached, too." She pointed towards a large gash in his neck and then up at the ceiling, where there was evidence of blood spatter. "As I said, whoever stabbed him would have been drenched in Morton's blood. Yet, there are no bloody footprints anywhere."

"Like before?"

"Yes, George. It's why I said you needed to be here."

"Anything else?"

"There are also signs that Morton's bladder let go."

That explained the smell. "Any dismemberment?"

"No. By all accounts, this was a frenzied attack designed as an ambush. It was a quick in and out. They even left the door open, which is why he was found. Or so DC Zhang tells me."

"Have you counted the puncture wounds yet?" She nodded. "How many?" George asked.

"Thirty, at least. Though I can't be sure at this stage; there's too much blood. I'll have a clearer picture during the post-mortem."

Thirty? Christ. George exhaled slowly. Was this a victim of particular significance, or was the killer escalating? The young crime scene photographer from before was looking at photos on her camera. "Are you doing the post-mortem?" She nodded. "When?"

"Tonight. I can fit you in at six. There goes my Easter."

He hadn't even realised it was Easter Sunday. Nor had he remembered Good Friday. The case had consumed him. "Any idea when Morton died?"

"Rigor mortis hasn't been completed yet," Lindsey said. "I've taken his temperature, but because of the door being left open and the chilly night, I can't be accurate. But I'd say five or six hours ago."

That would make the time of death between 10 pm and 11 pm the night before. "OK, thanks."

He found DC Zhang on the phone in the kitchen, standing with his back to the door, staring out of the window into the back garden. A metal swing was standing there, its seat swinging in the wind. "Yeah, love, I'll be home when I can." He must have felt George's presence as he turned and held up an apologetic hand. "OK, love. I love you. Bye. Bye."

George smiled. "Sorry, sir, the wife gets worried when I'm on call."

CHAPTER TWENTY-FOUR

George grunted but didn't answer. He was worried about Isabella. She always answered her phone.

"On your initial inspection, did you find any evidence to suggest that he had company?" George scrutinised the kitchen. There were no cups or glasses out. If Terrence Morton had received a visitor, he hadn't offered them anything to drink.

"No, nothing," Zhang said. "Initial statements taken by uniform suggest Morton had only just pulled into his drive when a car pulled up behind him."

"A car? Really?" said George.

"Yeah. Whoever it was left the car for five minutes and then returned and left in a hurry." Zhang shuddered. "Clearly the killer."

"What sort of car was it?" This may be the best lead they had so far, but only if the cases were connected.

"A blue Ford Ka. But it was too dark for any of our witnesses to record the reg."

George leafed through the statements. They were handwritten and a nightmare to read. "Did anybody offer a description?"

There was a severe look on DC Zhang's face. "No, sir. It was too dark."

"OK, thanks, DC Zhang. We'll take official statements later, and I'll send some officers door-to-door. Did you find a mobile phone on him?" George asked.

Zhang shook his head. "Sorry, sir."

George knew he had one. In fact, he'd tried calling him earlier. What time was that? He checked. 2.09 am. "The killer must have taken it," he told Zhang as he searched his contacts for DS Fry's number. He removed his mask. The smell of sweat mixed with aftershave suffocated him.

"Morning, sir," Josh said with a yawn once he'd finally got through. "Everything OK?"

"Josh, I need you to get your laptop and do a trace on this number to see if it's still active," George said, ignoring Josh's question. "I think it's turned off. If it is, get on to EE and ask them for a data download. I'll get a warrant from DSU Smith. I called the number this morning at 2.09 am, but it went to voicemail. That means it was on, and somebody turned it off."

"Whose number is it?"

"Terry Morton's."

"He was probably in a mood with you, sir. Especially calling him at that time. He probably turned it off."

Shit! He hadn't told Josh that Terry had been murdered. "He can't have answered it, Josh. He's been murdered. The time of death was between 10 pm and 11 pm last night. The killer has his phone. I'm at the crime scene now."

"Holy shit! Poor Terry. But that means the killer turned his phone off? I'm just putting you on speaker whilst I get dressed."

George could hear him tumbling about. He didn't think Josh had a partner but was unsure. "Exactly. I need cell site analysis so we can find out where the culprit was at the time I called. We also have a vehicle—a blue Ford Ka. No reg. I'm going to wake Tashan up now and get him down here to collect CCTV. Call Yolanda for me and get her into the office. I need her on ANPR."

"On it, sir," Josh said. "Do you need me down there?"

"No, Josh. I'll call you after I've spoken with DSU Smith."

George shook Zhang's hand and told him he'd speak with DCI Shelly Arnold later to take over the case as he left the crime scene. There wasn't much more he could do now, and he wanted to get home and shower away the stink of piss, sweat, and blood. DSU Smith answered immediately and said he'd provide a warrant.

The sky glowed in the distance as he left Morton's house. Not that it made any difference to the chilly temperature. He nodded to the policewoman at the cordon and headed to his car.

Before reversing and leaving the cul-de-sac, he looked down at Morton's house one last time. Why Morton? What did he have in common with Rawlinson and Kennings? Mark and Catherine were both adamant the killer was going after a type, an IC1 rich male in his fifties who was handsome and went to the gym. No offence to Terry, but he wasn't that guy. He never even pretended to be. So, what were the similarities? Their age, sex, and ethnicity. That was it. Yet, this murder had been starkly different from the first two. Were the murders really related?

The wild nature and the entry wounds suggested they were related. Lindsey Yardley was convinced. And so was he. Their assumed MO was wrong. His body shook as he drove out of Colton. They now had three victims, all with a very similar MO. It looked like they officially had a serial killer on their hands.

Chapter Twenty-five

"Fucking hell, Beaumont!" Detective Superintendent Smith bellowed after George entered his office. "They've only gone and named her the Blonde Delilah. You know what that means, don't you?"

George grinned, though there was no happiness in his grin. "Of course, sir. It means we have—"

Smith held up a hand. "Don't you dare, Beaumont? Don't you dare?"

Whether or not the super liked it, they had a serial killer on their hands. "Sorry, sir." George briefed him on what he'd seen at Morton's house.

"Fucking hell!" DSU Smith bellowed again. His office door was open, and several officers glanced nervously at them. "This case has now turned personal for the two of you. It's the same for the rest of your team. I might have to remove you all from the case."

DS Wood sat down, comfortable, but George held his ground. "With respect, you're wrong, sir. This is our case. The MO of Terry's murderer matches the other murders. Don't remove us, any of us. Sir, this is our case. I want to send some of our officers over there to do door-to-door. Somebody may have seen something."

Smith frowned. "I agree with you, but the Chief Super does not. DCS Sadiq has ordered me to remove DS Wood from the case—"

"What?" George interrupted. "You can't do that, sir."

"I can, and I am." Smith gave George a pointed look.

"But—"

Smith held up a hand. "Don't, George. DS Fry will be your deputy." George looked at Isabella, who shrugged. It was because of the argument. She understood.

"I respect your decision, sir, even if I don't agree with it," said Wood. "For the record, you're making a huge mistake."

Smith shook his head and gave a dramatic sigh. "This wasn't my decision. You two make a good team."

George and DS Wood nodded before she asked to be dismissed. She didn't look upset or even shocked. George wondered whether it was how she truly felt or whether she was putting her guard up. "Take the day off, Isabella. Get some rest."

"Sir."

"OK, George. I understand you're not happy about it, but it's above your pay grade. Mine too. I guess this means we have a fucking serial killer on our hands?"

George nodded, but a ping interrupted the flow of the conversation. It was an email from Calder Park.

"What now, Beaumont?"

"Unfortunately, sir, the DNA profile from the hair that was found didn't match anybody on the DNA database. We can't try and match the profile to Sanderson, either, as we didn't take one..." George wasn't deterred, however, because they could match the sample whenever they brought a suspect in for questioning. The good news, though, was that it was definitely female. He told Smith as much.

Smith was fuming. "Bloody hell, Beaumont! Who decided it was a good idea not to take a sample from Emily?"

"The DCS, sir."

Smith shook his head erratically. "Teach me to be off sick, won't it? For fuck's sake! I'll get on the phone with Shelly and let her know that from now on, the case is yours. Get uniform on door-to-door, too. I want this case tied up ASAP. I'm sick of it now; we can't have this woman running around wreaking havoc. Let's hope the press doesn't get wind of Morton's death. Speak to Juliette when you can and liaise. We can't have them linking this to the other two murders."

George gave a brief nod. "Yes, sir. I haven't seen or heard from Catherine for a couple of days. Is she OK?"

"She booked Saturday and Sunday off, Beaumont. It's Easter Sunday, and she doesn't work for the police any more, remember?"

* * *

"What was that all about?" DS Fry asked when George got back to his office.

"We officially have a serial killer on our hands," said George, looking over his shoulder at his Ds. "Didn't you know that DSU Smith's allergic to the phrase?"

Josh chuckled. "You'd think he'd be used to it by now. Is DS Wood OK? I saw her pack up and go home."

George got up and closed the office door. It would be common knowledge she'd been removed from the case soon enough, but he didn't want rumours flying around. He explained that because of the argument, she'd been removed

CHAPTER TWENTY-FIVE

from the case. George also explained they were all lucky not to have been pulled, as it had been one of their own.

Josh nodded his understanding.

"You're my deputy again. Keep up the good work, yeah?"

"Will do, sir."

Get the team together in Incident Room Four, Josh. I'm going to tell everybody before rumours start."

* * *

As soon as everyone was in the incident room, George stood up and greeted his entire team. The atmosphere was tense. Elaine had been crying. Tashan looked as if he was going to start. He felt immediately sorry for his team. He hadn't dealt with his own grief yet.

"Is it true?" Catherine asked, power walking into the incident room.

He nodded, surprised she was in. DSU Smith had told him she wasn't due in. She stifled a sob. "You OK, Catherine?"

She rubbed her eyes. "Yeah, we worked together when I was a DC, not that he remembered. The man had his quirks and an archaic way about him, but he was a good detective."

George nodded and faced his team in the incident room. He saw Catherine looking around. Who was she looking for? "Terrence Morton was a good guy. A decent detective. A father figure to some of you. We need to catch whoever did this. And soon. His wife, June, has agreed to speak with us tomorrow. As you can imagine, she's too shaken up to talk to us today."

"Where was she when Terry was murdered?" Tashan asked. "In bed asleep?" Every head turned to him.

"No. London. Morton told me June went to London to

announce their daughter Tessa's pregnancy. Apparently, June's parents are getting on a bit."

The depressed mood penetrated every space in the room. There was a lack of energy that was unlike his team.

"Come on, team. I know we've just lost one of our own, but we need to band together and catch whoever did this. It's what Terry would have wanted. He wouldn't have wanted this kind of atmosphere. Come on, let's go through the information we have."

"Where's DS Wood," Catherine asked.

George was going to leave the information regarding DS Wood until last, but now Catherine had mentioned it, it made sense to explain.

"Yeah, is she OK? I saw her leave earlier," DC Scot said.

George explained that because of the argument between DC Morton and DS Wood, she'd been removed from the case. George also explained they were all lucky not to have been pulled from the case, as Morton was one of their own.

"She's not a suspect, is she?" Catherine asked. She got up and joined George at the head of the room. "I want to apologise to you all. My profile was wrong. It happens. In my line of work, we provide an educated guess, and sometimes, that guess is wrong." She looked at Yolanda. "Great work on the CCTV." Then she looked at Elaine. "Well done for speaking with Mrs Shawcross. Great detective work." She looked at George. "I'm sorry, DI Beaumont." Then she addressed the entire room. "I appreciate that some of you may think I should be removed from the case because of my mistake, but I'm here today to prove that I shouldn't. Now we know it's a woman. We can use my profile and home in even more."

"What do you mean?" Tashan asked.

CHAPTER TWENTY-FIVE

"Now we know it's a woman. I can start and give you an idea of what kind of woman she is."

"Fine, Catherine," George said. "But first, I want to go through the details of the case with my team. You're welcome to stay."

She winked at him as she sat down, removing her laptop from her bag.

"So, Terry was found on his living room floor, near the entry into the hallway. There were thirty puncture wounds—more than either of our other two victims."

"Was it sexually motivated like the others?" asked DS Elaine Brewer.

George shook his head and explained everything that DC Zhang had told him about the door-to-door inquiries and the evidence from the scene provided by Dr Yardley. They were awaiting the phone records from EE and the CCTV from Colton. Yolanda had already spent hours looking at ANPR, but they were sparse around Colton. They'd only catch the car if they A, had the reg, or B, their killer, used the motorway to leave. "It's the entry wounds and the frenzied attack that make me believe the murders are connected." George also explained about the missing mobile phone and the blue Ford Ka, elaborating on the jobs he'd given Tashan, Josh, and Yolanda. "Our killer is escalating. Why? That's what we need to find out. DS Fry and I have had a conversation and believe we got our killer's MO wrong."

"What do you mean?" DC Jason Scott asked.

George fell silent for a moment. He pondered their new theory. The Blonde Delilah's victim selection was obviously IC1 males in their fifties. Whilst it made sense on several levels, on others, it didn't. Why did she kill Edward and Alec in such a way and not Morton? And why did she kill him in his house and not the others?

"Our killer is getting more adventurous," Catherine said. All eyes turned to her. "That explains your apparent change in MO. Has anybody read Emily Sanderson's novel?" There were a few nods and murmurs from around the room. "The Blonde Delilah kills the third victim in his home after he's put his wife in the hospital."

"And the fourth murder?"

Catherine smiled, her crimson lips threatening to take over her face, and shook her head. "The Blonde Delilah is caught before she could murder again. However, it's clear that once she is released at the end, she kills the lead detective."

"So what does this mean for us?" asked George.

"Nothing. Not really," she said. "It all depends on how deeply rooted the fantasy is. And whether or not Emily Sanderson is the killer."

"Go on, Catherine. Humour me."

"OK. Sure, DI Beaumont." She stood up and straightened her charcoal pencil skirt, which had obviously ridden up. She straightened out her white blouse, too. "A, your killer stops because her fantasy is over. If so, then it's possible she killed her intended target. B, she escalates and murders again. But this time, she makes the rules, not the book."

"Why does it matter if Emily is the killer or not?" Oliver asked.

"I was getting to that, DC James. To answer your question, it's my belief that Emily's fantasy would have been fulfilled by the three murders. She wouldn't escalate and murder again. She most likely didn't have any targets in mind and killed indiscriminately."

CHAPTER TWENTY-FIVE

"OK, let's consider that angle," George said. If Emily weren't guilty, then she wouldn't be on the run. "Elaine, I want you and Oliver to direct door-to-door in Morton's neighbourhood. Check if any of the neighbours noticed a strange woman in the area in the days leading up to his death, too. Take Sanderson's picture with you, but only use it as a last resort."

"Maybe Forensics will find something," said Jason, his tone hopeful.

George shrugged. "She was in and out, apparently. I know we say every contact leaves a trace, but she's extremely forensically aware. Other than a hair that might not even be hers, she has left nothing behind yet."

"They all make mistakes eventually," Catherine said.

George attempted a smile. "Let's hope so."

"That brings us back to what I said earlier," Catherine said, standing up. George sat down and let her speak. "Now we know it's a woman. I can start and give you an idea of what kind of woman she is, especially if it's not Emily Sanderson. It's clear to me we're dealing with a person who is cold and calculated. Intelligent and meticulous. The murders were well-planned and premeditated. It's also clear she is very well-versed on police procedure and extremely forensically aware."

George stopped listening and thought about what Catherine had just said. It was heading in the same direction as Mark's theory. He'd told George that their female suspect was 'forensically aware' but was also 'aware of previous cases.' Could she be a copper like Mark had suggested? Or a detective? Maybe she's a pathologist or a criminal psychologist? It could even be a SOCO or somebody higher in that chain of command. Mark also said she could even be an author as police procedure is straightforward to research. There are enough TV shows about it, too. *Shit.*

"A Crime Scene Co-ordinator, perhaps?" Catherine said, bringing him back from his thoughts. His team was discussing potential suspects.

George thought he knew somebody who was blonde, well-versed on police procedure and would be exceptionally forensically aware, but DC Scott's words interrupted his thoughts.

"What about a female detective? Detectives are very well-versed in police procedures and extremely forensically aware. They're also intelligent and meticulous. And it's not the first time a detective has turned out to be the killer." He was, of course, referring to Alexander Peterson, the Bone Saw Ripper, their old DCI.

"Absolutely, DC Scott," Catherine said.

"Ah, but being all of those things doesn't provide a motive to kill Terry Morton." He sounded deflated.

"You're right, DC Scott. Motive is everything. Can you think of anybody who was annoyed or angry with DC Morton recently? Somebody who is intelligent and meticulous? Somebody who is well-versed in police procedure and forensics? It could be a policewoman, a SOCO, a Crime Scene Co-ordinator, or even a detective. If you identify a suspect with those traits, my advice would be to bring her into custody."

Chapter Twenty-six

After a three-hour drive and what felt like an age—with even more time lost as they worked their way through various security checks, checkpoints, and X-ray machines—George and DS Fry could finally speak to and convince the relevant person to allow them both access to who George thought was one of Britain's most depraved paedophiles, Boris Jarman.

Despite accompanying him all the way to Northumberland, Boris had requested only George, which meant DS Fry was forced to wait outside until their conversation had finished.

"I was wondering when you'd come and visit me," Boris said, tapping his fingers on the table. "I've heard everything about the new killer you're chasing."

"Yeah? You know who it is?" George said.

"Is that why you're here?" Boris asked.

George dipped his head slightly and shook his head. The guy was playing games already. "I've driven a long way to come and speak with you. I got your message. Spill it."

Boris bent forward across the table, his face gleaming in the dull light. The man George had encountered earlier on in the year was entirely different to the one in front of him now. Once, Boris had been a tall, broad man with an overbearing presence; now, he looked as if he lacked energy. There was a deathly pallor to his cheeks, and his eyelids were swollen. It looked as if all the colours had drained from his body. His hair, including his beard, was tangled and unkempt, and he looked as though he hadn't slept a wink. And he'd lost a ton of weight, too. So much so, in fact, that the garments he wore drowned him, dangling from his shoulders and revealing a tuft of ginger chest hair. If he passed Boris in the street, George reckoned he wouldn't have recognised him.

"I'm ready to confess," Boris said.

"Confess to what?"

A smirk grew on Boris' face. "It was me who killed Anna Hill."

Finally. George breathed a sigh of relief. "Why are you admitting it now, after all this time?" George asked. He had to be careful how he played it—it wasn't uncommon for criminals to confess to a murder and then retract it later. If he antagonised Boris now, he'd risk it losing his cooperation altogether.

Boris shook his head. "Because you're still trying to get me to confess to the murders of Nicole Green, Joanna Cox, and Stacey Lumb. I had nothing to do with those broads. By admitting to killing Anna Hill, I'd get a shorter sentence, correct? You keep asking me for cooperation before my trial. Here it is. I'll plead guilty. But I'm being serious when I say she was the only woman I ever killed."

"Why should I believe you?"

The smirk on Boris' face grew wider. "Because of your killer, George. They snuffed out Alec Rawlinson and Edward Kennings, right?"

"Right."

"And I hear they snuffed out one of your own. DC Morton." The smirk somehow grew wider.

He'd only been at the crime scene this morning. "How did you hear about that?"

Boris shrugged. "You hear things in here, George."

"Where? How?"

"The walls." He smirked again. "When you spend a lot of time surrounded by three of them, they start speaking. I don't mind admitting it gets rather scary after a while."

"If you think the walls are talking to you, then perhaps you should see a psychologist?"

"Maybe I should. It might prove when I killed Anna; I couldn't possibly have formed the criminal intent. I should plead mitigation by diminished responsibility, shouldn't I?"

Was that why Boris had finally admitted to killing Anna Hill? An attempt at absolving his liability in the murder?

George slammed his fist on the table. "My, my, DI Beaumont. Losing your temper already? Patience, man."

"Stop fucking about Boris and tell me what you think I need to know."

Boris leant back in the chair and folded his arms. The smirk was gone. He commanded George's attention with one facial expression. "How's that son of yours? What was his name?" Boris tapped the table with his index fingers. "Jake? Jordan? Jack! That's it. How's he doing? Better than his mother, I hope?"

To George's surprise, he stood up and threw his chair at the wall. Boris was chuckling at his reaction. "You're wasting my time. You've admitted to murdering Anna Hill, yet you've provided no actual evidence you did it. I think you're messing about. You killed all of those women, didn't you?"

Boris clapped for a minute before halting. He leant forward again. George retrieved his chair and sat back down. Their gazes met. The tension was palpable. "No, I did not. But I think I know who did."

"If not you, then who?" George asked.

"How's my nephew? His trial's soon, yes?"

"I don't know how Peterson is," he lied. The less Boris knew about the extent to which George monitored Alexander Peterson, the better. He received daily calls from the governor of HMP Leeds. "You were about to tell me who killed those women thirty years ago."

"Ah yes, so I was."

George was getting nowhere with Boris and so shifted the dynamic of the conversation to focus it more on Boris. "Seen much of Mary?"

"Are you fucking kidding me? That ex-wife of mine wants nothing to do with me. I've written letter after letter and got fuck all back. My fault, though. I should have known those boys were underage, even though they lied to me. That's the problem with society." The smirk was back. "They lied to me, and I got locked up. Where's the justice in that? I was supposed to be released this month. Did you know that?" George nodded. "I did my time, Beaumont. But because of you, they won't release me."

"So that's why you're admitting to murdering Anna Hill?"

"Yes. I'll suffer for my sins, and then I'll be released. I can live the next thirty years of my life as a good man."

"You said Mary has answered none of your letters?"

"That's right, George. But I don't care. As I say, I've got thirty years to be a good man. You'll never get me back behind these walls."

CHAPTER TWENTY-SIX

He allowed himself to think about Boris on the outside. Could he really stick to a normal life, one that didn't involve fourteen- and fifteen-year-old boys? He didn't think so. Boris was a sick, perverted man. "You said you could help me with my recent case? They're calling her the Blonde Delilah."

"Glorious name. I'd love to get inside her—" Boris paused a beat and smiled. "Inside her mind, DI Beaumont."

An awkward silence ensued that George had no intention of breaking. He simply met eyes with Boris, not looking away.

"I can help you, but I want something in return. What I want is a statement from you about my confession, signed and dated. I'm sorry, George, that I killed Anna. I really am. I've been locked up in here for most of my life. Tell the courts that you believe I've been rehabilitated. Please, George."

There was an emotion in Boris' voice that George hadn't heard before. When they'd first met, Boris had sworn during every sentence and didn't care that they were questioning him about the four murders that happened back in 1994. He didn't seem bothered that he'd paid fourteen- and fifteen-year-old boys to have sex with him. Yet now, George was sure he saw the corners of the man's eyes glisten in the dull light. Was it all an act? "I'll need your information first, and then I can get permission from Detective Chief Superintendent Sadiq."

"No deal."

"If you want me to trust you, Boris, then you need to trust me." Their gazes met.

"Fine. You need to look at cold cases, DI Beaumont. I've heard of a case that sounds similar to yours. One in South Leeds. Indian fella. Look into it, and you'll see a connection. Trust me." He thought about the murder of his old colleague, Nathan Patterson, that DCI Shelly Arnold had been looking into. He'd promised DSU Smith he'd take a look, but he'd been too busy. He made a mental note to ask Josh to put somebody on it.

George wrote the information down in his pocket notebook about the 'Indian fella'. "Thank you."

"Look," Boris said. "I had nothing to do with Nicole, Joanne, or Stacey. But I knew Anthony Shields. Or Tony Shaw, as you now know him."

"Shaw was vindicated, Boris."

"So what?" There was no expression on his face and no energy left in Boris' tone. It was like he was on his last legs. "I was with Anthony the night Stacey Lumb was killed. The fact is, we both shared Stacey that day. We were together all night after she left. Neither of us could have killed her. But—"

"But what, Boris?" He was becoming angry again.

Boris untangled his beard and smiled. It was clear who had all the power; George wasn't sure he could change that.

"Anthony was there when I killed Anna. He watched it and even recorded it, I think. He'd heard about the killer wearing one of your forensic suits and how they used a saw to dismember the victims. We were off our fucking faces. It was bad, George. I'm not saying the drugs made it OK, but we were fucked. Ask him—"

"He'll just deny it. We have no proof he was involved." George swallowed hard. He hated admitting they didn't have any hard evidence on Shaw. "Why did you kill her?"

"It's the truth that Anthony was there. And it's the truth that I killed Anna Hill. I killed her, and her alone. Not a day passes where I'm not remorseful over her death. It eats me up inside. I'll speak with her husband, Timothy if you like. Apologise. Or her son, Thomas, was it? Please, George."

"Why did you kill her?"

"She reminded me of my wife. Mary. She was a natural redhead who dyed her hair black. She stopped wanting to sleep with me. Mary, I mean. When I started taking drugs and drinking alcohol, I saw Anna and wanted her. No, I needed her. But I couldn't afford her. So—so—so I took her. Alright?"

"OK, Boris. I'll take your statement and get one of my team to bring Shaw back in. Who killed the others?"

"Well, that's just it. I think it was Hill himself. He was always around because he chaperoned his wife. The poor woman was selling herself because he couldn't provide for her. I'd seen him speaking with every girl repeatedly. I saw many in his car. He'd disappear for an hour. But he'd always be back for Anna. Stacey Lumb got in his car the night she was murdered. It was the last any of us saw of her. Shaw will corroborate. I promise."

Chapter Twenty-seven

Terry's wife, June, was in her mid-fifties with a pallid, stunned expression that showed George she was clearly still in shock. Yesterday morning, she'd been informed that her husband had been killed, murdered in their home whilst she was in a London hotel room. According to the Metropolitan Police family liaison officer that George had spoken to, June had taken it badly; it was only today, a day later, that she'd felt up to answering some questions.

As it turns out, June had filed for a divorce, which was news to George. It meant Terry could have been seeing somebody else, and when June was asked, she referred to a hotel booking for the Holmfield Arms Hotel on Denby Dale Road in Wakefield and how she'd accused him of having an affair. But he'd wanted to stop proceedings and wanted her back, adamant he wasn't seeing anybody else.

She'd last spoken with Terry on Saturday after the argument with DS Wood. He'd gone for a drive to calm down.

Then the poor woman had broken down as she admitted Morton used to beat her. If she spent too much money, he'd hit her. If they argued, he'd beat her. It was a shock to the detectives, especially as they'd worked with Morton for a while, but it did give George an idea.

CHAPTER TWENTY-SEVEN

"I've had an idea about the MO, Josh," George said. "Maybe the Blonde Delilah kills cheaters and abusers. Think about the statements you gave me the other day."

Josh nodded. "Makes sense."

"We're missing something, though, something important," George added.

Then they asked her whether she could think of anyone with a motive to harm her husband, but she couldn't.

* * *

Timothy Hill had been mentioned twice now, and so they decided to go and visit him. As luck would have it, George knew where Timothy Hill lived. His large house was in Alwoodley near the reservoir, on the same road as DSU Jim Smith's but set back from the road. Instead of it being rendered white, like the others, Hill's house had exposed golden bricks that glowed warmly in the spring sunshine.

Josh whistled softly. "Guy hasn't done too badly for himself, has he? This place must be worth a fortune."

George smiled, acknowledging his new deputy's opinion. "Tim's an investment banker." George had already done all the necessary searches on Timothy Hill already and knew that it had only been since Anna's death that he had done well for himself. In the years leading up to her death, they'd been skint.

It was raining. Again. Pulling their jackets around them, they made for the cover of the porch. As there was no bell, George thumped the door and stood back. It was solid and painted a glossy navy blue.

A young girl with long blonde hair opened the door. She couldn't have been over sixteen.

"Hello. How can I help you?" she said, her smile hesitant. George thought she had an Australian accent. She was tanned and wore a tartan print pinafore dress above a black roll-neck crop top. Josh was staring at her exposed midriff, and George had to cough to get his attention.

"Well?" she questioned. Despite being inside, she wore a pair of white, smooth leather Docs. The heat blasted George from the doorway. She raised her brows.

They held out their warrant cards. "I'm DI Beaumont, and this is DS Fry. We'd like to speak to Timothy Hill if he's in?" George said.

Her face crumpled with worry. "Are you the police?"

"That's right. Is he in?"

"He is."

"Can you get him for us?"

"Sure. Wait here, and I'll get him."

As they watched her prance up the stairs, George wondered why she'd made that exchange so tricky.

When the young woman reached the top of the stairs, she said, "Mister Hill, the police are here. They say they want to talk to you."

A man's voice replied, but it was too muffled for the detectives to hear.

"They haven't said," the girl responded. "They're waiting outside."

A short moment later, a tall, thin man in an expensive navy suit walked down the stairs. He adjusted the watch on his wrist—a TAG Heuer Chronograph in obsidian. George had always wanted one.

"Mr Hill?" George asked.

He nodded. "What can I do for you, gentlemen?"

"Can we come in? We have some news to share," George said.

He nodded awkwardly and asked them to follow him into a double reception room that was decorated entirely white. There was a bottle of twelve-year-old Macallan Whiskey on the low coffee table, with three glass twist tumblers.

After the trio sat, Timothy asked, "Now, tell me what this is all about?" He didn't offer them tea or coffee, but then this wasn't a social call.

"That your daughter?" Josh asked, pointing towards the hall.

Tim hesitated. "No. My PA."

PA? Somebody was going up in the world. He wondered what DS Wood would have thought of it all.

"We're here to inform you we have a suspect in custody who we believe murdered your late wife, Anna."

A look of relief washed across his face. "After all this time?" Tim said. "Thank you. Thank you for coming."

"But first, we need to ask you some questions regarding her death."

His dark eyes turned frosty. "You just told me you had a suspect. Anna died over thirty years ago. I gave my statements back then. Why, after all this time, do you want to talk to me now? I have nothing more to add."

"Do you mind if we record this?" Josh asked, placing George's Dictaphone on the coffee table.

"Fine. Of course. Go ahead."

"Thanks, Tim. May I call you Tim?" Tim nodded. "OK, so it wasn't common knowledge at the time that Anna was a prostitute. It is now."

Tim frowned, closed his eyes, and then gave a curt nod. "Yes.

I was—I was embarrassed. A banker not knowing what his wife was up to." George and Josh shared a look. "No one mentioned it, and I did not volunteer it."

"We understand, Mr Hill," Joshua Fry said.

George nodded and added, "A customer murdered her. He's admitted to it."

Tim scratched his dark beard. "Good. Lock him up and throw away the key."

George noticed he didn't ask who the culprit was. If he were in Tim's situation, he'd have wanted to know who killed his wife. "Do you recognise these names? Nicole Green, Stacey Lumb and Joanne Cox?" He watched Tim for a reaction, but his dark brown eyes barely faltered.

"Are those names supposed to mean something to me?"

Joanne Cox was Lorraine Cox's cousin. Josh had researched Lorraine's family and background already. "Do you recognise any or all of those names?" asked George again.

"No, I do not think so, and I am pretty good with names. It helps in my job."

"What about Lorraine Cox?"

There was a slight hesitation, but otherwise, Tim appeared unflustered. He shook his head. "Sorry."

For now, George dropped that line of questioning. He'd come back to it, though, but first, he wanted to get the basics out of the way. If he started accusing Tim of killing them, he was liable to kick them out.

"Mr Hill," George said, then hesitated. He wanted to keep the guy onside. "Would you take us through the events of that day Anna was murdered? I appreciate it was a very long time ago."

"As I already told you, the authorities took my statement,"

he said. "It has been over thirty years. I could not add to it."

George smiled. "I've read the original report, Tim, but I'd like to hear it in your own words if you don't mind."

He sighed, then glanced at his TAG Heuer. "If you insist, although I have to be off soon."

Josh attempted a smile and received a nod.

George held his hands out, palms up, and said, "Whenever you're ready."

"It was before Christmas. I was at work. Anna had Thomas. No, wait, our neighbour had Thomas. She used to leave him with her. When I came home, she was not there. But our neighbour was. If I remember right, she was worried Anna had not called for Thomas."

"That must have been awful for you," remarked George.

He nodded. "Yes. Truly awful. I phoned the police, but I could not report her as missing until twenty-four hours had elapsed."

"Did she often disappear?" George asked.

"No. Never. I mean, she was always out of the house. If I gave her an inch, she took a mile."

Josh made a note on his tablet. Nothing against Josh, but he missed DS Wood's methods already.

"You said earlier, Mr Hill, that Anna left Thomas with a neighbour?" Josh asked.

"Yes."

"Why was that?"

"Have—Have you not read my initial statement?"

"Of course, sir. I just wanted it in your own words." Josh attempted another smile.

"Fine. She used to go to the shops. We were—" Tim looked down at the wooden floor. George could see the fear in his eyes.

215

Something about those days terrified him.

"What's wrong, Tim?"

Tim smiled. "Look around you. Look what I've achieved. I did this without Anna, but I wanted to achieve it with her. Those days are a reminder of my failures. We were poor. Very poor. We could only have the heating on at certain times. I was working every hour I could to provide, and I failed, did I not?"

Tim took a deep breath before continuing. "We had no refrigerator, and so Anna had to shop twice a day, so I—so we had fresh meals."

"That must have been very difficult for her," George remarked. He thought about his mother. From the research he'd done, he was a similar age to Tim's eldest son, Thomas. He just assumed his mother had everything she needed to bring him up, that his dickhead father had provided for them. He'd taken his childhood for granted, like so many others.

"Anyway, Anna left Thomas with our neighbour to go shopping Monday to Friday."

"Tell us what happened that evening after you got home," Josh asked.

Tim hesitated and looked at the wooden flooring once more. "I got home to find our neighbour with Thomas. I called the police. What else could I have done?"

"You didn't go out and look for her?" Josh asked.

That comment had hit a nerve. George saw the slight change in posture, the vein quickly popping up at the surface. Tim took another deep breath. "How could I? I had Thomas."

George nodded. *Fair enough.* He could have left Thomas with the neighbour, though. "You said Anna handed Thomas over to your neighbour Monday to Friday." Tim nodded. "What normally happened when you got home?"

CHAPTER TWENTY-SEVEN

"We would usually have half an hour of family time together before I took Thomas to bed. Then Anna would cook my meal, and we would do the usual husband and wife activities."

George smiled. "When you first got back, and Anna was missing, what did you initially think had happened?"

Tim looked confused. Was it the question or the backtrack? Probably both, which was why George had done it. "I er—I cannot remember. Sorry. I certainly did not think she had been murdered, then decapitated."

Then something clicked in Tim's mind. "Wait. Does that mean you have caught Jack the Butcher?"

George raised his brow. "Why is that who you thought had killed her?" asked George, knowing full well it was. Tim's initial statement had his concerns logged about Jack the Butcher.

"Well, does it? Have you caught him?"

George didn't answer. He could see Tim fighting with himself. Silence was the oldest trick in the book, and it worked nearly every time.

"You must have done. Apparently, the murders he committed were pretty horrific. They all followed a pattern. I remember reading about them in the newspaper, which is why I thought he had got Anna." He shivered. "It was awful to think of Anna like that. Being cut up with a saw."

"It must have been very traumatic for you."

He nodded. "I had therapy to help stop the nightmares."

There was a brief pause as George collected his thoughts. "We cannot comment on an investigation, Tim, as I'm sure you understand. However, we wanted to inform you of officially opening the case."

Tim swallowed. "You're reopening the case?"

"Naturally," said George. "Did you hear about the Bone Saw Ripper?"

"The copycat?" he asked, even though George thought Tim knew it was.

George played dumb. "Copycat?"

Tim swallowed again; his thickly muscled neck made the swallowing look difficult. "Yes. I think Peterson copied Jack the Butcher, correct?"

If only you knew, George thought. "I'm told you used to drop Anna off when she went to work the streets in Holbeck?" he asked.

Tim looked like a deer in the headlights. Did they have him? "What? No. I—I did not know what she was doing. As I told you, I gave her an inch, and she took a mile. I was often left at home with Thomas whilst she frolicked about. I had my suspicions she was seeing somebody else, but I did not know she was being paid for it."

You're lying, George thought. He could see it in Tim's eyes. Should he push? *No.* It was clear to George Tim hadn't murdered Anna, but he was still making his mind up about the others. He moved on but was still curious about their relationship.

"What was your relationship like with Anna?"

He scowled. "How is that any of your business?"

"Humour me." George smiled.

"We were falling out of love, to tell you the truth."

"How so?"

He inhaled. "She had put on a bit of extra weight after the pregnancy. It had affected our sex life, as had the tearing and the constant worry. I also thought she was cheating on me. It made things difficult."

What a wanker. Women sacrificed their bodies when they gave birth. "Constant worry?"

"She didn't want to get pregnant again. It was a shame, as I really wanted a large family." His phone beeped, and he glanced down, his memories of the past now broken.

"Thank you for your honesty regarding your late wife," George remarked. "We're also here for another reason."

He nodded. "Go on."

"Where were you between the hours of 12 midnight and 3 am on Thursday?"

"In bed, probably. Where else would I be?"

"Well, you tell us, Mr Hill," Josh added.

Tim furrowed his brows and held up his hands. "Well, what? What do you want me to tell you?"

"The truth would be a good start, Tim," George said.

"I am telling you the truth."

"Lorraine Cox is saying otherwise."

There was a slight hesitation, but otherwise, Tim appeared unflustered. He asked, "What did Lorraine say?"

"I thought you were 'pretty good with names', Tim?"

"Let us not play games, Inspector. Do you want me to withdraw my cooperation?"

"Certainly not, Tim. But you lied to me earlier when you said you didn't know Joanne Cox and Lorraine Cox when you did."

Tim got flustered. "Right, I am telling you, I only know Joanne's name because she was Lorraine's cousin."

"Was?"

"Yes. Was. Jack the Butcher killed her. And you know he did, Inspector." His mobile phone rang, and he got up to answer it. "Excuse me, detectives. I will be just a moment."

George studied Tim as he took the call out in the hall. He

was a rich, confident, well-spoken man who clearly spent a lot of time in the gym. Women would probably describe him as handsome. Hopefully, he'd seen the Blonde Delilah on the television. He was the kind of guy who would make her list.

"I will be in when I can, Ali," he was saying. "Look, I appreciate that, but I am currently engaged.... I will be in the office when I can... Fine..."

Tim returned, ending the call with a beaming grin. "Is that everything, detectives? That was work. I really must get back to the office."

"Answer our questions honestly, Mr Hill. Then we'll get out of your hair."

He sighed and sank back onto the sofa. It groaned under the weight of his muscle. "What was the question?"

"Where were you between the hours of 12 midnight and 3 am on Thursday?" George asked.

He hesitated. Was he really going to lie? "Fine. At Lorraine's," Tim finally said. "I was there from 8 pm Wednesday night and left her house to go to the office at 7 am Thursday morning. Why?"

"Did you have your phone on you?" Tim nodded. "Who is your provider?"

"Vodafone."

"Thank you, Tim. Now, we need to go back to Nicole Green, Joanne Cox, and Stacey Lumb."

"Why? I already told you I don't recognise the names."

"Yet you know of Jack the Butcher? They were the names of his victims. Each one was a prostitute. They worked with Anna." Tim scowled once more. "And we have intelligence that suggests you knew them, too. Intimately."

Tim's eyes widened. "Me? Why would I have any business

knowing prostitutes intimately?"

"Because you needed to fill your time whilst Anna worked," Josh said.

George nodded, watching as Tim stumbled over her words. He bared his teeth. "I–I don't fucking think so! Don't you dare?"

"Where were you on the nights Nicole, Joanne and Stacey died?" George checked his pocket notebook and gave him the dates and times.

Tim clutched his phone and thought about calling somebody. "You are making no sense. Whoever told you this crock of shit is lying, OK? And as for the dates, I do not know. It was over thirty years ago."

He was grasping at straws, trying to avoid the situation. George said, "Can you think of anything that would help us with the investigation?"

"Anything at all?" Josh added. "It could help steer the investigation elsewhere?"

He shook his head. "No. I know nothing. Nothing at all. I am a decent man. I have always worked hard and was always home for my family. Never in my life have I paid for sex." Tim repeated the last sentence, almost like he was convincing himself.

"We're sorry, Mr Hill, aren't we, sir?" Josh said. "Unfortunately, we have to ask these questions, even if they're uncomfortable."

Tim had turned pale. His eyes were focused on the dark screen of the television. They'd lost him.

"We have a witness, Mr Hill, who told us they saw you with Stacey Lumb the night she was murdered. The problem is, they were with their friend. It's more of a problem for you than us."

Josh was laying it on thick. They hadn't spoken with Shaw yet, but they soon would. They wondered whether he'd confirm Jarman's story.

"What?" He stared at George, shock all over his face. "Not possible. Did their friend corroborate his story?"

George grinned. It was forced and uncomfortable, but they were on tape. If he lied using a facial expression, then the tape would never know.

Josh was nodding his head.

Tim dropped his head into his hands, then suddenly stood up. "Get out. Get out, now!"

Josh said, "I'm sorry, but we still have—"

Tim shook his head, then pointed at the door. "Leave. Now!" He was shaking, and his face was red. There was a look in his eye that George didn't like.

"We will leave when we're finished with our questions, Tim," George said. His tone oozed calm, and he locked eyes with Tim.

"Am I under arrest?" Tim asked, moving towards the hall.

No, but you might be once I start and do some digging, George thought.

"No, this was a voluntary interview. I thought we were clear about that?" Josh said.

"Then I think you had better leave now." Tim got slowly to his feet and wavered for a moment. George had the suspicion he might be about to pass out.

"Fine. Absolutely." George smiled. There was no point in continuing. Once they had more evidence, they could bring him in under caution.

Tim walked to the door as if in a trance.

"Thank you for talking to us today, Tim," George said. "I'm sorry for the bad news and the shock." George grinned as he said it.

"I am absolutely fine," he choked, clutching the door handle and showing them out.

"OK. If you change your mind, call us." He handed Tim his business card. "We can send a Family Liaison Officer around."

Tim didn't reply; he simply slammed the door.

Chapter Twenty-eight

She knew where Justin Broadchurch met for beers with his friends every Wednesday night in the city centre. Like the others, she'd stalked their social media accounts, though he hadn't accepted her message request. She knew he was married, but then so had some of the others. Perhaps he didn't have a messenger app installed?

The young blonde turned the phone off and placed it in her bag, replacing it with a fresh one; there must have been something wrong with the profile on that one.

She assumed the profile she'd created on the new phone might have put him off, especially considering the picture and bio were so like his daughter, Cassandra. She was wrong. Within half an hour of sending a message, she got a bite, and a quiver of excitement fluttered through her stomach. She'd caught him, hook, line, and sinker. All she had to do now was reel him in. And she knew exactly how to do it.

The blonde started the chat. As she'd suspected, they'd hit it off. She could see him furiously tapping away, ignoring his mates as they each left, one by one.

"I'm only free tonight or tomorrow night, as I'm going abroad for a month," she eventually typed. His wife worked Thursday nights, and so she knew Justin would have to see her

CHAPTER TWENTY-EIGHT

tonight. It was all part of her plan.

"Tonight?" he replied.

"Yes," she said. "I'm out in Leeds. What are you up to?"

"I'm in Leeds, too." There was a pause. "Want to meet up?" A winking face emoji.

She smiled but didn't reply. The young blonde watched him from across the bar. His eyes were glued to his phone, expecting her reply. She wouldn't. Not until he messaged her again.

The other men had managed half an hour or so before messaging her. Poor Justin lasted five minutes.

He'd last even less once she had him tied to a bed.

* * *

"How was your morning, George?" Catherine Jones asked the following morning, offering him a cup of coffee. George smiled and took a sip. It was excellent coffee, and he wondered where she'd bought it from.

"There's been another murder. Justin Broadchurch."

"Holy shit. Cassandra's dad?"

"That's right," George said. "Killed last night in a B&B in Headingley whilst tied to the bed. Lots of stab wounds. Phone taken. Something lodged in his arsehole. You know the story. Dr Yardley is still there now with her SOCOs. We need to catch the killer, Catherine. And soon."

"I know. It's shit, but my profiles can only help you narrow down your suspects."

"Well, I wish they could hold up a sign saying: 'this is your fucking killer!'"

"You're funny, George," she said, placing her hand on his

arm. "Get up to much last night?"

He thought for a moment. Isabella had let him down, but he couldn't tell her that. Isabella had been struggling with her removal from the case, which wasn't unusual, nor unexpected, and so she had spent the night alone. "Not much. Watched a film. *Jurassic Park*. What about you, Catherine?" George asked.

She blushed. "Went on a date, actually."

"Oh, yeah?" George said. "Who's the lucky guy? Or girl?"

Catherine grinned. "Don't tell anyone but DCI Robertson."

"Wow, Alastair? Really?"

"Yeah, I love his Scottish accent. He asked me out a while ago before I got put on this case. Seeing him in the building and working on cases made me change my mind. You know I love a guy in a suit," she said with a wink.

George was glad she'd started seeing somebody, as it meant she might stop flirting with him. "Fair enough. He's a good—"

George's internal phone rang. "George, my office." It was DSU Smith.

Feeling highly agitated, George strode into Smith's office.

"I need an update, Beaumont."

George got him up to speed on where they were, ending with the murder of Justin Broadchurch and how they were waiting for the post-mortem results. "I need a warrant too, sir, for Justin's phone records. They've given us triangulation data from the last known location but won't provide anything else. DS Fry is working on it."

"Fine," barked the Superintendent. "We need to catch her before she kills again, George. We're getting desperate now. I'll get on the phone to the DCS immediately."

"Thanks, sir," he said, getting up to leave. They still did not know who the killer was, and that fact was grating on George.

CHAPTER TWENTY-EIGHT

* * *

"Hello, sir. What can I do for you?" DS Fry asked.

"How are we getting on with Justin Broadchurch's phone?"

"Still waiting, sir. The network eventually triangulated the last known location for me, which was the B&B room in Headingley. The phone was switched off from the network at 01:04 this morning."

"DSU Smith has provided a warrant. Get onto the provider ASAP, yeah?" George frowned. "We need to find out who the killer is, and soon."

"Yes, sir. Once I have the warrant, I can access messages, call history, and more detailed location history. It's a shame we don't have his phone. All of this would have been much easier."

George headed back to his office and pondered what Josh had just said. The amount of data they could seize from a phone repulsed him. He found it incredible that within minutes, they could download the content of an entire smartphone, but also found it scary how easily they could explore the owner's private data. Deleted or not, they could download location tracking, messages, and photos. And they didn't need a warrant for it. It felt invasive to see such intimate details of a person's life. But it wasn't just that. It was the fact that data taken without understanding could be misinterpreted and misunderstood. Only a month ago, his author mate Gareth had been brought in for questioning, and when they'd seized his phone, they were shocked by the internet history. Gareth had explained it relatively easily. He was an author and needed to know ways in how people could get away with murder, how people could be poisoned, or which vein or artery sprayed more blood once cut. They'd had a laugh about it after, but initially, DCI Robertson's team had taken the data extremely seriously but without context.

DC Jason Scott pulled him to one side, interrupting his thoughts. "Sir, I spoke with Alan Bainbridge, Justin's mate, this morning, and he said Justin was waiting in a pub for a blonde bird last night."

"You took a formal statement?"

"Of course, sir."

The pair walked to George's office. "Which pub was Justin waiting in?"

"The Crooked Clock in the city centre, on the Headrow. They all meet there every Wednesday, apparently. I've checked the other statements, but they all left before he met this woman."

"Great job. Email me the statement, and get down there, see if they have any CCTV."

"Will do, sir. I'll give you his number too, shall I?"

George checked his watch. "Aye. Thanks." He went to see Elaine Brewer. "Fancy coming with me to speak to a witness?"

Her eyes lit up.

Chapter Twenty-nine

DI Beaumont and DS Brewer pulled into the car park and exited, soon finding themselves in Leeds City Square. He spied the nude nymphs and the Black Prince as he walked vigorously towards the finance sector, where Alan Bainbridge worked.

A friendly young woman in a pinstripe suit greeted them at reception and quickly buzzed them through into a waiting area.

A minute later, a middle-aged man with red hair in a sharp, charcoal suit stuck out his hand. "Hi, Alan Bainbridge. Nice to meet you." He shook Elaine's first, then George's, as they both introduced themselves. "Please, follow me to my office." His accent had a hint of scouse, George thought. He and Elaine followed as Alan led them into a generous office space and closed the door.

"I thought I'd clarified all the details with Detective Scott? But, please, how can I help?" As he faced George and Elaine, he dabbed a bead of sweat from his brow. The guy was clearly busy.

"You were his closest friend, is that right?"

Alan nodded. "Yes. For years. I just don't understand. What happened? Was it that blonde lass who did it?"

"That's where we're hoping you can fill us in. He was killed late last night or this morning. And what do you mean by a blonde lass?" George replied. Alan gestured to the three seats around a small coffee table. "Shall we sit?"

"Of course. Sorry."

Alan slid into a padded chair, and George and Elaine took the other two. "Coffee?"

"Please," he said with a smile. He waited for Alan to make the call to his receptionist, and when Alan said back down, George said, "Tell me about this blonde lass."

"Well, there's a killer on the loose. The Blonde Delilah? I've seen her in the newspapers." Alan thought for a moment and lapsed into silence. "I should have tried to stop him. He told me he was staying to meet up with a lass. It wasn't—it wasn't until later that he told me she was blonde."

"What time did you speak with him?" asked George, inviting Alan to continue. The other men had informed nobody of their encounters with the Blonde Delilah. It was progress.

"About 11 pm. Let me check." Alan pulled out his phone. "Look, via a WhatsApp message at 10.55 pm."

"May I see?" George asked. Alan handed over his phone. On it was an image of Justin with a blonde woman in his lap. He couldn't see her face or any identifying features. "Can we have a copy of this image? And can you provide Justin's mobile number?"

"Of course." DS Brewer took Alan's mobile and screenshotted the WhatsApp message, and forwarded both that and the original image to her own mobile. Then she screenshot Justin's contact page. It was the same number they already had. She forwarded it, anyway.

"Do you know anything else?"

"Only that he was thinking of meeting her one minute and almost transfixed the next. The woman must have charmed him. It wouldn't take much, though. His marriage is in tatters."

Elaine nodded sympathetically. "Can you explain what you mean by tatters, please?" she said.

"Just that his wife wasn't giving him what he wanted at home, and how he wanted a woman who could both suck cock and be an excellent mother to Cassie." He grimaced when Elaine frowned. "That's how Justin talked about women. No offence," Alan added quickly.

"None taken," she said, a slight smirk appearing on her lips. "I've heard worse. Comes with the job."

"Justin could be a bit of a dickhead. He cheated on his wife a lot. I've been there during the fallout. He'd always apologise with a bunch of flowers, saying he'd never do it again. Young blondes were his favourite. Hence the image he sent me, I guess."

"What was Justin like as a person?" Elaine asked.

"He was great but had a bit of a temper on him. It was very short, though. When he got mad, he got very loud. It was worse when he was drunk. I've known him to smash stuff up. But she never accused him of laying a finger on her."

"Were they getting a divorce?" Elaine asked.

"Oh. I don't know. I think Marie put up with Justin because she was comfortable."

"Comfortable?"

"He had money." Alan cocked an eyebrow. "Our boss, Tim, pays well. Very well." He shrugged as he spoke. "I'm making Justin out to be a wanker, but he isn't. Or wasn't." Alan looked down at the table. "He was a good guy. I'll miss him."

"Can you tell us anything else about this blonde woman?" George asked.

"Just a call from Justin half an hour later asking me for B&B recommendations. He told me not to wait up and that he might be late to the office. He sounded happy. There was a lot of giggling."

"Feminine giggling?" George asked.

"Oh yeah. Justin was a homophobe, unfortunately. I won't go into details, but yeah, she was a she, not a he. Justin loved women. All women." Then Alan fell silent. He'd said too much.

"Could he have been overcompensating?"

Alan laughed. "Are you telling me the Blonde Delilah is now a man?"

"No, of course not, Alan," George said. "We have to ask all kinds of questions. It's just routine."

Alan raised a brow. "I'm sure." He met George's eyes, and when he spoke, every word was carefully weighed. "To my knowledge, Justin was a straight man. He was a known cheater, and by all accounts, his wife, Marie, didn't care."

"That's very helpful, Alan. Thanks."

"Sure. Anything else?"

"I have a question," Elaine said, straightening her chair. "Cassie, is what, sixteen or seventeen? And Justin was with Marie for five or six years before his death. Was he seeing anybody between those two periods?"

"Yeah. A few women. Lass named Lorraine for a while. Our boss pulled him, though. Apparently, they were seeing each other, and so Justin left it." Timothy Hill was their boss. George already knew that. Was Lorraine, Lorraine Cox? Could Tim be involved in the murders somehow? If so, how? "I can't remember the others' names. Sorry."

"That's alright. Anything untoward there?"

"I don't think so. I'm sorry." His dark eyes were sombre as they regarded the detectives. He'd already told them too much, and Alan knew it. George got up to leave. "Before—before you go, was it quick? Did Justin suffer?" Alan's hand balled into a fist, and George could see him shaking.

"I can't answer that, I'm afraid," George mumbled.

Alan nodded and stood up to shake George's hand.

"Detective, there was one other thing." Alan looked troubled as George raised his brow. They hadn't stopped shaking hands yet. "It's probably not even worth mentioning."

"Even the tiniest details help," Elaine said.

Alan hesitated. "Look, I'm sure it's nothing. He'd been getting a few messages recently from women on Instagram and Facebook. At first, he thought it was Marie winding him up or even trying to get evidence to put to a divorce solicitor. He was paranoid about that."

"OK, we can look into it." The problem was, they needed Justin's phone for those details—the one piece of evidence they didn't have. Their killer was very meticulous and had taken all mobiles with her. "If he was paranoid, why did he engage with the blonde?"

"Marie worked Wednesday and Thursday, and there's a strict rule in place about no phones. It's why he trusted she was who she said she was. That's why I said it was nothing. I shouldn't have mentioned it. Sorry."

George handed him a card. "If you think of anything else, Alan, then please call me."

Alan took it, staring down at the card for a second. "Thanks, Detective. And, please—please find out who did this to my friend," he whispered.

Elaine answered before George could speak. "Don't worry, Alan, we will."

* * *

"Just an update, sir," George said to DSU Smith over the phone. "We still haven't found Emily Sanderson. It's like she's vanished into thin air."

"I've got a bad feeling about her, Beaumont. A terrible feeling."

"I agree, sir. Justin's post-mortem confirmed he died late on Wednesday night or in the early hours of Thursday by exsanguination, and his identity was confirmed by dental records. A lot of the knife wounds this time were inflicted post-mortem, which is different. We're waiting on the data from Justin's network provider."

"Got something for you, sir," DS Fry said as he seemingly popped up from nowhere. He'd left his office door open.

"Yeah?" George turned to him. "Putting you on speaker, sir. Josh has some info."

"I've found some interesting material on Justin Broadchurch's phone records," Josh said.

"Justin's?" George frowned.

"Yes, sir. There are some rather interesting conversations between him and a woman named Catherine."

"Catherine? Such as?" Josh had George's full attention.

"Text messages. Catherine suggested she was free Wednesday or Thursday night only as she was going abroad for a month. Justin seemed keen and messaged back. He wanted to meet her that night. They both shared that they were in Leeds, and he asked her again whether she wanted to meet that night, with a winking face emoji and everything. She ignored him. Five minutes later, he messaged again, and they agreed to meet at the Crooked Clock in the city centre, on the Headrow."

"Which is where Justin was with his mates. Gotta be the killer, right?" George frowned. "Catherine, who? Does it give a surname at all?"

"Check the previous messages," came Smith's booming Geordie twang. "Did she ever give a name before?"

"No, sir, she didn't," Josh said.

"Gotta be a fake name then, right? To throw us off the scent?" His heart calmed. For a moment, he questioned whether Catherine Jones was the killer. She had the knowledge and the means. But not the opportunity. She'd been on a date the night Broadchurch was murdered. Or so she'd said. He made a mental note to check it out.

"It's also unusual as this exchange is done solely through text messaging. I assume her other exchanges with her victims were done via WhatsApp, or Messenger, and the like."

"Untraceable, you mean?" Smith said impatiently.

"Yeah, exactly."

"This case doesn't get any easier, does it?" Smith bellowed.

"No, sir, it doesn't," George added.

Chapter Thirty

They got into George's Honda, drove the half mile to the nearby pub, and Josh took a seat while George fetched a couple of beers.

"How are you, boss?" Josh asked as George sat down opposite him, ominously quiet. "Personal life going well? Or would you rather not talk about it?"

"It?" he replied with a smile before raising his eyebrows. "And less of the boss. We're not at work now, Josh."

"Sorry, George. Habit," Josh said. "And you know what I mean. Mia. And Jack, I guess. Must be tricky having a young child as it is, never mind having one being a detective."

"Mia... we're not together," he replied shortly. "To tell you the truth, I don't see Jack as much as I hoped. Being a detective takes away most of my free time, as you say. I have him tomorrow on my day off. All day. And overnight. I do my best, mate."

"You do your best with everybody, George. We can all see how hard you're working to solve this case and how hard you work to solve all the others."

"Thanks, mate. Means a lot. The situation with Mia is complicated, to be honest." George wasn't sure why he was sharing his personal business with his subordinate, but it sure felt good to get it off his chest. "She wants to get back with me, but I—I don't think I do. We broke up a year ago. She broke up with me, in fact, because she wanted to be with—" His lip trembled as he finished his sentence. "With Adam Harris."

"That must have been terrible for you, George." Josh remembered the Miss Murderer case like the back of his hand. It was an awful time for a lot of people.

George shrugged. "It was worse when she told me she was pregnant, then spent the next nine months apologising. She's so sorry for what she did, and I can see it in her eyes. I believe her. But it doesn't make me want to give her what she wants any more like I used to. Instead, I've begun to—"

"Resent her?" Josh butted in.

"Yeah. I even asked her for a DNA test once Jack was born. It destroyed me inside because if I wasn't Jack's father, then I'd killed Jack's father."

"You didn't kill him, George," Josh said, patting him on the shoulder. "You saved two lives, as well as your own. Your job is to preserve lives at all costs. I know it's easy for me to say, but you need to stop beating yourself up over it. You did the right thing."

"I know it was the right thing, but I lost it, Josh. I should have stopped. I still—I still struggle with it now. His face haunts me. I'm not even sure whether I deserve to be a DI and be in charge of a team any more. I'm conflicted inside."

"We can see the conflict in your eyes, George. When you're at work, it's obvious. You don't want to be—"

"Is that what this drink is all about then, Josh?" George interrupted.

Before Josh could respond, he was displeased to see Catherine Jones approaching. Josh knew George and Catherine had a history and had been initially shocked that DSU Smith had allowed George to continue working on the case.

"Can I join you?" she asked.

Josh would have liked to continue his conversation with George in private, but it wasn't as if he could object, so he smiled up at Catherine as George nodded his consent.

"So, what are you two talking about?" Catherine asked as she sat down. "The Blonde Delilah?"

Josh smiled to hide his annoyance at the intrusion, and George nodded again. It was so unlike George to be quiet, so forlorn. He wondered how Catherine knew where they were and nearly asked as much when Catherine began a new conversation.

"I still can't believe she's a woman. I was so convinced otherwise. Sorry guys, I really am. I feel like I've cocked up the investigation."

"What?" George said. "No. You haven't. We were all convinced the killer was male. As you said, your profile was an informed guess." He thought about Mark and how easily he'd guessed their killer was female. Catherine wasn't as experienced as Mark, though.

She placed a hand on George's arm and grinned, clearly delighted he'd taken her side. Josh didn't trust her. Though not blonde, to him, Catherine personified Delilah, a flirty, deceptive and sexually attractive woman. A seductive femme fatale. If George and Mia were trying to salvage their relationship, then Catherine was definitely attempting to impede that.

"Found anything else out?"

"Text messages from the killer to Justin Broadchurch," George said. "They set up a meeting."

"Says her name's Catherine," Josh added, doing his best to

hide his annoyance. "You're not our killer, are you?"

She wasn't fazed by his accusation and laughed as she said, "Catherine? Got to be a fake name, right? To throw you guys off the scent?"

"But how would they know to use the name, Catherine? We've not mentioned you to the press, and you don't work for West Yorkshire Police any more," Josh said with a shrug.

"Terrence Morton," Catherine said.

"What?" George asked. "Terry?"

Catherine told them about her contact within the press, who told her Morton was leaking information. He'd been an informant for years, earning thousands of pounds yearly.

"Hence being a DC for all those years. You think you know somebody," George said before getting up for another drink. "Another round?"

Catherine smiled and asked for a vodka tonic, but Josh shook his head. He hadn't touched his beer.

"Any news on Emily Sanderson, Josh?" Catherine asked once George was at the bar.

He shook his head. "No. Nothing. She's disappeared."

"But she's still suspect number one?"

"She's a suspect, sure," Josh muttered.

"But she's at the top of your list, right?" Catherine pressured.

"I don't think we have a suspect at the top of our list," Josh snapped, aware that he was allowing his irritation to show. He took a deep breath and smiled, deciding it wasn't worth pissing off the Chief Superintendent's lapdog. George had also come back with the two drinks. With a more measured tone, he added, "We have DNA we need to match to a suspect, but unfortunately, we didn't take a DNA sample from Emily

Sanderson when we brought her in for a chat. It doesn't match anybody currently on the DNA Database, nor the Contamination Elimination Database."

"Perhaps that DNA sample you found belongs to a previous customer?" Catherine replied.

"You're probably right, Catherine, and we're wasting our time. DSU Smith asked me to keep an eye out for any DNA which matches the DNA from the hair we found at our new scenes. So far, we have nothing. We're barking up the wrong tree."

Josh thought George looked defeated. His shoulders were slumped, and there was darkness in those green eyes of his. "Maybe we should stop discussing the case," Josh said. "It's—"

"What? Dragging the conversation down?" George asked.

"Yeah, it is," Catherine agreed, finishing her drink. She stood up. "Another, George?" She pointed at his pint glass, and he nodded. "Josh?"

"No. Thanks." Whilst he didn't want to leave his friend alone with Catherine, he certainly couldn't stand to be in her presence for much longer. "I'm heading off in a minute." He turned to George. "You coming?"

"Sorry, mate. Can you take a taxi? I want to stay and have another drink."

As Josh left, he saw Catherine sitting close to George, their legs touching, her leaning into him, smiling, and playing with her hair. Finally, he heard her say, "Are you hungry?"

* * *

"Starving," George said. "You want to eat here or somewhere

else?"

She desperately wanted to take him somewhere else, somewhere private, where she could have him to herself. She wanted to be the starter, the main, and the dessert. "Depends on what you fancy?" she asked with a wink.

"The grub's pretty good in here, to be honest. Shall I get some menus?"

Catherine immediately felt sick. She'd never forgotten her feelings for George, despite them not speaking after she left Elland Road. She thought she was making her feelings clear to him but was not having much success. Catherine tried hard to turn up wherever he was, hanging onto his words, smiling, touching, flirting, while he appeared oblivious to the attention she was giving him. "Sure. Sounds good."

They discussed the case whilst they waited, George, draining his pint glass at a rate that Catherine couldn't keep up with. He seemed down to her, his eyes as dark as his expression. "Are you OK, George?" she finally mustered up the courage to say.

"Yeah," he shrugged. "Why wouldn't I be?"

"I overheard you and Josh talking earlier whilst I was waiting for my drink." She smiled and patted his hand. "I'm sorry. I didn't mean to eavesdrop. Do you want to talk about it?"

"You're the one who looks upset, Catherine. Are *you* OK?" If Catherine was being honest, she was rather upset, but what had upset her had nothing to do with George's obliviousness; it was the conversation the two men were having about George's ex, Mia, she'd accidentally stumbled across. Catherine knew there was no reason for her to feel jealous, yet she felt that way, regardless. She'd heard it directly from the horse's mouth that they weren't getting back together. But Mia was the woman he'd got with after Catherine had left Elland Road, the woman who he'd chosen to have a child with. And no matter how hard she'd tried with George, he seemed against noticing her feelings, as if the closeness they had developed had existed only in *her* mind, and she cursed herself for allowing herself to grow fond of him. Catherine thought for a moment as she downed the rest of her drink. Maybe she needed to take a step back from him, as it would have been mortifying to have revealed her feelings, only to be rejected.

But then he smiled at her and placed his own hand on her arm. "You can talk to me, you know?" he said as the main courses were delivered to their table.

"I'm just shocked by what I heard, that's all," she said, attempting to draw out the truth. She needed to hear it from him, and him alone. "You and Mia. That you're getting back together after what she did to you."

George stopped eating his burger and took a large gulp of his beer. "Me and Mia?" He sounded surprised. "There is no me and Mia. We're amicable because of Jack. That's all. After what she did to me last year, I—"

It was her turn to sound surprised. "Really? How'd she take it?"

He paused, considering. "Badly. But someday, she'll meet someone else, someone who's not a detective, someone who can give her the time and attention she wants. I'm worried he'll take over as Jack's father, and for a little while, it was that terrifying thought that nearly made me get back together with her. But I got over it, and as for her and me, it's over. And I can honestly say I'm not as sorry or as upset as I should be. To tell you the truth, it's a relief."

Catherine smiled. "After what she did to you, it was the right thing to do, and you shouldn't feel guilty for feeling the way you do." *Especially if you love me as I love you.*

She was right.

"Yeah? Aren't you the type of woman who thinks second chances should be given?"

George was right, and she told him as much. She also added, "However, it's got nothing to do with me. After the way she treated you, you're better off on your own than trapped in a terrible relationship." She paused. She was thinking of a way to phrase her words to favour her. It didn't work for her if George gave Mia a second chance, but it would suit her if George gave her a second chance. "Maybe you should even think about starting a good relationship? Give somebody else a second chance, instead?"

"A good relationship. Yeah, I think you're right."

Her heart hammered in her chest. She shuffled closer to him, her bare thigh against his. Catherine took in those green eyes of his. "You got anybody in mind?"

"What?"

"I'm asking if you fancy anybody?" She smiled.

George halted abruptly. "Do I fancy anybody?" He thought for a moment, his words slurring. "Yeah. Yeah, I do, actually." He immediately wished he'd not said those words.

"Somebody you want to begin a loving relationship with?" Catherine didn't say that she wanted something of a relationship with George.

"Somebody I want to begin a loving relationship with?" George nodded his head. "Yes."

"Somebody close?"

George hesitated before nodding. "Thank you, Catherine. You've helped a lot tonight."

I could help you a lot more if only you'd let me, she thought.

Catherine interrupted the silence with a faintly embarrassed laugh. "Thanks, George. That means a lot. And anyway, you've helped me far more than I've helped you."

"How?"

It was Catherine's turn to hesitate. "You had my back when others didn't," she replied vaguely and paused, unsure what to say next. "This case has been hard for me, too. I wanted to make a name for myself but ended up fucking everything up."

"You can't blame yourself," he said, draping an arm around her back and over her shoulder. He squeezed, and at that moment, she felt happiness. She felt content. It's what she'd been missing in his absence. "We're friends, Catherine. I was always going to have your back."

"Friends?" Catherine looked away from him; afraid her face would betray her devastation.

He hesitated. "Do you not want to be friends?"

No. I want to be more than friends. I want to be everything to you, everything Mia could never be, not in a million years.

"I—I thought—"

It must have dawned on him what Catherine was about to say because he immediately removed his arm and turned to face her. She hoped he was going to confess his feelings for her. "Catherine, I need to be honest with you. I'm over Mia. The fact is, I've fallen for someone else. Hard. I can only hope she feels the same way."

Did that mean he'd found somebody else, or did he mean her? His words were vague, and so she said, "Then you should ask her if she feels the same way."

Catherine immediately regretted her words. If it wasn't her, then she wasn't ready to hear about George's new love interest. But if it was her, then it was an acceptable risk.

"You're right, Catherine. I should. In fact, I should do it right now."

He turned to her, and she was swallowed up in his emerald-coloured eyes. George squeezed her hand and smiled. His lips parted, but she got there first, sliding her manicured nails through his thick hair and pulling him close, putting her lips to his.

Then she heard the words she dreaded to hear. "Stop, Catherine. I'm sorry if you mistook my words. I meant I've fallen for somebody else."

Chapter Thirty-one

Timothy Hill had charmed Emily into a date that evening. She'd found him on social media and was surprised that Emily, who was a nineteen-year-old blonde student, was actually real and had replied to his messages. Not that he wasn't glad of it, because he was: the younger the girl, the better. Adrenaline rushed through him as he thought about what he'd get her to do in the hotel room he'd booked.

As a handsome banker with a gym bod, he wasn't short of messages on the app. Most were from desperate young women, obviously wanting him to be their sugar daddies. But Emily had been different. He'd chased her as soon as he'd read her profile and seen her profile picture.

Tim stepped into the reception area of the InterContinental on Crown Point Road, noticing the receptionist wasn't there. The place was dead, and he assumed the receptionist had gone out for a smoke. It didn't matter; he'd checked in earlier and had the key card in his back pocket. He checked out his reflection in one of the windows, spiked up his blond hair and ran a hand over his freshly shaved chin. Tim tossed the single rose into the air and caught it, watching himself in the mirror once more. He thought he was looking good for fifty-five, and every step he took exuded self-confidence.

When Emily entered the reception area, she stood by the desk, looking around. Prim and proper in a suit jacket and pencil skirt, she wore shiny red stilettos, adding to her height. Her blonde curls cascaded down the front of her chest, hiding the cleavage that he so desperately wanted to see.

She didn't look as young as she did in the pictures, which disappointed him slightly, but he was still old enough to be her father, which was good enough. Emily turned, meeting his eyes. There was a nervousness about her, a nervousness she gave away by her awkward posture. That, and the look on her face. She looked like a deer in the headlights.

He gazed back and gave her a smile. Emily was young, lovely, and inexperienced. But after he broke her tonight, she'd be his whenever he pleased. He knew she'd be addicted to him once he broke her.

Her cherry-coloured lips parted in a smile. "Hi, Tim." She extended a manicured hand.

He took it and bowed his head to kiss the back of her hand. Next, he whipped the rose he'd concealed behind his back and offered it to her. "For you, Emily."

She blushed as she took it. "A flower for me? I don't think I've ever been given flowers on a first date before. Thanks."

"After you, Emily. Our room's just back there."

Tim watched her hips swing in her pencil skirt as she walked ahead of him to the room. She smelled like sweet fruit. It was an expensive perfume he was sure he knew. It was intoxicating but also suffocating. He was sure the scent had been his second late wife's favourite.

She reached the door, and he draped an arm over her shoulder, sliding his finger across her cleavage as he opened the door. He felt her shudder. "Shall we, Emily?" Tim attempted to lace his fingers into hers, but she dodged his hand, twisted around him, and gently pushed him into the hotel room.

"You know, you've barely changed from the last time I saw you," she said as she closed the door and locked it.

"We've met before?" he said, hesitating.

"Yes." She twisted her head to the side as her crimson lips curled high, threatening to take over her face. "The last time I saw you was over ten years ago."

* * *

"Hello, Father," the Blonde Delilah said. It was probably the first and only time in her life she had seen genuine concern on her father's face. It certainly was a surprise. "Yes, it's me. Your daughter."

He glanced around the hotel room, and the blonde assumed he was assessing whether he had an advantage. After all, he'd never had an issue with controlling his daughter before.

Tim turned to the young blonde and moved toward her. His arms were spread open as if he wanted to embrace her. She would not fall for it.

"So, you're not called Emily then?" She shook her head. "My precious daughter, it's so good to see you."

"Don't you fucking dare come near me!" she spat venomously, her hand raised. A warning. She thought about bringing out the knife, but the look on her face must have been terrifying and clearly had done the job as Tim stepped back, maintaining his position next to the bedside cabinet, saying nothing. The tension could have been cut with a knife.

She studied her father. He hadn't changed since she'd last seen him more than a decade ago, though his face had aged accordingly. He smelled of stale sweat. It was a scent she remembered. A fragrance that made her feel sick.

"Poor Timothy. You just couldn't help yourself, could you?"

Her father wore a puzzled expression. "What? What do you mean? I've no idea what you're talking about."

She rolled her eyes and groaned, stepping forward, the knife behind her back held steady.

"Don't demean me! You abused me. But that wasn't the first time you'd abused somebody, was it? I know what you did, Timothy. I know all about the women you raped and killed. At least they weren't your daughters, though I suppose one was your first wife." The blonde fought to keep her emotions under control, but the feelings she had harboured for years wanted to break free. It would be effortless to lose control now. But she couldn't allow the monster who had once been her father to see that; she wouldn't allow it. "And then, after the murders, you took poor Thomas too, didn't you? You had whetted your appetite with him. And then that was just the start."

"Please. I don't know what you're talking about."

And it begins, she thought, *the swift personality change.* As a child, she'd seen it often. Once ignorance stopped working, his next tactic was an attempt to gain sympathy. Even after all these years, she knew only too well how her father reacted. All she had to do was keep pushing him, make him aware that all was lost, and then he would become angry. Perhaps he would resort to violence. Then she could defend herself.

"Please listen to me. You must understand, Princess. I'd lost your mother, and I was drunk. I didn't know what I was doing."

"Don't you dare use my mother as an excuse! You fucking depraved bastard. You knew perfectly well what you were doing to me, drunk or not."

"No, Princess, I didn't..." He eased himself forward, away from the cabinet.

"Stay the fuck where you are, pervert!" Despite storing up so much hatred for him, she found it hard to believe it was possible. Those feelings she'd stored had nearly destroyed her. "You're a pathological liar, Timothy. You knew exactly what you were doing. Not once in your life have you stopped to think about any of your victims or about how they felt."

The young blonde trembled with rage, her crimson nails digging into the plastic shaft of the knife. Her insides roiled, and she felt cold and empty. All she wanted to do was puke, but she wouldn't give him the satisfaction. "It's awful, you know? When you first started, I was far too young to realise what you were doing. You say my mother's death caused you to abuse me? What a perfect excuse. Tell me the truth, did sleeping with your little girl comfort you?"

He fell to his knees and shed a tear but said nothing.

She knew it was a crocodile tear. "You disgust me. At first, you said we were doing nothing wrong and insisted it would be our little secret. I believe, or I want to believe, that at first, it was just a cuddle in bed together and that I comforted you. Yet, it didn't take you long to touch me, did it? When I protested, you forced me on my back and cuffed me to the bed. Our little secret, right?"

"No, that's not what happened. Please—"

"Shut the fuck up! On my ninth birthday, you told me you were going to give me a present. After cuffing me and fucking me, you told me everything we did was natural; that every father and daughter did it." The blonde shuddered. "My mother had died only weeks before, and the first thought on your mind was how you could abuse me. It was sick!"

"You're wrong. I was drunk. It wasn't my fault. Can we stop this?" He smiled. "I love you."

She laughed a guttural laugh that caused Tim Hill to stop smiling. "You never loved me. Did you even love my mother? Have you ever loved anybody? You didn't even love Thomas' mother. All you've done is tell me I was wrong, how it wasn't your fault. I've had no apology; I had no concern about how I felt. I knew something was wrong, even at nine. I desperately wanted to tell someone. But how could I? I still didn't understand it myself. Eventually, I did."

She thought back to the day she'd confided in her friend, Meera. She could still picture Meera's jet-black hair, her dazzling wide brown eyes, and her innocent smile. When Meera answered her, her own life had almost crumbled.

"Do you know what my friend said? She told me her father did it to her, too." Her hands shook as she thought back to the day she'd slaughtered Meera's father. It was still a cold case, one she'd gotten away with, one they'd probably never solve. It had been her first kill. And she'd become a serial killer when she killed Alec Rawlinson.

"You men are always the same; you disgust me! It's like what you can't get from your wives or girlfriends. You take from us. In my own story, I was nine years old, my mother had died, and I needed comfort. I needed you, Father because I had no mother. And what did you do to me?"

As if her accusations were unfounded, he said, "No. It wasn't like that."

"Of course it was. For Meera, her mother had stopped

playing with her father's 'willy', and it was her job as his daughter to play with it. That's what she told me. Does that sound familiar?" She noticed the expression in his eyes. As suspected, his mood was changing. "So, tell me, how did you feel, abusing your young, powerless daughter?" She glared at him but didn't give him a chance to answer. "In fact, don't bother. I've heard enough of your lies and excuses. But the word powerless is important here, Tim."

Despite her father's wrath escalating, she stepped closer to him. She could see he was losing control. Whilst silent, his mouth formed a grimace; his fingers were clenched. It wouldn't take long for him to snap completely.

"Look at you, getting angry." She didn't care about provoking him. "There's nothing more you can do to harm me." He spat on the floor; he was making her task easier.

The blonde's voice lowered to a whisper. "What sent me over the edge was the night before I left home. You've no idea how frightened I was that night. Something had snapped inside you that night. I remember it, clear as day. I was at home, and you'd been drinking all night with your mates in celebration of your promotion. I guess you kept the fact you raped your daughter away from your boss. Right? Anyway, I remember being woken up because my bedroom door had shot open and crashed into the wall. I remember the light hurting my eyes as it flooded in. Then your swaying, drunken silhouette filled the gap."

She glanced at him. She wanted to kill him now but knew this was her last kill. This wasn't sexually motivated, this was personal, and she knew if she could make him feel the same fear that she herself had felt over a decade previously, then she'd be satisfied.

CHAPTER THIRTY-ONE

"You dragged the duvet from my bed and ripped my nightie off. Then you stood in the doorway, filming it. Did Lorraine ever know? If she did, why she didn't stop you? I'll never know. I hated her, you know? Lorraine. You never told me she was a replacement for my mother because she wasn't, was she? I was the replacement for my mother." He shook his head. "Did you have any idea what I was thinking whilst you filmed me? You, a naked adult, standing there with a camera, knowing there was nothing I could do. Lorraine was downstairs. I tried to shout for her. I had nowhere to run, nowhere to hide. Did you even care? Did Lorraine?"

Her father's fists balled, ready to attack. "She knew nothing," he spat. He would be no match for her, not with what she had behind her back.

"Despite that, I tried to run away. Remember? I thought—I thought deep down inside that at least if I attempted to escape, then you might stop." She laughed. "How wrong was I? You dragged me by the hair and pulled me back to the bed. I still have the scar on my shoulder blade where you used your lighter on me. Whenever I'm naked, it reminds me of that night." She laughed once again and pulled down her collar to show Tim. "A constant reminder, Tim. As if I needed one." She fought hard to hold back her tears. She was successful.

"Princess, stop!" He wasn't begging any more; his words were instead a warning.

She laughed at that. "I'm not that little girl who you can control any more. It's my turn. Lay down on the bed on your back and close your eyes."

"Absolutely not."

"Why? I want you like you were that night, Father. On your back, cuffed to the bed. For all you know, I have a camera on me, ready to re-enact what happened."

He took a step back. "Stop. I don't want to hurt you, but I will."

"You're not going to stop me!" She paused long enough to regain her composure. "Lorraine's as good as dead, anyway. Once I'm done with you, she's next." She didn't know why she was about to explain to him what she was going to do to Lorraine but was glad she'd stopped. It was probably something to do with wanting him to realise her feelings, past and present, though. All she knew was that she wanted to hurt him before she killed him.

"After burning me, and you forced my head down and forced yourself down my throat. Do you know that I wanted to die, Father? I certainly thought I was going to, especially when you had your cock in my mouth."

The young blonde desperately tried to hold it all together. She was shaking with anger. Her eyes were red, swollen from the tears that had suddenly burst through the dam. She clenched her fingers around the handle of the blade, wanting to leave because she felt sick at the sight of the man, but knowing she couldn't. She had to see it through. This was to be her last kill before she stopped forever.

With spittle flying from her mouth, she shouted, "Karma! You're going to get what you deserve!"

Chapter Thirty-two

"Why did you do it, Tim?" He said nothing, so she continued. "Nicole Green, Joanne Cox, and Stacey Lumb? Why did you kill them?"

"You weren't even alive back then. I don't have to answer you, *girl*!" screamed Tim.

The young blonde knew her father's anger had almost reached the point where he was likely to attack her, which was what she wanted. She closed one hand around the handle of the blade.

"You must have been relieved when the police charged Boris Jarman for the murder of Anna Hill. I bet you thought they were going to charge him for the other murders, too?" Tears welled in her eyes as she thought about the time she'd overheard her mother, Rosie, and father talking about his late ex-wife, Anna. Rosie had accused him of killing Anna and accused him of wanting to kill her, too.

"Did you kill my mother like you killed the others?"

"No. Your mother died in a car accident." He held his hands up in surrender. "Honestly."

"But you don't deny killing Nicole Green, Joanne Cox, and Stacey Lumb?"

"The police think it's Jarman, Princess, so it doesn't matter what I say to you right now."

"Maybe not, but if you don't answer for your actions to the police, then I'll make sure you answer for your crimes. Do you want to know how I found out?" Silence. "I found out because I checked you out; got you investigated. It turns out you were with Lorraine Cox before Anna Hill, and she dumped you for Edward Kennings."

A devilish smile flashed across his face. "She didn't dump me, so wherever you got your information from was wrong. She married into money so we could both be financially secure."

"Regardless, you're still a dirty, disgusting pervert!"

"So, what are you going to do about it, Princess?" Tim pointed towards the door. "You locked the door, and I have the key card." He took a few steps towards the en-suite. "It's obvious to me now why you're here. You've killed the other men, right? And now it's my turn?" She didn't answer. "I've heard about them in the news. A couple of them looked big and strong. You must have surprised them. Did you interact with them via social media like me?" She said nothing and continued to watch him. "Yes, I see now. You lulled them into a false sense of security, acted like a little tart, and offered up a taste of your succulent fruit. Now that your act is up, you're screwed. You're no match for me, little girl."

She stared deep into her father's vile eyes. "I never said I killed them, so don't put words into my mouth. And maybe I'm no match for you, but I might be. I'm not the little girl you abused any more. You should be ashamed of yourself. When you raped me, you may as well have killed me. At first, I thought you'd robbed me of my future. I was wrong. Killing you was my future. And now I've met somebody who completes me. It's time to end this for good."

"Whatever future you've built will be gone if you kill me!" shouted Tim. "Leave now, and you'll never hear from me again. That's what you want, isn't it?"

A bulbous tear fell from her eye. "It's not enough. Only killing you will stop this repeated cycle."

"Please. Princess. You don't have to do this."

"Of course I do!" she shouted. "I've dreamt of this day. When I left home, I'd often draw violent sketches showing how I'd kill you and write violent stories, going into great detail about what I'd do if I ever saw you again."

Tim stepped forward. "I've had enough of this, my sweet." He had a letter opener in his hand. "If you were going to kill me, you would have done it by now. You were always a disappointment to me." Tim pointed to the door. "Get out of this hotel room before I do something you'll regret. Like I've said before, you're really no match for me, little girl."

"Maybe not," she said, "but I will fulfil my fantasy by killing you."

Tim stiffened, and an expression of evil crossed his face. He bared his teeth as his eyes narrowed. He looked the way he'd done that night over a decade ago. The blonde felt sick. She closed her eyes for a second to combat the nausea when she saw a flicker and heard something move. The light changed to shadows beyond her closed eyes. She didn't need to open her eyes to know her father had moved.

Timothy feinted to his left, towards the en-suite and then sprinted forward and forced her against the door, holding the letter opener to her throat.

* * *

The tension in the room was intense, and the young blonde desperately wanted to stab the pervert right in the fucking neck. Instead, she said, "Don't do anything stupid, Father."

"It's a bit too late for that, Princess."

"Let me go."

"Why would I do that? You've threatened me repeatedly," said Tim.

"Because I realise now I'm no match for you," she said.

"What about the accusations? I've abused and killed no one."

She glanced at her father. "Why can't you just admit it? Then apologise?"

"It's your word against mine, sweetheart. I don't need to admit it, nor do I need to apologise for anything."

"Please. That's all I want." A burst of pain shot through her neck where the letter opener had slightly pierced her skin.

"You're a silly little girl. I told you, didn't I, that you weren't much of a match for me?"

"You did," she said, "and now I realise I made a mistake."

"Let's be honest here," said Tim. "You're not leaving this hotel room unless you've paid the price. Now, you can rather get down on your hands and knees like a good little girl, or you can leave here in a body bag. Do you understand?"

"I understand, Father. But for me to get down on my knees, I need you to let me go."

Tim looked down at his daughter and slightly released his grip on her. She held eye contact, not daring to break it. "Please?" she whispered.

He let go, and the blonde fell to her knees on the carpeted floor. "Why did you kill those women?" she asked as Tim began unzipping his trousers.

"Because I wanted to," Tim said. "Nicole, Joanna, and Stacey were whores, just like my ex-wife, Anna. They got what they deserved. They got to suck my cock. Just like you, you little whore! Now, if you'd be so kind, Princess?"

A sudden scream took Tim by surprise, and the young blonde thrust forward with her knife. He hadn't seen the attack coming. The sharpened blade cut through his penis, straight through his pubic bone and into the prostate gland just behind it. The force of the thrust pushed Tim onto the bed behind him. There was blood everywhere. The shock made him drop the letter opener. Before it clattered to the floor, the blonde stood up and was over him, bringing her right arm down and forcing the knife straight into Tim's neck.

The young blonde continued to rain knife blows down on her victim, her porcelain skin soon freckled with crimson.

Chapter Thirty-three

The frosty April chill had given way to a warm Friday mid-morning as George Beaumont sat on a beach towel, sipping his takeaway coffee. He was watching Isabella play with Jack on the white sands of Blackpool beach, enjoying a well-deserved day off. He felt a swell of pride within and a mix of love, which warmed him better than the coffee. She was great with Jack. Great with him, too. They hadn't had a chat about their situation, but he knew he couldn't keep it from everybody much longer. Occasionally, Jack would turn to find his dad, and his little arms would reach out to him, his blond curls framing his rounded face, his piercing emerald eyes checking for his dad's presence. George loved that his son recognised him, loved that he wanted him for comfort.

With his free hand, George waved at his son, a huge smile going with it. Isabella gently waved Jack's hand in reply whilst she giggled. "Is that your daddy over there?" she crooned.

There were a few other families on the beach. A couple of young girls set off towards the water in chase of another little girl, whose mother looked on nervously from her own towel to his right. He could understand. He wondered what Jack would be like when he was older, whether he'd like the beach as he did or hate it like his mother, Mia.

CHAPTER THIRTY-THREE

Sipping more coffee, George protected his eyes from the glare of the sun with his free hand. It was still low in the sky, and he cursed himself for not grabbing his sunglasses from the Honda. George needed the coffee; his tongue felt like sandpaper, and his lips were dry. His head felt foggy, and a hangover headache gnawed at him. He cursed the beer he'd drunk the night before.

"Something on your mind?" George hadn't seen Isabella and Jack approach. He'd been lost in his memories from the night before and hadn't heard her. "You were miles away, you OK?"

Catherine was on his mind. His first love. He hated admitting it to himself, but she'd had him hooked from the first second. But she'd cut herself off from him after leaving Elland Road, leaving him pining like a puppy. George had rung her and texted her constantly and had even shown up at her house. Her roommate told him she'd moved out, and soon Catherine had changed her number. Yet, from last night, it seemed she hadn't lost her feelings for him.

He thought back to the moment he told her to stop and the look in her eyes when she realised she'd misread the situation. She was angry and hurt and stormed off. He'd tried messaging and calling her, but she'd switched her mobile off. Yet, he didn't feel guilty. Last night, he'd got a taxi home and had called Isabella, asking her to come over. She was the one he loved. She was the one he wanted to be with. Catherine had her chance and had disappeared.

George grinned. "I was thinking about you and what we could get up to tonight, too."

Isabella handed Jack over and sat down on her own towel. "Not tonight, I'm afraid. I can't." She saw the disappointment in his eyes and kissed him on the cheek. "You have Jack, remember. Anyway, did you get me coffee too?" She looked around expectantly, smiling when he pulled out the extra cup.

"Jack seems to be enjoying himself during his first time at the beach. You're so good with him. Thank you."

"My pleasure. I love spending time with you both. And anyway, he's a mini-you. What's not to love?"

George grinned once more.

"Are you—are you sure you're OK? Nothing on your mind?" she asked.

"Other than work?" He shook his head. "No," he lied. It's what Catherine had said to him last night about being in a good relationship that was now on his mind. That and Isabella Wood. She was always at the forefront of George's mind. She had been since he'd bought her a ring. He just wasn't sure it was the right time. Yet, they'd been together a year, after all. Did she feel the same way he did?

"You'll catch her, George. I know you will. I wanted to say thank you."

"For what?"

"I've heard the rumours about me," she said, blowing away a stray curl. "They think I'm the killer because I argued with Terry. I know it's why Smith kicked me off the case. You had my back. You were ready to defend me. Thank you, George." She kissed him on the cheek, and he put his arm around her. He was happy there at that moment, with his two favourite people. "And thank you for agreeing to come here today. It's been years since I visited. And I won't lie. I was pretty jealous that you went to the coast recently without me. Especially as you went with another woman."

"You don't need to be jealous, Isabella," George said. "I

have no intention of cheating on you. I love you."

"Good," she said, matter of fact.

"I forgot to ask. Are you working tonight?"

"No," she said with a smile whilst raising both brows. "Just busy."

"Too busy for me?"

"That's right, George. Too busy for you." She got up abruptly, and George noticed Isabella rubbed the burn mark she had where her left buttock met her left thigh. She'd never told him how she'd got it. "I fancy ice cream. You want one?"

"Sounds good," he said. "Vanilla, please."

He watched her walk to the kiosk, wondering what she was doing tonight and why it was such a big secret.

* * *

Back at home and with nothing much to do for the rest of the evening, George settled down and watched the F1 free practice session from earlier on in the day. He'd have to record qualifying tomorrow and the race on Sunday, but it was nice to sit on his sofa and get lost in something else for a change. Jack was asleep in his Moses basket.

Then his phone rang. He reached for it from the other side of the sofa where it was charging. It was Dr Ross. "Hi, Dr Ross. It's nice to hear from you. Hope you're well." Whilst he enjoyed working with Lindsey, there was something about the older man that comforted him.

"Sorry to call so late, son," Dr Ross said, his tone as friendly as usual. "Something was bothering me about the Broadchurch murder. So, I had a look. As you know, Lindsey found microscopic fragments of metal in his throat, a sign that the blade had been recently sharpened. She also looked at Rawlinson and Kennings and found the same. Now, because I wasn't involved until yesterday, I couldn't give you my expertise."

"Where is Lindsey, by the way? I thought she was dealing with it?"

"Yes, I'm afraid my young blonde colleague has not been in since yesterday. I believe she's feeling under the weather."

"OK. So what expertise do you have for me, doctor?"

"Well, in March, there were two murders with similar MOs to your set."

"Two? OK."

"And I thought I was going mad because of the similarities. Anyway, I checked my records, and lo-and-behold, I also found microscopic fragments of high carbon steel within the wounds."

"So what does that mean, Dr Ross?" George said, thinking about Boris Jarman. During his visit to HMP Northumberland, Jarman had told him to look at cold cases and had said, 'One in South Leeds. Indian fella. Look into it, and you'll see a connection. Trust me.'

"Well, after examining them under a microscope, I'm convinced they're from the same blade. No blades are truly the same. They're all unique. I'm positive, George, that the blade used to kill Rawlinson, Kennings, Morton, and Broadchurch, is the same one used to kill Viraj Patel and Nathan Patterson in March."

After thanking the doctor, George sighed and got up. They'd already had a serial killer on their hands after the death of Rawlinson. Mark had been right, after all. He needed a drink. He'd been doing so well recently, but the conversation with

Dr Ross had unnerved him, and he needed something to warm the ice in his veins, something to calm him down. He pulled down the whiskey bottle from his cabinet, and as he poured a thumb into a glass Isabella had bought him, he stopped. Jack. He was looking after Jack all night.

George tossed the whiskey down the sink as his phone beeped. A text message. He read it and immediately wished he hadn't.

"I'm coming to get Jack and take him home," the text message read.

Chapter Thirty-four

George sauntered down the steps to answer the door. He'd left Jack in his Moses basket. No doubt, Mia would want to pack up some of his stuff before leaving. She'd probably want another argument, too.

But it wasn't Mia who was standing there when he opened the door. It was Catherine.

"Not who you were expecting?" she asked.

She must have seen the look of shock on his face. He attempted a smile and said, "No."

"Disappointed?"

"What?" He didn't know what to say. "No."

"Tell that to your face. Should I come back at a more suitable time?"

"No, come in. I thought you were Mia," he said, opening the door for her to come in.

She didn't wait for him to move back and passed him by closely. He could smell her perfume and the shampoo in her hair. "Mia?"

"Yeah, I've got Jack. She's decided to pick him up. He was supposed to be sleeping over tonight, but I guess she changed her mind."

"She tend to do that a lot?" The venom in her tone was

unmistakable. George nodded. "How do you put up with it? Are you still in love with her?"

"No, it's not like that. She's Jack's mother. It's better this way than us not speaking. The kitchen's up the stairs and to the right. You fancy a hot drink?"

"Sure." She led the way, taking in the small flat. It lacked a woman's touch. It was something she could help him with, and she found she wanted to help him with it. Desperately. Why wasn't he interested any more? What had she done?

"How are you, Catherine?" he asked, clicking on the kettle.

"Look, I just wanted to apologise. It's why I'm here. You don't have to act all nervous around me. I'm not—I'm not just going to come onto you. Alright?"

"Alright. Thanks."

"Thanks?"

"For the apology. But there was no need. We'd had a bit too much to drink, and our wires got crossed. That's all."

"Yeah," she lied. "Wired crossed..."

She watched him pour the scalding water over the two tea bags and then added, "But for me, George, it wasn't crossed wires." She stepped towards him. "I meant to kiss you. I've wanted to kiss you from the moment I saw you again."

He turned to her, and she was swallowed up in his emerald-coloured eyes. George smiled. His lips parted, and he said, "I'm sorry, Catherine. I was drunk, and my sentences clearly weren't making sense. But I meant it when I said I've fallen for somebody else."

"But why her, whoever she is, and not me? What's wrong with me?"

"Nothing, Catherine. You're beautiful. Fun. Intelligent. Any man would be lucky to have you, but—"

"But what?" she interrupted.

"It was already too late for you. I met this wonderful woman a while ago."

"Well, who is it? Who's the lucky lady?"

"I—" Luckily for George, the doorbell rang, saving him from telling Catherine a lie. He couldn't tell her about Isabella. "That'll be Mia. Make yourself comfortable in the living room, and I'll be back soon. Can we finish this conversation then?"

She nodded as George left the kitchen, headed down the corridor and down the stairs.

* * *

"I don't want to fight with you, George, but I need to take Jack home. Now!"

"OK, Mia. Calm down. It's fine. If you need him, you need him."

"Oh yeah, of course. Because I need our son, you're so forthcoming. But when I need you, you tell me to sling my hook."

"It's not like that, Mia, and you know it. Our romantic relationship ended last year."

"What, and that's it? I made a mistake, George. One that I've apologised for. Repeatedly."

"I know, Mia, and I forgive you. In fact, I forgave you last year. But that doesn't mean—"

"Then why are you punishing me?" she asked. "You're punishing Jack, too."

"Jack's better off not hearing these kinds of arguments growing up, Mia. Look, I have a guest. Can we not do this now?"

"A guest?" She raised her brow. "Who?"

"Somebody from work. We're—She's here to discuss the case we're working on."

"She?" He nodded. "DS Wood?" He shook his head. A look of disgust spread across her face that was suddenly one of hurt. "You've let another woman in your house when our son is here. How dare you?"

"Mia. It's not like that. We're friends. We work together. That's it."

"Oh fuck off, George. Give me my son, and I'll get out of your hair. Leave you to fuck your work colleagues."

George nearly bit, desperately wanting to remind her she was the one who fucked work colleagues when he thought of Isabella. Better to be silent than a hypocrite.

"Fine. Jack is in my room in his Moses basket. Do you need anything else?"

"Just his bag."

"That's in the living room." Where Catherine was.

Mia stormed off upstairs, and George headed for the living room to retrieve Jack's bag. Hopefully, he'd get there before Mia entered the living room and realised who was sitting on his sofa. She knew all about Catherine. George had struggled when Catherine had initially left. She'd broken his heart. He'd once told Mia as much, much to her annoyance. They'd been drunk, and Mia had asked him about his exes. He shouldn't have said anything, but he hadn't realised what her reaction would have been. "I'll meet you in the kitchen, Mia," he said. "I've got some milk in the fridge. You may as well take it with you."

But as George entered the living room, he realised he'd made a colossal mistake. Catherine wasn't there, which meant she was still in the kitchen, and Mia had gotten there before him. *Shit.* He heard them greeting each other and Catherine asking her if she needed help to look for anything. He hazarded a step closer, worried about the fallout when his phone rang. "I'll be with you in a minute, Mia. It's work calling me."

"Hi Josh!" he shouted. "Everything OK?"

"Sir, we were called down to the InterContinental Hotel on Crown Point Road this afternoon. There's been another murder."

"Right, OK. Mia's collecting Jack as we speak. Where are you? I'll come and meet you."

"Back at the station, sir. We've found some video footage that the victim had taken without permission."

"Really?"

"Yeah. And we now know who the killer is, sir," Josh said. "She's on the video, clear as day. I can't believe it's her."

"Video footage. Of the killer?" The two women must have heard him because their faint chatter stopped.

* * *

"Who is it, Josh?" George asked. It could be anybody. Anybody at all. He'd thought for a while she may not even be blonde. Hair colour could be changed. Wigs could be worn. There was no way of isolating the woman's height from the footage they had. Was their killer even a woman? They had no DNA and no idea. A gust of icy wind blew through the flat's open window, causing the blinds to rattle, and he jumped. His heart was pounding.

"I'm sorry, sir, say that again. The line's pretty bad."

"I said, who is it, Josh? The killer?" They had no suspects.

CHAPTER THIRTY-FOUR

Word around the station suggested it could have been DS Wood because of her argument with DC Morton. But then, Lindsey Yardley and Catherine Jones had also been mad at Terry. Was it Isabella? She'd been home alone on Wednesday night, the night Justin had been killed. Or so she'd said. He'd watched Jurassic Park alone after she'd cancelled on him. Catherine had an alibi for the night that Justin Broadchurch was murdered. A date. He hadn't checked on it yet, though. Did Lindsey have an alibi?

"You want to know who it is, sir? The line's breaking again. It's…"

"Yes. I need to know, Josh. Please?" George asked, desperation in his voice. Were the three women innocent after all? Was it Emily Sanderson they were after? They hadn't found her yet, which was concerning. Or was it somebody else? An anomaly, somebody not already part of the investigation?

"It's—It's… sir." The line was scrambled.

"Wait, what? Who is the killer, Josh?"

"You'd better hang up that phone and get in here before I do something you regret, George," a sultry voice purred. "Now!"

As George hung up, he hesitated and looked around the living room. What did he do? He had a murderer in his house? It set him on edge. Panic exploded deep inside George. There was a murderer in his kitchen, with his son, a boy he loved so much he couldn't explain it.

The voice filled his mind. *You'd better hang up that phone and get in here before I do something you regret.* His phone rang. It was DS Fry. "Throw me the phone through the door, George," the killer demanded.

George obeyed her commands. His son Jack was in there, and his life was being threatened. Every instinct screamed for him to attack the assailant, to defend Jack. But he wasn't stupid, and neither was the assailant. By charging in recklessly, he could endanger all of them.

"What do you want?" he asked, his breathing a staccato, disjointing his words. He hazarded a step closer into the kitchen and saw the silver glint of a knife in the light coming from outside.

He edged even closer.

Enough to see the person who had his son at knifepoint.

A dark mass sat at the kitchen table, which was in the centre of the kitchen. Her hands were bound with cable ties. Tears were chasing dark streaks of mascara down her cheeks. She was shaking so erratically that her loose hair shuddered, quivering in the air as it fell down the sides of her face.

Chapter Thirty-five

The Blonde Delilah met George's eyes and grinned. She had Jack in one arm, nuzzled close to her breast, and the knife in the other. That sharp knife, with its silver glint, was too close to the other woman's neck, held out by a manicured hand. It was shaking. George raised his hands, palms facing her.

Wearing cherry-red lipstick to match her nails, the young Caucasian woman shook her head in warning. Her long blonde curls danced in the light. On the table was a black mass. A wig, he realised. She'd been the killer all along, the wig part of her disguise. She'd been staring him in the face all along, pretending to help when leading them down the wrong path.

Catherine.

She looked the same as she had the night they'd slept together all those years ago. Same outfit. Same hairstyle. Same makeup.

She met his furious gaze.

"What do you want, Catherine?" he demanded, his tone aggressive, his body stiff. Like a spring, George was prepared to explode into movement at the slightest provocation. With Jack to her chest, he didn't dare rush her. Especially not with the knife. Not yet.

"The game's up, I guess?" she asked. Her voice was calm and soft, yet it cut through him cleanly, slicing through the thrashing of his pulse in his ears.

"Give me Jack and let Mia go. Then we can talk, alright?"

Mia looked up at him, a subdued look in her eyes. He promised her she'd never be involved in one of his cases ever again, and yet here she was. A hostage. Again.

"You lied to me, George," snapped Catherine, brandishing the knife closer to Mia's neck. "She's the one you're getting back with, right? She told me as much as you were talking on the phone to Josh. But I love you. I always have. We'd be great together. You can see that, right? Just you, me, and Jack. All I have to do is get rid of Mia."

"Mia and I have been over for a long time," George said. His hands were still carefully raised in a placating gesture. The kitchen was small. If she didn't have his son to her chest, he'd have rushed her. Even with the knife, he was sure he could overpower her.

But with Jack between them, he swallowed his pride. "Give me Jack and let Mia go. *Then* we can talk, alright?"

"No, I can't give him to you!" The tone of her voice was as fierce as her stare. That knife was being gripped in her shaky grip; the blade splashing reflected street lights onto the tiled wall.

"Yes, you can. Once I have my son, we can go into the living room and talk. This is about me and you, right? Not Mia and Jack." He stepped closer.

She bared her teeth at him. "No! This is about Mia, too. She took you away from me."

"No, you're wrong, Catherine. If anybody did that, then it was you. You left the station, Catherine. What was I supposed to do? Follow you?"

"Yes. I loved you, George. I still do. Can't you see that?"

His heart was pounding so rapidly that his pulse was thundering in his ears. He saw her lips move, but he missed the words.

"What. Repeat it?"

"Yes, I wanted you to leave with me," Catherine said, grinning savagely. "That's exactly what I wanted. But you got with this whore instead. A murderer fucker. And you bred with her. How disappointing. The good thing is, we can bring up Jack together, you and me, George."

"And if I say no?"

Slowly, she placed the knife to Mia's throat, drawing a bead of crimson. "You read Emily's book, didn't you? In fact, I know you did. You called me the night you were reading it. What happens in the end?" She wasn't looking at him; she was looking at Mia.

"The detective dies." George stared, unable to think of anything else to say. He couldn't believe what was happening. "Then leave Mia and Jack alone. Get that knife away from her. And anyway, why kill me when you've already killed a detective?"

Catherine seemed to take personal pride in what George said, raising her brow and sneering at him. "DC Terrence Morton was personal and not involved in my fantasy, George. It also got that pretty DS out of the picture. I couldn't tell who it was you were fucking, to be honest. Isabella Wood or Emilia Alexander?"

At her words, George's heart raced, and his body started shivering. His glance flicked to Mia and the knife. He swallowed when he saw his son begin to stir, too far away for him to get to. He knew he could take her down, yet something was stopping him. He thought about his son and about the ring he had for Isabella in his wardrobe. Despite the circumstances, he kept his voice as calm as possible. Everything he did now was for his son's sake. A single tear snaked down his cheek, and George decided to ignore the question. "How was Timothy Hill connected to your fantasy, Catherine?" He was quivering with anger whilst ice oozed through his veins. "And Justin, Edward, and Alec? Did they reject you, too?"

"The men I killed thought they were untouchable, George." Her sneer widened. "I made them pay."

"Pay? What for?" he asked, though he dreaded the answer. He was going to pay for refusing her advances; was it the same for the other victims? He stared at Mia, who didn't have a clue what was happening. It was evident in the way her wide eyes were fixed upon him, silently begging him to protect them, to get her and Jack out of there.

George wished it were that simple. Catherine was a cunning woman with skills, experienced in killing, and keen on violence. She also had Jack. They were all in greater danger than he first thought.

Catherine cocked her head to one side and grinned. "Alec Rawlinson cheated on every partner he had, including his wife, Christie. Edward was a paedophile. Justin was abusing his daughter and had been since her mother died! They were scum, and they had to pay. Have you figured out how I led them to their deaths?"

George didn't answer, but with every sentence, he took a tiny step closer. Next to Catherine was Jack's Moses basket. She'd need to put Jack down soon, especially if she was going to kill George.

CHAPTER THIRTY-FIVE

"You know, George, most killers are narcissists. They'll share with you the ins and outs, and they'll tell you their story with a straight face. They'll show no emotion as if they're reading a bedtime story to their child. Killers are proud of what they've done. And make no mistake, so am I."

Again, George didn't answer, letting her speak. Whilst she was speaking, she was waving the knife around, but at least it was away from Mia.

"So I'm going to do just that, my love. Share the ins and outs with you. I pretended to be sixteen- and seventeen-year-old girls," she said with a shrug. "When I lured Justin to his death, I made myself look like Justin's daughter, Cassie. The B&B weekend girl, if you remember? Justin was a sick bastard. They were all sick, to be fair, each and every one of them. I should be given a medal for what I've done. I enjoyed the torture and suffering I put them through, at any least." She was imagining it—he saw the faraway look in her eyes that told of the pleasure she got from killing. "It sends shivers through me just thinking about when I plunged my knife inside them."

George risked another step and said, "And Hill?" He explained what Josh had told him about the video footage. Her smile faded, replaced by a darkened gaze as her focus returned to him.

"You probably aren't aware, George; few people are." George shrugged. "My name, before I changed it, was Amber Hill. Timothy was my father."

Chapter Thirty-six

"Your father?" His eyes were wide. "Why did you kill him?" he asked.

"What do you want me to say, George? That I did it because my mum died when I was nine, and my father started sexually abusing me?"

"I didn't know you were—"

"What, abused?" she interrupted. "Why would you? I went to great lengths to hide it and have done so for years."

"I'm sorry, Catherine, I swear—"

"I don't want your pity, George. I've killed him, and that was that. Well, until you found out."

"I'm glad I did. You're a victim, Catherine. Society has failed you. It's created a serial killer."

"No, George. I was a victim. *Was*. But Timothy wasn't. You probably don't know because it sounds like you haven't watched the video, but he was Jack the Butcher. He killed those prostitutes thirty years ago. Guess you could say I was a chip off the old block after all!" She puffed out her chest and smiled serenely.

George took a moment to take in the new information. *Tim Hill was Jack the Butcher. Christ.* "So your motive was revenge? You lied about the lust murders?" George frowned. Revenge

CHAPTER THIRTY-SIX

was the oldest motive in the book.

"Exactly. Revenge. But remember, I'm a damaged woman, a woman abused as a child by a man who should have done everything in his power to protect me, love me, and care for me."

He thought for a moment, never taking his eyes from her. "I understand that. But not the others. Tell me why you killed them."

"You realise I can't let you leave here alive? You know that, right? So telling you is irrelevant."

"Why? Josh knows, which means DSU Smith knows. I wouldn't be surprised if a team were on its way now." George's phone buzzed inside Catherine's pocket as if to prove the point. "See. They're worried about me, and they know where I live. It's hopeless for you. Give up, give yourself in, and plead mitigating circumstances. You're a victim, Catherine."

"If it's so hopeless, then I'll kill you all. Take you all with me." She tightened her grasp on both Jack and the knife. "Then I won't be a victim, will I?"

"Tell me why you killed the others? Maybe I could help you tell your story," George said. He wanted to move the conversation away from them all being murdered. George looked at the knife and tensed. "But first, let Mia and Jack go."

"You deserve to know why you have to die, I suppose," she said, ignoring his pleas. I'm sure you remember Nathan Patterson."

George did. His old colleague, who he found out, has been murdered recently. Had Catherine murdered him? He ran through his options. Jack wasn't safe, especially if George rushed her. Whilst he stood a chance of winning, Jack and Mia would get hurt. It was too much of a risk.

"Did you ever wonder why I transferred?" Catherine asked. George nodded his head. One minute she was there, rocking his world, and the next, she'd disappeared. "I had to leave the station because of the abusive behaviour from your buddies."

"What abusive behaviour?" he asked.

"You were protected from it. The new Detective Sergeant. The golden boy." Her face darkened, and her sneer turned into a snarl. "Smith protected you and told you I was transferring because of our relationship when, in fact, I left because Nate Patterson raped me."

"I'm sorry about that, Catherine. I had no idea. Honest."

"I know you didn't, my love. But because of your selfish friend and my bastard of a father, you are going to be punished, too. It's unfair but necessary."

"It's not necessary. Tell me how to make it right, Catherine. Please. Let Jack and Mia go. They're innocent."

"How can you make any of this right, George? Do you know how it feels to attempt to take your own life? I've suffered so much at the hands of people who were supposed to love me. The pain became so unbearable that I didn't want to live." She paused, and George could see the grief on her face, the haunting memories that seemed to cleave her in two. He could easily have rushed her right then, the knife in her hand momentarily forgotten, but he didn't. He needed to hear her out, especially if he was partly to blame for who she'd become. "It's driven me crazy all these years, and I had to make sure I got justice one day."

"And you got justice. So give it up. Let us go. Confess what you did. Plead mitigating circumstances. What Tim Hill did to you was—"

Anger flashed through her at his name. "But I've killed

others, George! It's why I killed Viraj Patel. He was abusing his daughter, my friend, Meera Patel." Her fingers tightened around the handle of the knife. "You see, that's the difference between me and this whore!"

George flinched, his mouth open. "What?"

"She was fucking a murderer, George. I'd never do that to you. So tell me who the better woman is. Tell me!" He saw her tense and stepped back. He saw a flash of anger in her eyes. The blade of the knife slipped through Mia's blonde hair, up towards her ear. "You're making me sad by not answering me, George and the only way to make me happy is to smile. Shall we make Mia smile for all eternity?"

Mia whimpered, and George said nothing. She pressed the knife against the back of Mia's skull, painting her hair crimson. "I'm a desperate woman. Remember that, George."

"I'm sorry about all of this," he said desperately. "But please, don't punish Jack or Mia. It's not their fault. Let them go. I'll happily take their place. Let them go. Please." It was as close to grovelling as he could get, but if she required it, he'd go down on his knees.

She grinned at his pathetic apology, and a fresh wave of panic roared through him. George gulped as blood ran down Mia's neck. Fear had frozen him. He couldn't save her or himself. Mia glanced up at him, her lip trembling; she was innocent in all of this.

After a minute, the answer came. "I'm a serial killer, George, like my father before me. I can't seem to control myself. So no. We all die."

"But why kill people now?" George dared to ask once more, moving the conversation along. "You were abused years ago. All you had to do was tell me. You had my number. It's the same one I have now. We could have put Nathan behind bars. I would have—I would have protected you." The thought of Nathan Patterson raping her made him sick to the stomach. Despite her killing these men, she was a victim too. His fingers itched to grab Catherine by the throat and squeeze. She was within distance, but she still had the knife to Mia's jugular and Jack in her other arm.

"That's nice to hear, but it's far too late." She raised her chin and took a deep breath. She placed Jack in his Moses basket and stepped next to Mia.

"And why DC Morton?"

She smirked at him before a loud laugh erupted from her mouth. "Why not?" When it didn't get a rise out of him, she continued. "Terrence Morton was a misogynistic arsehole—"

"A misogynistic arsehole who you killed in cold blood. Was he part of your plans, or did he just piss you off once too many times?"

She laughed and said, "You're a hypocrite, George. You killed the Miss Murderer in cold blood. You'd disarmed him, yet you continued to bring that rock down on his skull. How dare you sit there on your high horse and lecture me?"

"I did it in self-defence, and not a day goes by that I don't think about what I did. I've shown remorse, Catherine. You've shown nothing."

"You know, George," she said, ignoring his remark, "you're right. I have shown zero remorse. But I don't have to. I've removed abusive men from society. People will root for me. I deserve a fucking medal!" She paused, licked her lips, and took a calming breath. "The only tears I shed will be when I slice through your carotid. I meant it when I said I loved you."

George smiled. "I'm sure there will be people out there

rooting for you. Sadly, I won't be one of them. And why all the violence? Let us go."

"Violence doesn't exist in human society only; it is a manifestation of the need for survival in all things living, George," she said. Foxes are violent towards chickens because they need to survive. I learnt about the natural order of the world early in life."

"And your violence was through a need to survive?"

"For better or worse, human beings are animals and are part of nature," she said. "We kill and eat other living beings. For some reason, it's quite easy for us to accept this kind of violence since it is linked with the survival of our species. Yet, when we use violence elsewhere, it's suddenly an issue. I was violent because I needed to survive. You said it yourself during the case, George. You thought it was a man because the crimes required strength and a different mentality."

"You could have come to me, Catherine. I would have helped you."

"No, you wouldn't. There was no proof. There never is. It's my word against theirs. You couldn't have brought them to justice. Have you ever heard of the term 'bottom of the pecking order'?" He nodded. "What I bet you don't know is that it derives from roosters raping hens. Roosters are known to force themselves savagely upon hens. They are bigger, stronger, and have sharp spurs that they use. The roosters force themselves upon the hens at the bottom of the pecking order. In fact, sometimes a rooster will mount a poor hen several times in a single day and will peck her and slash her, leaving her bleeding with her feathers torn off."

George risked another tiny step, and Mia flinched; her watery eyes were fixed on him, pleading.

"I was that hen for years, and my father the rooster. I was that hen again when Nate Patterson decided he wanted to fuck me because he was jealous of you! It took me a while, George, but I decided I wasn't going to be a hen any more but was going to be the fox. Those roosters needed to be brought to justice. All of them. That was why I searched through social media with fake profiles. I wanted to find those men who were disgusting, the ones who took advantage of vulnerable people, the ones who reminded me of Nate Patterson and Tim Hill. I killed two known abusers in Patel and Patterson, to begin with. And in between finding my father on there, I found some disgusting, despicable abusers, and I killed them too. So give me my fucking medal!"

"You don't deserve a medal," he said, taking a noticeable step closer to Catherine. "What you are is a cunning, treacherous woman. And I will do everything in my power to make sure you rot in prison!"

"You have no power, George. I am the one in control here. Before we all die, I need you to answer my question. If you don't love Mia, and you're not interested in me, then who is this new woman in your life?"

"What?"

"You told me there was somebody else. Who?"

"That's none of your—"

"Business? Yes, it fucking is! I'm the one holding the knife. Tell me, or Mia dies first."

Something snapped within him.

George launched himself at the woman, pulling her left arm with his dominant right, pulling her towards him. They collided, and he crashed into the tiled wall behind him.

Chapter Thirty-seven

Mia shrieked and stood up, running for Jack despite her hands being bound. She was off balance, but despite her bounds, Mia gripped the wicker Moses basket by both handles and tried to leave the kitchen. But Catherine was up, having landed on George, his body reducing the impact of her fall. She lunged for Mia, but George tripped her. She swore as she fell and bounced off a chair.

Holding Jack in his basket, Mia sprinted into the corridor and down the stairs outside the house. A gust of wind buffeted George as he stood and blocked the kitchen door. Catherine slashed out with the knife.

He stood firm and raised his hands before him; fiery pain erupted across his outstretched palms. Blood dripped to the floor.

Catherine's screams drowned everything out as the young blonde stopped slashing and tried to pursue Mia and Jack. George pushed her back, and she bared her teeth at him. George didn't care as Mia and Jack were behind him now. He was a physical barrier between them and this mad woman.

Then Catherine slashed again, forcing him to step back into the hallway as another gust of freezing air blasted in. It was still freezing for late April. Catherine slashed again, catching him high on the chest but not very deep. His white shirt turned crimson.

Behind him, the sound of sirens screeched in from the open front door.

George smiled and advanced on Catherine. She had a snarl locked on her face. He had the advantage if he stayed near the door. "You've lost, Catherine. Give it up. Those sirens are for you." His hands burned where they had been slashed. Dark blood oozed out, smearing his trousers where he'd firmly pressed them against to try and stop the bleeding.

In desperation, Catherine grabbed a cast iron skillet that was hanging above the stove and threw it at him. It crashed onto the tiles behind him before it bounced onto the floor with a clatter. George picked it up, but Catherine used the moment to sprint to her right, George's left, around the side of the table, and near to the door.

But Catherine had made a mistake. She'd gotten too close to George, and with a bloodied palm, he forcefully grabbed her wrist. "I said it's over, Catherine," George said.

Catherine seized her chance. With her knife, she attempted to slash George with it again.

But the attempt was feeble, and George deflected it with a swing of the skillet, knocking the knife from Catherine's lethargic fingers. With a strong hand, he raised the skillet high in the air before crashing it down against Catherine's head with a sickening thud.

Thud, crash. Thud, crash. Thud, crash.

He hit the Blonde Delilah with the cast iron skillet again, and again, and again until her face and head were nothing but a bloody mess. He only stopped when he heard the sirens, now deafening, and the door battering on its hinges.

CHAPTER THIRTY-SEVEN

The sound of the kitchen door crashing against the kitchen wall, shuddering in its frame, and then slamming shut in the wind woke him from his vision. Catherine was slumped on her knees, still held firmly in his grasp, the skillet in the air, her eyes pleading.

Thud, crash. Thud, crash. Thud, crash.

George was confused; he thought he'd really killed her. He looked around. Catherine seized her chance once again and punched him in the nose. Disoriented, he fell back against the tiles as out of his nose flowed a crimson river.

She sprinted away, and George knew he needed to get after her, so he got up from the floor. The adrenaline had dulled the pain, but he swayed as he did so. The knife and skillet lay where they had fallen. He contemplated picking one up and chasing after Catherine, but he assumed she'd be long gone by now.

Instead, he immediately left the kitchen, his eyes straining to see down into the inky blackness outside. He saw nothing but knew the Delilah must be waiting for him in the shadows.

Then he heard a sob from behind him, from his bedroom. George swallowed. He was sure Catherine had gone outside. Had he been wrong? His heart was in his throat. He headed towards the bedroom as a flash of blue lights illuminated the inky blackness outside.

Slowly, George made his way down the corridor, taking each step lightly, the beating of his heart in his ears. The door opened with a faint creak. And then a black mass crashed into him.

It was Mia, crying and shivering. She had removed the cable ties and had Jack in her arms. George enveloped them with his arms, smearing her back with crimson. "I'm so sorry, Mia.

Are you alright?"

She sobbed in his arms.

"Mia, I need you to tell me if you're hurt." He felt lightheaded and could feel his pulse in his temple. He was sure it wouldn't be long before he collapsed.

"I was so scared, George. She had Jack!"

"I know, Mia. None of this is your fault," he said soothingly. "You're safe now. I promise. Did she hurt you?"

"She punched me in the face and kicked me when I was down. She—"

The sound of footsteps caused Mia to pause.

George's nerves erupted again, and he stood up, pushing Mia and Jack behind him. But as he glanced down the hallway, he saw a familiar man wielding a torch.

Relief flooded him.

"DI Beaumont? Sir, are you there?" His team had arrived. "Are you OK, sir?" DS Fry asked.

"I'll live," George said with a grin. "Catherine?"

"Don't worry, we've got her, sir," Josh said. "Elaine has her in cuffs outside."

* * *

"Beaumont, how are you?" DSU Smith said. He was smiling, but George knew their conversation was going to be a difficult one.

"I'm sorry, sir. For the situation. Please accept my apologies, I—"

"It's not your fault, George. Catherine Amber Jones had charmed everyone, including me. The DCS is fuming. He's taken all the responsibility. You never answered my question."

CHAPTER THIRTY-SEVEN

"Sorry, what question, sir?"

"How are you, Beaumont?"

George sighed with relief. "I've been better. My hands hurt," he said, holding up his bandaged hands. "Sleeping was difficult last night, even with the meds. And my chest hurts. They want me back in tomorrow to check for infection."

"That's good, son. What about mentally?"

George knew this was going to come up, and he was prepared for it. But he needed to know something first. "Alex Peterson, the Bone Saw Ripper, told me I had a rotten seed in my team, one I needed to weed out. Now that he's passed away, I need to know. Was that rotten seed Terry Morton? Was he the one accusing me of abusing my position for a sexual purpose?"

Smith paused for a moment before he said, "You know I can't tell you that, George."

"Why not? It's just for my peace of mind. It doesn't matter as it went no further, but I'm paranoid there's somebody on my team out to get me."

"It was Terrence Morton, yes. We take all claims seriously, but there was no evidence, as you know. I'm sorry, George. We had no choice but to investigate."

"I understand." A wave of relief flooded through him. "Thank you, sir. Thank you for being honest with me."

"You're welcome. Anyway, you never answered my question," Smith said.

He assumed it was the question of his mental health. "To be honest, I'm struggling, sir."

A look of shock mixed with relief flooded across Smith's face. Then he smiled. "Thank you for being honest with me. I respect a man who can tell the truth. Go on, tell me. I'll do whatever I can, George."

"I think I need a few weeks away, sir. Clear my head. Or get my head straight, at least. Mia's been—been involved in my cases twice now, in fact. She could have lost her life at either time. It's not fair to her."

"So you two are back together?" Smith said after George had stopped speaking.

"No, sir. We're still co-parenting Jack. But I confided in you before how she was struggling. She was making good progress, according to Cathy Hoskins, but I'm worried this is going to make things worse. I need to be there for her. For Jack, too."

"OK. I understand. I think you need to decide about your future, too. To be blunt, Beaumont, you need to figure out whether being a detective is for you. I think it is, but I'm not the one deciding. You are. In our line of work, it's difficult to separate work and home. Do you think I've got my shit together, Beaumont? Well, you're wrong. I still struggle. It's why I don't work weekends unless I have to. You'll get there as I did, but I never went through this." He stood up and moved around his desk, placing a hand on George's shoulder. "I respect you, George. For what you've been through and for how you conduct yourself. You're a good man. But you have a family now. Take a couple of weeks and decide."

"Thank you, sir. But I haven't told you everything." Smith raised his brow and pulled the other guest chair to face George before sitting down. "It happened again. Or I thought it did."

"What did?"

"I had Catherine by the wrist. I told her it was over. She went to attack me with her knife, and I deflected it with a skillet she'd thrown at me. I remember raising it high in the air and then crashing it down against Catherine's head. There was a sickening thud. A thud, crash. Thud, crash. Thud, crash.

CHAPTER THIRTY-SEVEN

Exactly like when I hit Adam Harris. I kept doing it, bringing down the iron skillet again and again until her face and head were nothing but a bloody mess. I only stopped when I thought I heard the police break down the door and enter my flat. Yet I'd done nothing. Catherine was slumped on her knees, her eyes pleading, and I noticed I held the skillet in the air. I thought—I thought I'd killed her."

"But you didn't, George. You didn't harm her at all. Look, nobody blames you for what you did to Adam Harris. Your job is to preserve life. And you did that—"

"But I didn't, sir. When I should have taken Adam into custody, I killed him. I still think about the families of Adam's victims and how they said nothing. I'm convinced their silence means they blame me for killing Adam. They didn't get any answers, nor did they get justice. I don't blame them."

"You're wrong, George. About everything. Erika Allen's fiancé came to me personally to ask that you be spared an investigation, as did Emma Atkinson's. Both men were on your side. They never blamed you for anything. Nor did Eileen Abbott's family. Her sister and two nieces appreciated the fact that you went back to the house, as something didn't feel right. You stopped Adam from defiling her body further. I know you didn't want to go to the funerals, and I appreciated that decision because of what happened. But I did. I went to all three with the DCS. Everybody I spoke to praised you for your actions, but it wasn't only them."

"What do you mean, sir?"

"I'll save the best 'til last, OK, son?"

"OK."

"But I spoke with Elizabeth Anderson's parents. You solved a cold case, one that had been playing on their mind for years.

It didn't matter to them that Adam Harris was dead—what mattered was they knew who took their daughter away from them. And think about Eve Allgood's mother. The trauma of us reopening the case, and asking questions, was terribly difficult for her. Yet she appreciated the truth. You won't know this because I haven't told you, but Marie Allgood passed away whilst you were dealing with the Bone Saw Ripper. Olive invited us, but I knew you were struggling. I went alone. Olive told me how Marie's health improved once she knew the truth about what happened to Eve, but that terrible disease eventually took her life. Marie wrote you a letter a couple of weeks before she died." Smith got up from the chair, rifled through his bottom draw and came up with a manilla envelope. "I wasn't going to give it to you, as I didn't think it would do you any good. But from what you just told me, you need to hear it."

"This is what you saved for last?"

A bright smile lit up his face. "No, George. David Clark. The icing on the cake. He contacted me last week. He's been out of prison for nearly a year and wanted to meet you. To say thank you. You see, George, you saved that man's life. He told me he was considering suicide. I can't imagine what he must have been going through, being forced behind bars for a crime he didn't commit. And think of Mia and Jack. You saved them, too. And yourself. Adam Harris was armed and dangerous, and you did what you could."

"Thank you, sir."

"That's my pleasure, George. I'll arrange sessions with a police psychologist for you. Wait here."

As Smith left the room, a tear fell from one of George's eyes. He'd been holding everything in for so long, thinking that everybody hated him or was disappointed in him for his conduct. From what his superior was telling him, he'd been wrong. Very wrong.

George opened the letter, read the four paragraphs, and cried.

Dear Detective Inspector Beaumont,

It is with a mixture of great sadness and delightful happiness that I write this letter to you. I have been told I do not have many weeks to live, and as I could not relay my wonderful thanks and huge appreciation for what you did for Eve and me last year, I wanted to write this letter to you.

First, I want you to know that I do not blame you for what you did. In fact, you did what any person would have done. You protected your loved ones as well as yourself. I was thrilled to hear that professional standards agreed with all of us that you acted in self-defence. When I say all of us, I mean just that. All of us. The families of the victims. And even the victims themselves.

David Clark was a victim. And because of you, the gross miscarriage of justice was corrected. I will not say rectified because an innocent man lost years of his life. But I want you to know that I asked David for forgiveness, and he gave it to me. I want you to know that I do not feel as if I deserve forgiveness like you. I also want you to know that you deserve forgiveness, too—forgiveness from yourself, Inspector. I do not need to forgive you because I never blamed you. Nor did anybody else. You were the one who brought my daughter justice, just as you brought other daughters and their surviving family members justice.

So instead, I want to say thank you, George. Thank you for what you did and how you conducted yourself. Thank you for being good enough to ask for forgiveness when you never required it.

Marie Allgood

Chapter Thirty-eight

Catherine had refused a solicitor. Apparently, a cocky smile rested upon her face until Joshua had shown her the footage they'd retrieved from the InterContinental Hotel on Crown Point Road.

She told them about her motive and how desperately she wanted revenge on Nathan Patterson and her father, Timothy Hill. They'd both abused her, sexually and mentally. She wanted her story to be told, in her words, without a filter, and despite admitting everything to George, she didn't admit to killing anybody except Timothy Hill.

They discussed Emily Sanderson and her novel. In the year after being raped by Nathan, Catherine told the detectives she was just trying to survive. She felt suicidal and refused to ask for medication, not wanting to talk about the abuse she had suffered. Then one day, everything changed. After reading Emily Sanderson's book, she had clarity. And once she formed the plan in her mind, she had a purpose—a reason to live. The plan felt wrong but also felt so right. Killing Timothy was her initial goal, but when she struggled to find him, she thought about killing others. She was a victim of sexual assault. Society had let her down.

Josh asked her about the murder weapon, and Catherine

played dumb. He explained what Dr Yardley had found. Microscopic fragments of carbon steel in the victims' throats indicated that the blade that was used during the murders had been recently sharpened. The fragments were matched to a specific blade which was collected by SOCOs from DI Beaumont's flat. Elaine disclosed further evidence proving the blade was used to inflict harm upon DI Beaumont by way of DNA analysis and the fact that those microscopic fragments were found inside George's wounds. Catherine's prints were the only prints on the handle of the knife.

Catherine played with the two detectives, suggesting the knife could have been George's as it was his flat, but Josh disclosed more evidence. Josh explained forensic analysis was done on the chef's knife, which resulted in a forensics specialist finding microscopic blood particles lodged in the slit between the blade and the hilt. When they analysed the DNA, they matched samples taken from Viraj Patel, Alec Rawlinson, Edward Kennings, Terrence Morton, Nathan Patterson, Justin Broadchurch, and Timothy Hill.

Despite this evidence, Catherine continued to play with the two detectives, suggesting her prints may have been on the knife, and the DNA might have belonged to the victims', but if they couldn't put her at the crime scenes, then they had no evidence at all.

Josh disclosed evidence that proved she was in the room where Alec Rawlinson was killed. A blonde hair—initially assumed to be from a patron of the B&B—when analysed, matched the DNA profile taken from Catherine when she was booked in on the night of the attack. She hadn't been on the case until after Alec had been murdered and so smiled intensely at Josh as he explained.

Of course, Catherine had an answer for that. Hotel rooms were dirty, and she was sure she'd stayed there before. She could probably provide a receipt.

They explained they'd also spoken with DCI Robertson for her alibi the night Justin Broadchurch was murdered. He told them Catherine had left at 9.30 pm. Elaine then disclosed the CCTV evidence they had of Catherine in the bar that same night. It was a simple coincidence, Catherine had said. Was she not allowed to be in the same bar as one of the victims without being the murderer?

But Josh and Elaine had her. They disclosed more evidence. They had her purse, with various burner phones and burner SIM cards inside, and her own personal mobile phone. On each burner phone was a fake social media profile, with evidence proving she had contacted and met each victim, luring them to their deaths. But it wasn't just the profiles and messages on the burner phones that tied Catherine to each victim, as once analysis was done on the phones, they traced her movements by GPS on the days the victims were murdered, and the burner phones put her in the right areas at the correct times.

As expected, she ended the interview by stating she didn't know what was right from wrong and that she was a victim and mentally ill. She was living in a fantasy world—that her violence was mitigated because it was self-defence and preservation of life. Josh and Elaine laughed at her. She'd proven otherwise, yet Catherine continued to explain how she could easily plead mitigation by diminished responsibility because all she had to do was admit she couldn't possibly form the criminal intent to commit those crimes.

* * *

CHAPTER THIRTY-EIGHT

The marble pillars inside Leeds Magistrates' Court had always amazed George, but he preferred them when he could see them. Dozens of people were milling around, waiting. There was tension in the air. It had a nervous quality to it.

Catherine Amber Jones was unpredictable. He assumed, as did the press, that she would plead mitigation by diminished responsibility. She'd already told him that all she had to do was admit she couldn't possibly form the criminal intent to commit those crimes. She was mentally ill and had been abused by her father. It was certainly a compelling argument, but she knew what she was doing. She had criminal intent. They had enough evidence to prove it. George couldn't wait for the day the judge threw the book at her.

It was rare that he went to Leeds Magistrates'. Usually, he left it to DSU Jim Smith, but there was something about Catherine Jones that intrigued him. He also hadn't seen her or spoken with her since the night she attacked them. That, and he wanted to see how she'd react, how she'd plead, especially because she'd admitted to only killing her father in her interview with DS Elaine Brewer and DS Joshua Fry. He was surprised the Superintendent had agreed, especially after he removed himself from the case.

The doors to the courtroom opened, and so George walked down the corridor, following everyone else inside. He took his seat, revelling at the vast audience that was filtering through. As soon as they were seated, the doors were closed. The district judge was already ensconced on the bench.

"Catherine Amber Jones, you are charged with seven counts of murder, contrary to common law. How do you plead? Guilty or not guilty?"

The tension was palpable, and it seemed the audience

couldn't take a breath.

She looked at George instead of the judge; a grin stretched across her face. "Guilty."

"Er, sorry, Madam," Catherine's defence lawyer said, scrambling around. "Sorry, Madam. Can I ask for the plea to be put again?"

Catherine's entire defence team was also scrambling around, trying to keep the plea from being released by the press.

But it was already too late, even as the judge shouted, "Sit down." Nobody was listening. "I said sit down."

The press was on their phones and tablets, firing off emails and messages.

Once the noise died down, the district judge spoke to the defence. "I take it from your reaction, Ms Linklater, that Queen's Counsel has not been instructed of Ms Jones's plea?"

"That is correct, Madam."

"Could you confirm your plea, Ms Jones? It seems your own counsel requires confirmation."

"Guilty," Catherine said.

"Do you have anything to say about your actions?"

Silence.

"There are family members of the victims in this courtroom who deserve an apology, Ms Jones."

Silence.

"I hereby sentence you to a whole life order."

George didn't judge success by prison time received, but a whole life order was an incredible result.

After, he called DSU Jim Smith, who was eager to hear how it went, from his Honda.

"How'd it go, George?"

George explained about her guilty plea and how she received

a whole life order.

"That's fantastic. Another lunatic off the streets."

"Lunatic, indeed," George said. "As Catherine was being led away, she stopped and turned to the entire courtroom. It looks like she didn't want anybody else's narrative being told, sir, only her own. To her, this wasn't about the victims but was about herself. Do you want to know what her last words to the judge were?"

"Go on, DI Beaumont."

"Her words were, 'Fuck you!'"

Afterword

Thank you, wonderful reader, for reading my third novel. Whether you purchased this book in paperback or eBook or read it through Kindle Unlimited, I thank you. As a self-published author, I'm so very grateful for your continued support. This experience has been extremely humbling so far, and I appreciate each and every one of you.

I moved away from my hometown of Middleton in this book, as Leeds is such a diverse area. The disorientating, suffocating streets of Headingley, around the home of my beloved Leeds Rhinos, made the novel enjoyable for me to write, as did situating part in Yeadon.

I love taking my family up to Yeadon, whether it be to the Tarn, or Multiflight Café Bar, watching the planes land and take off. I'm also partial to the food they offer, especially the fish and chips. You'll know the place I'm talking about.

I'm super excited to take you to more amazing places in Leeds as you follow George and his team, and I hope you enjoy George and Isabella's journey. If you enjoyed this book, I'd really appreciate it if you could leave a review on Amazon or Goodreads, or both. As a self-published author, reviews mean more people read my work.

George Beaumont will be back soon, and you can pre-order The Cross Flatts Child Snatcher on Amazon.

Thanks, and take care,

AFTERWORD

Lee

Also by Lee Brook

The Detective George Beaumont West Yorkshire Crime Thriller series in order:

The Miss Murderer

The Bone Saw Ripper

The Blonde Delilah

The Cross Flatts Snatcher

The Middleton Woods Stalker

The Naughty List

More titles coming soon.